BLACK SQUARES

Prince Mapp

info@blacksquares.com

Dedicated to my dad who overdosed on heroin at the age of 30.

CONTENTS

INTRODUCTION

Silky was the Prettiest woman Prince had ever seen. She was flawless. He was a young parttime Basketball star and a full time drug dealer from Jamaica, Queens, NYC. She offered him the chance of a lifetime to take his skill to the next level, and it wasn't the NBA. But the Baltimore Heroin Trade where he would become King. But not without a price.

In a Hustler's world dominated by men, there is no room for weak women, especially women who wanted to penetrate the steel curtain that lined evil streets. Silky was not one of them. Not only was she strong, powerful, and successful, but her beauty had placed her in a class all by herself. While visiting a supermarket in NYC, she ran into an up and coming hustler. Never seeing a woman who had him mesmerized before, he had taken a chance and approached the beautiful, older woman, and from that day on they became they most powerful Hustlers the streets of NYC and Baltimore had ever saw. Follow them into an exciting life of drugs, murder, and mayhem and see how a world dominated by men can be turned upside down by six inch stilettos and expensive manicured fingernails

Amir walked into his plush condominium after a long and exhilarating workout.

He finally checked his mail, something he never did, and he saw a letter from his daughter, Silky. He hadn't heard from his only daughter in over a year. She wanted to leave the country for a little while after being faced with so many tragedies back to back. Amir had given Silky her space. He let her move about the world without any interference. He removed his sweaty clothing, took a shower, got dressed in comfortable clothes and grabbed him a shot of Ciroc on the rocks. He sat in his favorite La-Z-Boy chair and began to read Silky's letter. To his surprise, the letter looked as if blood had been splattered on it. He quickly gulped his first shot of vodka and refilled. He didn't realize how much his hands shook as he held on tightly to the letter. His body began to tremble as a cold chill ran through him. It was a chill that he had become very familiar with; the chill of Death. He sat back in his chair and began to read.

Dear Dad....

CHAPTER ONE

"AUNT SARAH'S"
JUNE 1984

"Daddy, Daddy, can I go with you?" Prince asked excitedly.

"No not today Lil Man, I'll be right back."

"Why Daddy?" Prince asked as his eyes began to water. His father looked at him in shame, as he knew again, he would let his son down.

"Come on. Get your Jacket," his father said as he rushed out the front door. Prince grabbed his jacket and ran outside. He climbed through the back window of his father's 1979 Chevy Caprice station wagon. Prince looked back at his mother standing in the front door as she began to leave. She left his sight as he rode away with his father to a destination that did not matter to him. He just wanted to ride with his dad. At age 6, Prince didn't understand the arguments that had taken place between his mom and dad. He didn't know the substance of the arguments, but whatever it was, he hated to see his mother crying in the end. He knew that he should stay home and protect his mom, comfort her and support her, but he also knew that his dad was gonna stop at the penny candy store and buy his favorite cherry balls and gumdrops. As routine, his father exited the station wagon and spoke to his friends for a few minutes. His father always seemed to give his friends money. The same money that he told Prince's mom that he didn't have. Once he finished talking to his friends, he strolled into the penny candy store to buy Prince's cherry balls and gumdrops. Now it was time for their regular stop to Aunt Sarah's. Prince always heard his mom talk about Aunt Sarah. Nothing nice, and none of his brothers and sisters called her Aunt Sarah; especially after she tossed a brick through the front window of their house. It was wrapped in a red ribbon especially for his mom.

"Come on!" his father said, slamming the driver's door and heading to Sarah's house. "Now remember, don't tell no one we was at Auntie Sarah's, okay? No one! Or you'll never ride with Daddy again. You understand?" his father said sternly as he looked back at him.

"Yeah Daddy, I understand," Prince said with a mouth full of gumdrops. Once they entered the house it was always the same scenery; same people, especially his dad's brother, Steve. Sarah's house was nothing like his mom's house; mom's house was clean. Aunt Sarah's house was filthy. It was filled with garbage and half filled beer bottles that smelled like urine. Prince didn't really like this part of the trip because his father would always leave him with other kids who claimed they were his brothers and sisters. They would call his father "Daddy". Prince knew this was impossible, because the only brothers and sisters that he had were at home with his mom. He had a younger brother, Laron, who was 3 years old, three brothers and four sisters who were older than him.

"Hey Lil' Man, give me a five," a staggering man with a cracked voice said as Prince walked through the door of Aunt Sarah's house. His spooky eyes looked as if he was surprised all the time and Prince would always say to himself that his breath smelled like dog doo-doo. This was his uncle Steve; a tall light-skinned, thin man who always walked around Sarah's house without a shirt.

"Hi Uncle Steve," Prince said smacking his uncle's hand with his sticky gumdrop and cherry ball covered hands.

"How you doin Lil' Man?" Steve asked.

"Fine," Prince said as he watched his father disappear right before his eyes behind the assorted color beads that separated the living room from the dining room. Prince hurried away from his uncle, because he knew his uncle's next move would involve more touching and Prince refused to tolerate the smell that came off Uncle Steve. He proceeded upstairs where he had seen his friend and so called brother, Dennis dribbling an old basketball in the hallway.

"Hey Prince!" Dennis said excitedly and very happy to see someone his age.

"Hey Dennis," Prince said nonchalantly as he walked up the steps.

"What are you doing here?" It ain't Saturday," Dennis said referring to the fact that Prince only came by on weekends, so his dad and Aunt Sarah could play "house". Actually, Aunt Sarah and his dad played house everyday; but not until after they played "Doctor". At first, Daddy would remove his shirt and Aunt Sarah would bring in her Doctor's bag. Daddy would take medicine that his friend gave him at the penny candy store, open it up, pour the contents of a small white bag into a silver spoon; he would then pull out his cigarette lighter and for some reason unbeknown to Prince, he would cook the medicine. Aunt Sarah would take the medicine out of the spoon by drawing it up in a needle. She would then tie daddy's belt around his arm and stick the needle in his arm. For some crazy reason, Uncle Steve liked to stick the needle in his private area below his belt and Aunt Sarah did the same. The odd thing about "Doctor" was when they were given their needle, they didn't cry like Prince always did when he went to the doctor. Actually, they had the biggest, silliest smile on their faces and right after, his daddy and Aunt Sarah played house.

"Oh, I wanted to come with my daddy," Prince said, stretching the word "my" out.

"That's our daddy. He's not just your daddy. My mom says he's my daddy too. He just lives with you," Dennis said as he continued to dribble the semi-dead basketball in the hallway. "Hey wanna go out back and shoot some hoops?" Dennis said, referring to the milk crate that was cut out and nailed to a tree in their backyard.

"I guess so. Why, do you always wanna play basketball?" Prince said turning and walking back down the steps, jumping two at a time and running through the living room into the dining room, through the back bedroom and into the backyard. Prince knew this route very well. After all, it was the only way to the backyard and when his dad and Aunt Sarah played house that is the way they sent him. Both boys went into the backyard and they both giggled because they had seen their dad and Aunt Sarah naked, as Daddy jumped up and down on her as she yelled curse words telling their dad, "fuck me, fuck me, tear this pussy up Dennis," not noticing them as they ran pass into the backyard. Prince was confused at times, because he never saw his dad and mom play house at home. At six years old many thoughts raced through his mind; why was the other little boy named after his father? Ironically, Prince too shared the name. It was his middle name and he hated it; especially after his grandma would always say that it was the devil's name because Dennis spelled sinned backwards.

Dennis continued to dribble his ball in route to make a lay up into the milk crate. Dennis was a tad bit taller than Prince, but they both were six years old.

"I bet you can't make more shots than me," Dennis said, passing Prince the ball. Prince gladly took the semi-dead ball and dribbled it as if it were filled with air. Easily slicing the ball through his legs and behind his back, driving it towards the milk crate for a reverse lay-up.

"Oooh SHITTTT!" Dennis cussed and quickly covered his mouth hoping that his mother did not hear him.

"Dennis! You better watch your fucking mouth out there boy," Aunt Sarah yelled from the window that looked directly into the backyard.

"Sorry Ma!" Dennis yelled and giggled. He knew his mother didn't care if he cursed or not, but his dad didn't like it. He was still in awe at what he had just witnessed. He had played ball with Prince at other times, but never did he see what he had just seen.

"Prince, how did you do that move? Can you show me how to do that? Please? I mean, my mom said we are brothers," Dennis said seriously.

"You ain't my brother," Prince said sternly. "My brothers' names are Eddie, Tommy and Laron."

"Well, that's what mom and dad told me", Dennis said, trying his best to repeat the move he just saw. He didn't care about the brother stuff. He just wanted to learn that move.

"For your info, my brother Tommy taught me that move. He said one day I'ma be in the NBA just like Magic Johnson." Prince closed his eyes and imagined himself in Magic's shoes.

"Shoot me too! We're gonna be there together," Dennis said imagining being in the NBA also. "Hey Prince?"

"Yeah Dennis."

"Can we be best friends in the whole wide world forever? I mean, you said we ain't brothers right? So, can we be friends?"

Prince looked at the sincerity in his brother's eyes. He hadn't put too much thought into being friends with anyone in particular; especially somebody that lives in a "garbage dump" like the place where Dennis lives. After all, he had friends already. Where he lived he had plenty of friends. Plus, these trips were solely based on obtaining cherry balls and gumdrops. "I guess so," Prince said, finally giving in to Dennis' request; slapping him five.

"Yessssss!" Dennis said jumping high to the sky. Prince had agreed to be his best friend. It was his first best friend and for that matter, his only friend. All the other kids on his block weren't his friends. They made fun of the way his clothes looked. "Prince, I promise you, I will be your best friend forever and ever."

"Me too Dennis," Prince said with a smile. He began to like being best friends with Dennis. He grabbed the basketball and patiently showed Dennis what he knew. Surprisingly at six years old, they both were well advanced at the popular sport.

"Prince!" Dad yelled.

"Huh?"

"Let's go. Tell Dennis you'll see him later," his father said from the window, shirtless and sweating tremendously.

"I'll see you later Dennis," Prince said, dropping the basketball.

"Okay Prince, I'll see you tomorrow," Dennis said as he kept his eye locked on the milk crate. He squared up with his fingertips under the ball and put up a long three point shot. His release was perfect. It went high brushing against the leaves that hung from the tree and swoosh? Straight threw the milk crate. "It's gooood!" Dennis yelled and did a victory dance in his backyard.

"Good shot Dennis," his father yelled from the window.

"Thanks Dad," he yelled back, getting his own rebound as he watched Prince run into the house. Dennis stood alone in the backyard as tears began to well up in his eyes. He wanted to go with his dad for once, but he knew that would never happen.

Prince was glad to be home. A nice clean house with lights, a television and most of all, food. He missed his brothers and sisters too. Prince's mom always told him to be thankful and never take what he had for granted. "There are kids your age that are way less fortunate that you," she would tell him. Dennis, his best friend, was one of them. Aunt Sarah's house had no lights most of the time, no T.V. and no food. Now that he and Dennis were best friends, he wondered how Dennis ate, and did he get to watch television. The thought quickly erased from his mind when he heard his mom yell to him to wash his face and hands and get ready to eat dinner. Everybody sat at the table as mom brought dish after dish filled with fried chicken, cornbread, and mac and cheese and collard greens.

"Eddie, say grace," Mom ordered.

She was not a church going woman but she believed in God. She was blessed to have eight healthy children and provided for every single one of them. She worked for the rich white folks cleaning their houses on the weekends, and she worked as a school bus matron for special needs children during the week. Above all, Mom made certain that her children were all clothed and fed while Dad *talked* to his friends and *played* house and doctor at Aunt Sarah's.

"God is Good, God is Great. Thank you for the food we are about to receive, Amen," Eddie said, and before he was finished saying grace, everybody began digging in.

"Hey ma?" Eddie said, biting a piece of chicken.

"Boy, what I told you about talkin' with food in your mouth. Chew your food first," Ma said smiling.

"Oh my bad Ma," Eddie said, chewing his food first and continuing. "Ma, can I work with Ernie on the Mr. Softee Truck?'

"Who?" Ma said.

"Mr. Ernie, you know him; the one who drives the ice cream truck. He asked if I wanted a job for the summer. I could help you with the bills like Bubba does."

"I don't know about that Ed, I gotta see. You know there's some crazy people in this world. I'm going to have to do a background check," Mom said, raising her eyebrows.

"So that means yeah!" Ed said excitedly.

"No, it ain't yeah. I said we'll see."

"Okay Ma, that seems fair enough," Ed said.

"Prince, why aren't you eating your food? Don't you know its people in Africa starving?" mom said.

"Name two of em'. You don't know nobody in Africa mama," Prince said seriously as his siblings laughed at his statement.

"Boy you too smart for your years. Now how do you know I don't know anybody in Africa?" she said smiling.

"Well do you?" Prince asked.

"Shut up Boy!" Mom said laughing.

"I'm saving my food. I wanna save my food for my best friend. He doesn't have any food at home," Prince said.

"Who is this best friend and why doesn't he have food? Peanut seems to come from a hard working family," Momma said.

"Peanut ain't my best friend Ma. My best friend is a secret. I can't tell anyone his name, but I know he doesn't have food and sometimes his lights don't work and his T.V. looks different.

Right there his mom knew exactly whom he was talking about. She knew that her husband Dennis, took Prince to his mistress's house and she hated that. She knew that there were many other children out there that were related to her children. She wasn't stupid. She knew everything. She had many arguments and cried many nights but yet, she would not kick Dennis out of the house. She had sincerely loved him. He had once been a great man. He was the father of her beautiful children, but just like a lot of other good men, Dennis had fallen victim to a vicious drug that destroyed many families; Heroin. At first, he used the drug on occasion, but now he was a heroin addict who lived to get high. His priorities were drugs, his responsibilities were buying drugs and his major concern was using drugs. But even with all of this, his wife refused to abandon the man who gave her so many good memories as a teenager.

"Hey Papi," when you're done painting that door you can fix that back shelf for me too, por favor (please)." Papi ,the Puerto Rican store owner said to Dennis as he skillfully painted the store's back door. Dennis was a very talented man of many crafts. When it came to fixing anything, houses, cars, appliances, he was at his best. He made money by doing odd jobs for Papi at the Puerto Rican store and for other businesses around the neighborhood. He actually made good money for his skill.

Tonight, when he's done, he would get paid one hundred fifty dollars. His wife argued with him earlier that morning about backed up bills and he knew that she needed money badly. He had to make his decisions, give his wife the much needed money or he would go play house and doctor with Aunt Sarah. His decision was made. He was sick with the monkey clawing at his back and he desperately needed a hit. The bills would have to wait. Dennis finished up his work at the grocery store, was paid his money and was on his way. He stopped by the gas station and put ten dollars worth of gas and proceeded to see his suppliers for a couple of bags of dope. He noticed when he got to the spot that it was flooded with people as if it was New Year's Eve at Times Square.

"Step in line for Black Rain yall. Get your free Black Rain," the dealer yelled to the anxious crowd as he passed out free samples of the high-powered heroin. Dennis saw many people that he knew, but he refused to show himself. Since he had money he would stay in the cut until the traffic was clear, and then he would purchase the new grade of dope that was on display..

"How did all these people get here?" Dennis thought to himself as he sat and watched one after the other step up and retrieve their free goodies from the dealer.

"Boo!"

"What the fu...," Dennis said turning around quickly and startled as if he had seen a ghost. It was his brother Steve at his driver's window looking and smelling as if he hadn't taken a shower since the Vietnam War.

"Hey Dee man, what's shakin? Why you ain't on line?" Steve asked.

"Nah, I don't need nothin free, I'll buy my own when this crowd clears up."

"Oh you got money huh?" Steve asked raising his eyebrow.

"None of your damn business nigger! How is that shit anyway?"

"Man this is it! This shit here is the best shit I ever had. This is smack for real. I've been shooting dope for over twenty years and I ain't neva had nothing like this," Steve said shaking his glassine bag in his hand. "This some fine shit. I can't even do half a bag at one time. You gotta be careful with this shit."

"Aight, here. Go get me four dimes and buy you one. I ain't got no change, so bring my fifty dollars change back mother-fucker!" Dennis said to Steve as he passed him the money.

"Say bro, lemme borrow another dime. I got a girl waiting for me at Sarah's and she only does coke," Steve asked, gripping the money.

"Man, who the fuck do you think I am? I gotta give Ronnie some of that money. Man go the fuck ahead. I want my money back or I'm gonna whip your skinny ass," Dennis said sternly. Steve gave Dennis a devilish smirk and quickly walked away to cop their lethal drugs. Dennis sat back and thought again about the argument he had earlier with his wife. He knew she was one hundred percent right, but yet his addiction wouldn't let him make any other decisions. He badly wanted to leave the addictive drug alone, but yet it was impossible. Even his numerous stints in rehab weren't enough to deter him away from his addiction. "Man I gotta leave this shit alone, I got too many damn kids and a family that need me. Fuck it, today will be my last day fucking with this shit. I'm done." Dennis said as Steve jumped into the passenger's seat with five dimes of heroin and two dimes of coke.

"Where is my change?" Dennis said, holding his hand out.

"Here man. Damn. You act like I'ma steal from you Bro."

"Man fuck that Bro shit. You a dope fiend and I don't trust no dope fiend."

"So that means you don't trust yourself ?" Steve asked. Dennis thought about the question that was just asked and softly answered "No".

"Look, I gotta stop and give Ronnie some bread," Dennis said.

"Okay. How's Ron doing anyway?" Steve asked.

"She's good, man. She's doin good," Dennis said, pulling away from the curb. They pulled up to the house, it was early Saturday morning; the kids were up and Prince was in front dribbling his basketball while Ronnie swept the front porch. Dennis got out of the car and tried to playfully steal the ball from his son.

"You can't hold me Dad," Prince said as he crossed the ball over and sliced it through his father's legs causing him to do a 360 degree spin.

"Oh shit. Dennis, did you see that? How old is that boy?" Steve yelled from his window amazed at what he saw from a six year old kid.

"Yeah, that's my boy. What do you expect?" Dennis said proudly. The truth was he didn't teach his son how to dribble. It was his other son, Tommy who taught his younger brother the moves.

"Hey Ronnie?"

"What?" she yelled back.

"Here, take this until I come back," Dennis said, handing her fifty dollars. "Papi still owes a hundred dollars. I'll pick it up from him later," Dennis said walking towards his car. Ronnie knew he was lying. She knew that Papi had given him one hundred and fifty dollars. Afterall, she and Papi had a very good friendship. She had known Papi for over twenty years and they both knew that Dennis had the potential to be a good man if he left heroin alone.

"Dad! Dad!" Prince yelled, dropping his basketball and running towards the car.

"Wassup Lil fella?

"Can I go? It's Saturday. You said, I mean you promised you'll take me to the penny candy store."

"Not today Lil' Man. I gotta take care of some important business. I'll be back. I'll take you later," Dennis said and he saw his son's eyes begin to water.

"Get in boy. You betta stop being a cry baby," his father yelled. Prince paid his remark no mind as his frown turned into a smile and he ran inside to get his book bag and came back out and jumped through the station wagon back window.

◆ ◆ ◆

Before heading over to Aunt Sarah's Prince was adamant that his dad stop at the penny candy store. Dennis was against stopping at first since he was so sick, but quickly changed his mind when he saw his son in the rear-view mirror.

"Here Prince, this is a ten dollar bill. This is for you, only spend one dollar..."

"I know Dad. I get nine dollars back," Prince said cutting his dad off.

"Yeah make sure he gives you nine dollars back," Dennis said as his son had already jumped out the back of the station wagon. He entered his paradise where he was surrounded by clear shelves filled with every candy you could name. Prince went to his favorite section, the penny candy section.

"Hey Mr. Pete!"

"Hey Lil' Man, what can I do for you today sir?" Mr. Pete asked.

"I got ten dollars and I want twenty-five cherry balls, um I mean fifty cherry balls and fifty gumdrops; and I need nine dollars back. Oh yeah, Please."

"You got it young man. Just don't eat it all at one time, or I'ma have to use these," Mr. Pete said as he lifted a pair of rusty pliers and showed Prince.

"What's those for," Prince asked worried.

"To remove any rotten teeth." Mr. Pete said and scooped his order, giving him a few extras and placed them in a brown paper bag. "Here you go young fella, enjoy your day."

"Thank you Mr. Pete. I'll see you later," Prince said grabbing his candy and his change and running out of the store.

"Damn boy what took you so long?" an agitated Dennis said to his son as he jumped through the back window.

"Nothin'," Was all Prince said, popping a cherry ball in his mouth.

"Can we go now?" an impatient Steve said and Dennis gave him a look that could kill which quickly calmed Steve's tone.

Dennis, Steve and Prince arrived at Sarah's house. As usual, she was at the door anxiously awaiting their arrival. She couldn't figure out to save her own life why he brought that spoiled-ass brat with him, but she knew not to express her feelings because she knew Dennis didn't play games when it involved Prince. Prince was Daddy's Lil' Man and no matter what his flaws were, he loved his children unconditionally. He loved Sarah's son, Dennis too, but he wasn't sure the little boy was his son.

"Hey yawl, what's going on?" Sarah said excitedly. She looked terrible. Her face was dried out and cracked. Her lips peeled with dried blood in between cracks and her neck was the same color as Dennis' car tires. She smelled like urine and her eyes were banana yellow. She was literally walking dead. She was happy to see Dennis because she too had the monkey on her back. She hadn't had a fix since the wee hours of the morning and Dennis was here to save her life.

"Where's Roxy at Sarah?' Steve asked.

"Man, fuck that broke bitch, she stole some money outta my purse and the black bitch ain't give me nothing for staying here last night. She Neva got dope and all she does is smoke that cocaine," Sarah said angrily as she tried her best to fix her hair as Dennis walked through the door.

"So you kicked her out because she didn't have no dope, huh? I know you lying about the bitch stealing money outta your purse cause you ain't have no money to steal. Before I left you were begging for two dollars to buy a beer. Remember that?" Steve said in a harsh and convincing tone.

"Listen, fuck you and fuck that freebasing bitch, Roxy. Neither one of yall gotta get high in my house. This is my shit and I kick out whoever the fuck I want," Sarah said stomping her crusty feet on her dirty floor.

"Yeah, yeah, you win Sarah, lemme get your works," Steve said quickly changing the subject and mood.

"Oh, they are right here baby. You got somethin for me Steve?" Sarah said seductively, quickly changing her tone when the conversation came to drugs.

"Hell yeah, I got somethin' for you sweet mama. This Black Rain is the shit. All three of us could share one bag and be high as a kite," Steve said.

"Nigga I," Sarah said pointing her dirty fingernail at her chest. "I can't share no bag Steve. You know that. I need one for myself."

"Listen both of yall shut the fuck up and close the damn door," Dennis said as he walked into the bedroom.

Prince hurried up the stairs to see his best friend, Dennis. He went from room to room looking for his friend. He finally found him sleeping across a pile of dirty clothes in the back bedroom.

"Hey Dennis, hey Dennis, wake up!" Prince said lightly, shaking his best friend.

"Huh?" Dennis said, squinting his eyes.

"It's me, Prince. Get up, I got something for you."

"What you got Prince?" Dennis said as he sat up.

"Come on. Let's move some of these clothes." Prince began to shove the dirty clothes to the side while Dennis stood and pissed inside a 40 ounce beer bottle, as if it were a regular routine. When he finished, he looked over at Prince who had cleaned an area that was covered with clothes and garbage. He was opening his book bag and pulled out a big ball of aluminum foil that was almost the size of the book bag.

"Here, take this, "Prince said, passing Dennis the ball of foil.

"Ooooo Shit!" Dennis said excitedly as he opened up the foil and saw the fried chicken, home fries, scrambled eggs, cookies, macaroni and cheese and fish sticks. He then pulled out two containers of Hi-C drinks and a brown paper bag full of penny candies. Prince ripped the paper bag so it laid flat on the floor and began to split the candy in half. He put twenty-five cherry balls in his pile and twenty-eight in Dennis' pile (the few extra that Mr. Pete had given him) and he gave Dennis the remainder of his gumdrops. He knew that his dad would take him back to the penny candy store. Before Prince was finished splitting the candy, Dennis was finishing his first Hi-C drink and staring wide-eyed at the candy. The aluminum foil was completely empty.

"Hey Prince, thank you. I was so hungry. I hadn't eaten in days," Dennis said rubbing his stomach and smiling.

"Today is Saturday. I told you I would be back," Prince said handing him his share of the candy.

"Prince, you are my best friend in the whole wide world. I love you man," Dennis said giving his best friend a brotherly hug.

"No Dennis, we're not best friends anymore," Prince said, and Dennis' face immediately saddened.

"We are brothers! You and I have the same dad and my mom says that makes us brothers. As long as I have food, you'll have food too okay?"

"Okay bro. Okay," Dennis said as a tear ran from his eyes.

"Here take these. These are my favorite clothes. If my mom finds out she will probably kill me; and these are my favorite underwear. They're Spider-Man underoos. They are new. I got them for Christmas. I want you to have them, okay? Prince said handing his brother the clothes. The book bag was empty. "Now, I have one more thing. You gotta make a promise that you don't share with anyone."

"I promise!" Dennis said, raising his hand proudly as if he were a boy scout.

"Here, take this." He handed his brother the only money he had in this world; the nine dollars worth of change that Mr. Pete had given him.

"Ooooh dip, how much is this?" Dennis asked.

"It's nine dollars. It's all yours."

"Wait. Hold Up," Dennis said undressing, exposing his private parts because he wore no underwear. He quickly put on the clean Spider-Man underwear and stuffed the nine-dollar bills in his crotch area. He put on the clean pants and shirt and sat back down. "I gotta hide this money or else Mommy will borrow it and I'll never get it back. She owes me two zillion dollars," Dennis said as he and his brother laughed.

"Hey, let's go shoot some hoops," Prince suggested.

"Are you nuts? I ain't getting my new clothes dirty," Dennis said pointing at his clean shirt and pants.

"So what do you wanna do?" Prince asked.

"How about we sit right here and enjoy our candy?"

"That sounds good to me," Prince said as they both began to pop cherry balls and gumdrops.

"Awe mannnn thank God for Black Rain," Steve sang as he nodded, almost touching the ground and bouncing up quickly.

"Hey Dee, you wanna hit me baby?" Sarah asked. She needed another hit because the first one wasn't enough for her.

"Yeah, come over here," Dennis said as he emptied the contents of the bag into the spoon so it could be cooked and made liquid.

"Baby, I don't have any more veins, my arms, my legs they don't do nothing for me Daddy. I see both of yall high as hell and I'm okay but I don't feel like you."

"So where do you want me to put it?"

"I don't know, I don't have any more good veins. I may have to shoot in my pussy'" Sarah said.

"Well shit, I ain't standing around to watch this shit. That gonna blow my high. I already smell you with your clothes on," Steve said nervously.

"Shut the fuck up Steve, don't start. Just give us two minutes okay baby?" Sarah said to Steve as he already was leaving the doctor's office and heading into the living room.

"You ready Dee?"

"Yeah, sit down." Sarah sat on the end of the bed and took her pants off exposing her pussy. Dennis walked towards her not looking in her direction as he filled the syringe with the high potent substance. He reached Sarah and began to prepare for surgery.

"Now where is your vein at? Where the fuck am I supposed to shoot this shit?" Dennis complained.

"Right here on the side of my pussy lips baby," she said rubbing her clitoris, getting Dennis aroused.

"I see I'm gonna have to stick my dick in here when I'm finished shootin ya ass up, " Dennis said as he looked face to face with her pussy.

"You know that's right Daddy. Ain't no nigga fuck me like you honey," Sarah said with her eyes closed as Dr. Dennis, slowly injected her vagina with the potent medicine. Sarah leaned her head all the way back as the greatest feeling she has ever felt ran through her body. A single tear ran down her cheek as she went into an instant nod.

"God bless you Dennis. God fuckin bless you," was all she could say as the devil helped her ease the pain that she possessed in her life. She stayed in her nod for the next twenty minutes.

Sarah Payne used to be the most beautiful woman in South Jamaica, Queens. She came from a decent family and her grandparents had left her the house that she lived in. It wasn't until her first child's father; Earl came into her life when she was exposed to the lethal drug of heroin. At first, she would sniff a bag on occasion and it would not bother her state of being. She worked a good job and received a healthy salary as a transit worker for New York City. Earl had cleaned up his act and left her and took their kids. She met Dennis at her train station. Dennis was the most handsome and respectable man she had ever met. She quickly fell in love with him, even though he was already married. She quickly tried to have a child by him in hopes that he would leave his wife, Ronnie. That never happened. Soon she began to rely more on her growing addiction as a way to get away from the pain she felt of not having a steady man in her life to stay with her at night. She became jealous and began to disrupt the everyday living at Ronnie's house. Her first episode was throwing a brick through the front picture window with a white piece of paper taped to it. It read "Die Bitch". Ronnie had no idea where it came from until she started receiving calls. Telling her about Dennis' habits and his side family. Broken hearted, Ronnie threw Dennis out and he moved in with Sarah. This is when Sarah got her wish. Dennis had been where he belonged, at home with her. It was shortly after he moved in with Sarah that he began to sit around smoking weed and drinking Colt 45.

"Hey Dee, you want some of this?"

"Nah, I'm good. You need to leave that shit alone before you get hooked," Dennis said, taking a small sip of his beer and a hard pull of his joint of weed.

"No baby. I am not gonna get hooked. It only takes the edge off, that's all.

"You see I just take a hit in the morning and one at night and that's it," Sarah said.

"That's a hit everyday, Sarah. You're gonna be just like the rest of those zombies walking around here dead."

"Never me Dee, never me. Besides, have you heard what a little pinch would do the to your sex drive?" Sarah said seductively as she sat on his lap facing him. He looked into her face and she was beautiful.

"My sex drive ain't good enough for you bitch?" Dennis said.

"Oh hell yeah! I can't complain at all Big Daddy," Sarah said holding the straw that held the heroin up to Dennis nostril.

"Fuck it. I guess one time ain't gonna kill me," Dennis said, as he inhaled the drug.

"Now see. I told you that it wouldn't be too bad," Sarah said unbuckling his pants.

"Fuck it. Hit another nostril baby," Dennis said.

"You sure Daddy?"

"What did I say?" Dennis commanded.

"Okay baby," Sarah said as she lifted another hit to his nostril. This time Dennis' reaction was different. He quickly rose from the chair knocking Sarah on her heels and ran towards the bathroom. He threw up everything he had eaten that week.

"You okay, Daddy?" Sarah said following him into the bathroom.

"I think so," Dennis said leaning over the toilet as a great sensation ran through his body. He had never felt so good in his entire life. He felt great. He felt strange. He felt untouchable.

"Now it's time to test out the myth of the infamous 'dope dick'," Sarah said as she began to undress showing off her flawless petite body. Dennis made his way back to the bedroom while undressing at the same time. He lay on his back in the bed and watched Sarah's naked silhouette standing in front of him. His dick had risen and was harder than a roll of quarters. Sarah straddled him, he closed his eyes as she began to moan as she rode him until it became dark outside and yet, and he still did not come. He was tossing Sarah all over the room. He had her moaning and cumming. It was the best sex she ever had. Three hours had passed and he finally exploded inside of her. Nine months later Dennis jr. was born. He had been conceived while both parents were under the influence of heroin. In fact, he was born with traces of heroin in his system. Six years later, Sarah and Dennis were addicts conquered by heroin and sniffing wouldn't do anything for them. They needed to shoot the powerful drug into their veins or they wouldn't feel a thing.

◆ ◆ ◆

"Yall finished in there?" Steve yelled from the living room ready to use Sarah's works for the final bit of dope he had left.

"Yeah, I'll be right out Steve," Dennis said putting his pants back on. "This is it," Dennis said to himself.

"What's that baby?"

"Nothin. I was just talkin to myself," Dennis said referring to him being done with heroin. He had a family at home and he wanted them back badly. He loved his wife and she loved and missed him. He had been tested for HIV earlier that week and by the grace of God he was negative. He went into the dining room carrying the syringe to give his brother, Steve.

"Hey man. Since Roxy ain't come back, I still got this coke over here. I was told if we mix it with the smack it's FIRE!" Steve said in a crackling voice.

"Yeah but this shit is too potent to mix with anything," Dennis said.

"Yeah but I think the coke will make it smooth. I only got a little bit of smack left. I gotta mix it with something," Steve greedily complained. He held the heroin in his spoon showing how much he had left. He took out the clear glass vial of cocaine and poured it on a piece of paper that sat on top of the television. He crushed it, and sprinkled on the spoon mixing it with heroin.

"Here Dee, shoot this in my neck for me Bro," Steve said as he too was running out of the veins to shoot in. Dennis absorbed the drugs into the syringe and gave the tip a light push making a drop of water seep out.

"Yo man, what the hell you doin?" You wastin my whole Goddamn bag, you stupid mother fucker," Steve said as if he wanted to kill Dennis.

"Shut the fuck up Steve. Here, here are two whole bags for you to keep. I'll shoot this in me," Dennis said as he wrapped his belt around his arm and pulled it tight with his teeth. He searched ever so carefully with precision for the biggest vein in his arm and calmly inserted the deadly mixture into his arm. Instantly his heart started to beat an alarming rate and his eyes swelled up with tears streaming from both of them. His life began to flash before his eyes as he saw his many children that stood before him. He saw his wife smile on their wedding day. He saw how beautiful Sarah looked when they first met. He fell into a complete nod and looked as if he was sucking his own dick.

"See bro, I told you that this shit was fire. Right Dee?" Steve said smiling at the effect that the dope and coke made on his brother. He couldn't wait to nod the same exact way. "Hey Dee, how you feelin bro?"

"Hey Dee! Dee! Dee! Dennis! Sarah! OH SHIT! Sarah," Steve yelled.

"What the hell is wrong with you Steve?" Sarah yelled coming out of her nod.

"It's Dennis. He ain't fuckin movin. He ain't fuckin movin man," Steve yelled as Sarah came running into the dining room

"Get some ice. Dennis Baby get up. Daddy, please wake up baby. You're gonna be alright. What did you do mother fucker? Get some fuckin ice," Sarah yelled hysterically.

"Bitch you ain't got no electricity. Where the fuck am I gonna get ice from?" Steve yelled.

"Breath Daddy. Please don't die," Sarah yelled in panic as she ran outside yelling for help.

"Prince and Dennis Jr., both stood in silence without emotion as they stare as the man they both called dad; the purchaser of the cherry balls. He sat in his chair with his head still in his lap, which was his regular position. This time the position would be permanent. Something was wrong. They didn't understand. Sarah was crying. Steve was crying and the two six- year olds stood and watched as the paramedics effortlessly tried to revive a dead man. Dennis was dead. He had overdosed on heroin and cocaine and his life had come to an abrupt end at the young age of 30..

CHAPTER TWO

Crowes funeral home was located on Sutphin Blvd and Lakewood Avenue.

This is where Dennis was finally laid to rest. The Macks, Dennis' parents, had financed the ceremony. A thing they had repeated once before when they buried Dennis' brother, Daniel who fell victim to the same vicious drug. Surprisingly to Ronnie, the funeral parlor was packed. She didn't realize that Dennis had so many friends and Children! They were all over the place, crying women holding their babies, falling all over the casket. Ronnie couldn't believe her eyes. The cat was out of the bag. These children had resembled hers and Dennis had lived many lives, with many different families. She had thought it was only she and Sarah. It wasn't. When the tally was complete, Dennis had fifteen children by five different women. . Ronnie sat in the front row with her in-laws and her mom, Lilly Byrd. Lily Byrd sat there in front only to support her daughter. She didn't care if Dennis lived or died. In her heart, he had destroyed a good family. She looked over at her daughter who was deeply distraught over a piece of shit nigger. She had not talked much since Dennis' death and she began to lose touch with reality. Lily made it her business to look after her daughter and her grandkids. She would go to her grave seeing that they were all right.

A swift change in attention went from Dennis' casket to the front door of the funeral parlor. A frail looking man in slacks and a white dress shirt and a thin woman in a black dress appeared as everyone stared at them.

"What are they doing here? They are the ones who killed him." Murmurs and whispers traveled through the overcrowded funeral parlor as if everybody had the same thoughts on their minds. Not Ronnie. She knew that Dennis had made his own bed and dug his own grave. Literally. Actually, she felt bad for Sarah, after hearing that she had lost her children to foster care. She remembered her first encounter with Sarah, a working woman who was very beautiful. Today she was not that woman; she was torn. Her skin looked rugged and her hair was thin and shiny; the characteristics of someone with Hepatitis C. Yet, Ronnie did not blame her. She had the right to be here. She too, just like everyone in the parlor had truly loved Dennis. Sarah and Steve walked past the many onlookers and stopped in front of the casket where her soul mate, the love of her life, her best friend laid to rest peacefully without a care in the world. She bent over so only the dead could hear her.

"Dennis?" Sarah said. "I know you can hear me baby," she said as tears streamed from her face. "I know that you're in a better place now. I never seen you in a suit before," she smiled. "You look like you gained fifty pounds," she said rubbing his cheek. "Dee, I wanted to tell you that I love you and so does your child. Don't worry, I'm gonna clean up and get my babies back. I wish I could have them with me so they could see how handsome you look. I'm so sorry Dennis. It was me who led you into this terrible life. It was me baby, my selfish, stupid self. I promise you though Dee, I'll be with you as soon as God permits me. I don't want to be here without you. Dee, why do you have to leave so soon? Oh yeah, I gotta tell you, today I was tested again. I was told that I am HIV positive. I couldn't believe it. When you told me you were negative, I knew that I was good. But when I found out that Steve tested positive last week, I knew there was a possibility that I had gotten it from him since we share the same needles. At least, you don't gotta suffer. Shit, I ain't gonna suffer either Daddy. You take care up there, you hear me? When you see my mom and dad, tell them I said hi and I will be with them soon. I love you Dennis Mack. Take care," Sarah said, as she kissed his lips and walked away, as if nobody else was in the room. Steve took one last look at his younger brother, placed his hand gently on Dennis' forehead and followed Sarah out of the parlor, without acknowledging his parents. Ronnie watched them walk out quickly as they left the funeral parlor probably going somewhere to ease their pain.

"Yeah, you and that dusty home wrecker get the hell outta here faggot," Lily Byrd cussed.

"Ma, now is not the time or place. Plus you've been drinking. Let them be,". Ronnie whispered to her mother.

A few more relatives and friends paid their respects to Dennis. They all said their final goodbyes, gave their sympathies to Ronnie and began to leave the parlor. Prince who was dressed in a three-piece suit and tie, the same color as his father's, walked up to the casket. Barely able to see in it but yet he was able to look into his father's face. Prince closed his eyes and said a prayer that his sister Deb taught him and he began to say his farewells to his dad.

"Daddy? Mommy said when you leave here you're going to heaven. I hear it's nice up there. When I went to church on Easter, the preacher said Heaven is the best place to be. If that's the case, then why are we here? Why didn't we start out in Heaven first?" the six year old asked and continued. "I hope you get to have your car up there, because Heaven is a really, really big place. You're gonna have to drive around. I was hoping that we could go back to Aunt Sarah's to see Dennis. His mom just left but he wasn't with her. When I rode past the house with Grandpa, the windows had wood on them. I think Dennis moved Dad. Anyway, I went to Mr. Pete's store with Mommy and he gave me one hundred cherry balls for free. I asked Mommy do God let you eat candy and she yeah. So here," Prince said, taking out a handful of sticky cherry balls out of his vest pocket and stepping on the stand that held the casket to place them in his father's suit jacket pocket. "Oh my bad Dad," Prince said as he took his cherry balls back from his father's pocket and ate them. "I took two back so you got forty-eight cherry balls. You can share them if you like. The other ones I got are for my brother, Dennis. Mommy said that this ain't the last time I'll see you; so

I hope that I'll see you soon, Dad. I'm not sure I want Mommy crying when I leave for heaven so don't rush me. But, if you get a chance, ride back from heaven and get all of us. We can fit in your station wagon. Mommy drives it. She looks funny driving it. Well Dad, I gotta go. Peanut's mom is taking us skating today. She doesn't like to wait. See you soon Dad, " Prince said as he slapped his father's crossed hands. He jumped down and sat back next to his brothers and sisters who had broken down in hysterical tears. He looked over at his mom who was distraught and crying uncontrollably.

"Don't cry Mom. You said that Dad's in a better place," Prince said as he put his tiny arm around his mother's neck.

The funeral ended. Dennis Mack was finally laid to rest in Pine Lawn Cemetery, in Long Island, New York. Later on that night, family members and select friends met at Ronnie's house for food and drinks to reminisce about the good and bad times of Dennis Mack's short life.

CHAPTER THREE

The Amelia Warner Child Care Services was located in Farmingdale, Long Island.

It was a well-respected establishment that catered to traumatized children. It's founder, Amelia had opened the establishment because she had been a child who grew up in a drug addicted household. Through the help of others who genuinely cared, she was able to become a successful businesswoman. Her agency was highly recommended and no child went unattended to. Every child there was treated like her own with lots of love. Dennis was brought there the day his father overdosed and was waiting to meet his new temporary family.

"Dennis, Hi my name is Robin Anderson. I'm a social worker and I just wanna see how you're doing okay?" the brown skinned lady who was dressed in a two piece suit said.

"Where is my mommy?" Dennis asked without any emotion.

"Well sweetie, that's what I'm here to talk to you about. Your mom is very sick, she's gonna get better; but until she does, we're gonna make sure you're okay."

"Where are my brothers and sisters?" Dennis asked, referring to his other siblings whose father had taken immediately after Dennis's overdose.

"They're in a good place and with God's will, you'll be with them too. Okay?"

"Uh huh," Dennis said.

"Tomorrow, we're gonna take you to meet some really, really nice people who will treat you very nice until we can get you back with your mom, okay?"

"Where's Prince?"

"I'm sorry. I don't think I know who that is," Mrs. Anderson said looking through her paperwork. "Is he your friend?"

"Yeah! He's my best friend in the whole wide world. He's my brother," Dennis said proudly.

"Oh. If he's your brother, he's with another family, Honey," Mrs. Anderson said.

"Noooo. Not that brother. We don't have the same mommy," Dennis said getting agitated.

"I'm sorry sweetie; I didn't understand you. I believe he's at home with his mom. I'll find out for you, okay?"

"Okay," Dennis said, closing his zipper to his Spider-Man book bag that Prince had given him the day their father died.

'Is that your book bag? It's a nice bag.

"Yeah, it's mine."

"Do you want me to hold it for your mommy?"

"No! I'll hold it. My stuff is in here."

"Are your toys in there?" she asked.

"I don't have any toys. My mommy's gonna buy me some toys when she gets her check," Dennis said.

"Oh, that's nice," Mrs. Anderson said. "I'll be back to get you early in the morning, so make sure you get a good night's sleep," she said as she patted Dennis' hand and walked away. It crushed her heart to hear him tell her that he didn't have any toys. She did her best to keep her emotions hidden. If she could, she would take him home herself. She stepped into the hallway as tears streamed down her face. There it was, probably the brightest six year old she had ever met in her twenty years as a social worker and his life has already been filled with so much trauma. She knew the statistics. She just hoped that he would not end up in a jail cell or six feet under before he was sixteen years old.

Dennis shook his head from side to side. This had to be the sixth person that made him promises this week. He had no idea what the next day would bring, but he looked forward to seeing Mrs. Warner later, who promised him ice cream and cookies. He reopened his book bag and recounted his nine single dollar bills once again to make certain that his life's saving was still intact. It was.

◆ ◆ ◆

Dennis sat on his race car bed in his newly decorated bedroom filled with every toy that a child would want or need. He had video games, a basketball, a football, a soccer ball and a whole wardrobe of brand new clothes. He looked at his larger than life television in amazement and watched cartoons. He couldn't remember ever seeing a color T.V.. They had a television at his school, but he barely went. He waited for the two unfamiliar people to enter his new room. They were outside his room whispering, but little did they know. Dennis could hear every word clearly.

"He's really quiet, Marv. Do you think he will like us?" the nervous white woman said to her husband.

"Don't worry Jane, we'll be fine. He doesn't know us yet. Give him some time to get used to us," Marv said.

"I sure hope you're right, Honey. I sure hope so," Janice said entering the room with her husband behind her.

"Um, hi Dennis, is everything ok?" Janice asked.

"Yeah," Dennis said, not taking his eyes off the basketball pictures that hung in his bedroom.

"You like those pictures Dennis? You like basketball?" Marvin asked.

"Yeah"

"You see that picture right there of the tall handsome guy driving the ball against Magic Johnson?"

"Yeah. I love Magic Johnson," Dennis said looking back at Marvin. Then he took a double look back at Marvin. "Ooh dip. That's you?" Dennis said excitedly.

"Yup kiddo, that's me," Marvin said and continued. "I used to play for the New York Knicks; at least until I blew my knee."

"Wow, that's you Mr..."

"Uh uh Dennis. It's not mister anything. It's Marvin or Marv."

"And you can call me Janice or Jane. It's completely up to you," Janice said politely. Dennis began to let his shield down and realized that his temporary family wasn't that bad.

"Do you like all these neat things you have around the place?"

"Yeah," Dennis smiled.

"Well, they're all for you. There's a basketball court downstairs. Anytime you're ready we can go," Marvin said.

"You got a milk crate on the tree here?" Dennis asked.

"Yeah somethin' like that," Marvin said smiling.

"Can we go now?" Dennis asked excitedly.

"We sure can Lil' Man," Marvin said, soliciting a smile from Janice.

"Well I guess this afternoon's plans are final. You guys go and shoot some hoops and I'll have a great big lunch made for you guys when you get back."

"That sounds like a winning plan to me. How about you Dee?" Marvin asked.

"I'll get the ball," Dennis said, grabbing his brand new basketball. He laced up his brand new Converse and put on his Spider-Man book bag.

"Hey, where are you going with the books?" Marv asked.

"They're not my books. It's things in here my best friend gave me," Dennis said proudly.

"Well, I guess I gotta grab my bag too," Marv said as he skipped to his room. Janice smiled as she saw Marvin having the time of his life. He had been married to Janice for ten years and they could not bear a child together. Marv, at one time, was a star on the New York Knicks. After suddenly blowing his knee, he had become depressed. It wasn't until he met Janice, the love of his life, that he started rebuilding his knee and his life. He had many obstacles that he faced; he being a black man, and Janice being a white woman. A beautiful white woman, whose body resembled Jennifer Lopez and a face like Jessica Alba, but people did not accept their love, especially her father. Her father was a respected multi-millionaire banker who wanted his daughter to marry a white Ivy League member. However, Marvin King had not done badly for himself either. He was a self-made millionaire, from smart investing earlier on in his career. Now Marvin had a son; well almost. A little gentleman, who he could spend quality time with, shared his talent by teaching him the game of basketball and most of all, love as a family. Marvin came from his room dressed in sweats carrying his Converse backpack filled with a sport bottle, knee pads and his best friend, Bengay rubbing cream, for after.

"You ready Dee?"

"Yup!"

"Let's go," Marvin said, leading his foster son out of the door.

"Be careful and have fun you guys," Janice said sitting on Dennis' bed as she watched her hopefully, new family walk out of the door.

Janice Rothstein was born in suburban Long Island. She was the only child of wealthy parents and very wealthy grandparents. As a child, she didn't want for anything. Janice's life began to change when she turned thirteen years old. She began to notice changes in her body instantly. Her bottom began to stick out and her perfectly erect boobs were bigger than her teacher's. The abrupt transformation in her body had not been a good thing. All the kids in her school always made fun of her. Some whites went to the extreme by calling her a 'white girl in a nigger's body'. Her parents began to notice her instant growth and immediately hired a nutritionist to monitor her weight and growth. Unfortunately for her parents, Janice's body had the characteristics of a bona-fide black woman. White men were intimidated by her and black men were attracted to her. Janice had her first sexual experience with a boy named Brad. Their parents arranged him for her and it only lasted sixty seconds. She hated everything about Brad, from his pointy nose to his little dick. Instead, she loved Donelle, the love of her life, whom she snuck around with. She eventually ended up getting pregnant by Donelle. She decided to tell her parents. They were ecstatic and full of joy until she confessed that the father was a black man. Donelle was paid a substantial amount of money to stay away and Janice was taken to the family doctor. The abortion had taken two hours and Donelle had disappeared forever.

Today, Janice was happily married to Marvin the love of her life. Her grandfather had left her one hundred million dollars in his will. Because of her abortion at a young age, she could not have children. No amount of money could make her happy; but today she felt joy. Dennis had brought joy to her life. Marvin was the key to her heart and together they made her life complete.

The two ball players, young and old, went down in the elevator of the luxury apartment building, to the state-of-the art indoor gymnasium. When they reached the NBA style basketball court, Dennis stared at the lighted scoreboard in amazement. He had never seen anything like it except for the time he caught a glance of Magic Johnson when they had electricity at home. In his new sneakers and shorts that his parents brought him, he quickly picked up the basketball and started dribbling.

"What do you know about that rock?" Marvin asked.

"This ain't no rock, it's a ball."

"Yeah, you're right, but where I'm from, we call it the rock," Marvin said.

"Oh okay. I guess it's a rock then," Dennis said shrugging his shoulders. He didn't care, he just wanted to play ball. He began to dribble the ball towards an unoccupied rim.

"Use your fingertips Dee."

"Huh?" Dennis asked puzzled.

"Use your finger tips when your dribble, like this," Marvin stole the ball from him and began to demonstrate the proper way of dribbling a basketball. "See, when you use your fingertips, you have much better control of your dribble," Marvin said and passed him back the ball.

"Like this?" Dennis asked as he perfectly demonstrated what he had learned.

'Yeah Lil' Man. Exactly," Marvin said, surprised at how fast Dennis was learning.

"Hey Marv. How's it going?" a thin white man in shorts said as he walked on his way to play indoor tennis.

"Hey Jim. How's it going?"

"Oh fine, thanks. Is that your boy? I didn't know you had a kid," Jim said, being nosey. Marvin paused as he looked at Dennis shooting the ball and replied; "Yes, that's my boy. He just turned six," he lied. He hoped that his lie would soon come true. He joined Dennis on the court and waited for the rebound to fall off the rim. Dennis shot the ball and "swoosh"! Nothing but net right into Marvin's hands.

"Wow! Good shot man. You were almost at the three-point line," Marvin said and threw the ball back so Dennis could shoot again. He caught the ball and was ready to take another shot.

"Hold up Dee," Marvin said, walking towards Dennis. "Let me see the ball." Dennis passed him the ball.

"Look at me. When you shoot the ball, form your elbow into a ninety-degree angle, like this," Marvin said showing, him what he meant and continued. "Line up your fingers with the seams and shoot from the tips of your fingers," Marvin said as he released a three-point shot and "swoosh", nothing but net.

"Here you try, but move a little closer. You ain't strong enough to shoot from this far," Marvin said squeezing Dennis' puny arms, making him laugh. Dennis grabbed the ball, positioned his elbow in a ninety-degree angle and "swoosh" right off his fingertips into the net.

"Good shot Lil' Man!" Marvin said proudly, giving him a high-five. He was amazed as was everybody else who stood around and watched. Here it was a six year old kid who could dribble and shoot the basketball with the same finesse as he; a professional ball player. Right there, Marvin knew that a STAR was born. He would do everything in his power to keep the young star shining. The two ball players played ball for hours. Marvin showed him things such as dribbling drills and opposite hand layup drills. Dennis had passed every single drill with flying colors.

◆ ◆ ◆

Two Years Later – 1986

"Okay class, remember, tomorrow we will assign your cubbies to place your art supplies in, okay?" Ms. Hairston said dismissing her class from their first day of 3rd grade. Janice and Marvin waited outside in front of the small private school. They didn't wanna stand outside the classroom when Dennis was walking out like the other parents. Marvin felt that he would be embarrassed. He was right. The kids walked out the front of the building with their parents to their cars, while Dennis decked out in his uniform walked out of the building by himself.

"Dee!" Janice yelled. Dennis' non-expression was quickly replaced with a smile when he spotted Janice and Marvin leaning on their Toyota Land Cruiser. They jumped in the truck, had taken Dennis to get ice cream and twenty minutes later they were parking in the underground garage of their luxury building.

"Afternoon Mr. and Mrs. King," the doorman said as he opened the door. "Oh hey lil fella, I didn't even see you behind them," the doorman said as Dennis walked through the glass doors.

"How are you and how was your first day of school?" the pleasant doorman asked.

"Oh, it was fine. I drew a portrait of my mother in art today." Dennis said running after Marvin and Janice to the elevator. They arrived at the door of their apartment, to an unexpected surprise. It was Mrs. Anderson from social services waiting for them with a grim look on her face.

"Mrs. Anderson? Hi how are you?" Janice asked nervously.

Her stomach quickly knotted as she felt something terribly wrong.

"Hello Mrs. King, I'm doing okay and how are you Mr. King?"

"Hi, how are you Mrs. Anderson?" Marv asked nervously.

"Hi Dennis. How are you?"

"Hi," was all Dennis said.

"Mr. and Mrs. King, do you mind if we have a quick word? Then I would like to talk to Dennis," Mrs. Anderson said.

"Okay sure. Uh Dennis, go and take your uniform off and put your play clothes on. There is a snack in the kitchen for you," Janice said.

The adults sat down in the living room.

"Would you like anything Mrs. Anderson?"

"No, I'm fine, thanks," Mrs. Anderson said, opening her briefcase, retrieving some paperwork.

"What is this all about Mrs. Anderson?" Janice asked impatiently.

Mrs. Anderson looked into the couple's eyes and saw insecurity. She looked back into her paperwork and said; "Sarah Payne has passed."

"Oh my goodness. That's terrible," Janice said as tears began to flow freely from her face.

"Man! I'm sorry to hear that. I mean, he's just a kid. How do you tell an eight year old that his only living parent will not be coming to get him? We've always told him that we're just holding him until his mom gets better."

"I know. It's sad, very sad. Mr. and Mrs. King, my supervisor sent me here to see if you guys want to legally adopt Dennis. A full evaluation has been done and it appears that you guys are a perfect fit for him. I came by to see if you wanted to make a life for that child, but first I have to speak with Dennis," Mrs. Anderson said.

"Wow," was all Janice could say. She didn't know whether to be happy or sad. She was completely overwhelmed. She has finally gotten her wish. It was unfortunate that it came at the death of another person.

"Let's get Dennis and see how he feels."

"Hey Dee?" Marv called.

"Yes?" Dennis yelled from his bedroom.

"Can you come in here for a sec?"

Dennis dropped the game controller and ran into the living room.

"Yes?" Dennis asked.

"Dee, Mrs. Anderson would like to talk to you, okay?"

"I'm leaving, aren't I?" Dennis asked sadly.

"Oh no honey. You're not leaving. I just wanted to talk to you."

"Oh okay," Dennis said as he watched Janice and Marvin leave the room.

"So, how are you? You are getting so tall," Mrs. Anderson said.

"Yeah, I know. I play basketball too."

"Oh yeah? That's great! Do you like your new school?"

"Yeah, I guess so. My teacher is really nice."

"That's wonderful. How about living here? Is everything ok?"

"Yeah. I just got my new game yesterday."

"That's nice, Dennis," Mrs. Anderson said, softening her tone. "Uh, Dennis?"

"Yes?" he answered.

"It's about your mom. She has passed on. She's in Heaven now. She's with your dad," Mrs. Anderson said. She waited for a response from the young child. He just stood there playing with his fingers with no expression. It seemed as if he was remembering his past life with his mom for the first time since the day he left. He had been having such a great time with Janice and Marvin that he hadn't thought about his mom's house. He actually contemplated calling Marvin and Janice, mom and dad. After all, they had been more of parents to him in the last two years than anyone else had ever been. When he was in his past life, he had gotten burned playing with a cigarette lighter and never even got a band-aid. Once when he was in the kitchen getting some cookies, while Janice was frying chicken, a drop of grease popped on his arm and Janice went ballistic. She immediately rushed him to their private doctor as if he had been shot. He looked up from his hands at Mrs. Anderson and smiled.

"She's safe now."

"Excuse me Dennis, I didn't hear you."

"My mom, she's safe. I saw on T.V., when the man said; when you pass on you're gonna be with God. He said that God will take care of you."

"Yes Dennis. That is true. She is safe now. The man on T.V. was right."

"Yep. One day we'll all be safe with God," Dennis said, as he got up and left the room. Mrs. Anderson wrote her final evaluation on the kid as his parents walked into the room.

"Well, how did it go?" Mrs. Anderson.

"That kid is amazing!" Mrs. Anderson said. She dotted her final "I" and passed the couple the adoption papers.

"Shouldn't we make sure that Dennis wants this?" Janice asked.

"Yes. You are right Mrs. King."

"Hey Dee!"

"Yessss!" Dee said, beginning to get aggravated and put his game on pause and ran into the living room.

"We need to talk to you and then you can go back and play the game. Okay?"

"Okay," Dennis said, sitting between Janice and Marvin.

"Dennis would you like to live here?" Janice asked.

"I do live here."

"No Dennis. We mean forever," Janice said not knowing what else to say.

"Yeahhhhh!" Dennis said excitedly. They didn't know it, but Dennis had prayed for this moment. He heard them talking before, saying that he might have to get placed back with child services. He asked God to keep him here. He loved his foster parents.

"Well today is your day Dennis. You won't be seeing me anymore. My job is done here," Mrs. Anderson said.

"Mrs. Anderson?"

"Yes Dennis?"

"Did you ever find him?"

"Find him? Who Honey?"

"My brother, Prince."

Mrs. Anderson quickly remembered their last conversation about Prince.

"Oh no. I'm sorry Dennis. I couldn't locate him. I haven't heard anything about him. I assume he's with his mom."

"Oh," Dennis said sadly. He left and came back with a white piece of paper.

"Here," Dennis said, giving Mrs. Anderson the paper.

"Oh, this is beautiful," Mrs. Anderson said looking at the picture that Dennis had drawn.

"Who is this beautiful picture of?" she asked already knowing the answer.

"My teacher said draw a picture of your parents. Marvin was too hard to draw, so I drew Janice. She's my mom and I love her," Dennis said and there was not a dry eye in the house. Marvin put his arms around his son and Janice. Mrs. Anderson moved towards the happy family and gave them a group hug.

CHAPTER FOUR

Ring! Ring! Ring!

"Hello?"

"Hello, can I speak to Tasha?"

"Who the hell is this calling my phone for my grand-baby?"

"This is P.I.."

"P.I.? What the hell is a P.I.? What's your real name?"

"My name is Prince, Miss," Prince said, getting agitated and about to hang up the phone on the bitter old lady.

"Grandma, Please! Give me the phone," Tasha said in the background and her grandmother threw the phone across the bed toward her.

"Hey Prince," Tasha said blushing.

"I told you my name is P.I., girl," Prince said smiling.

"Yeah, whatever boy. What are you doing?" Tasha asked.

"Nothin, I'm chillin. How about you?"

"I'm good. I miss you," Tasha whispered so that no one could hear her.

"I miss you too, Ma," Prince said whispering, making fun of her.

"Shut up boy!" she said jokingly.

"Yo what up? Round two or what?" Prince asked, refer-ring to his sex-capade with Tasha.

"I don't know. I gotta see. My grandmother leaves for work at 8 o'clock."

"Aight, I'll be through to get you at 8:30, okay?" Prince asked.

"I said, I don't know P.I.," Tasha said.

"Why don't you know? You wanna spend time with me, right?"

"You know I do," Tasha said.

"So what is it not to know?"

"It's my cousins. They might get me in trouble," Tasha said worriedly.

"Don't worry. We ain't gonna stay out late. I'll get you back before eleven."

"Aight, I'ma page you as soon as she leaves. Okay?" Tasha said.

"Okay Ma," Prince said as he rubbed his dick, just thinking about what would take place in his apartment later on.

"P.I., I'll speak to you later. My grandmother called for her phone," Tasha said with an attitude.

"Okay Ma. Give the old lady her phone," P.I. said laughing.

"You betta shut up boy. Don't talk about my grandma like that," Tasha said as she hung up the phone on the dresser and tried to ease out of the room.

"Come back in here Heifer!" her grandmother yelled.

"Yes Grandma?"

"What do you see in that long-headed boy?"

"Who Grandma?' Tasha asked acting dumb.

"You know who. That long-headed nigga who don't got no respect when he calls my phone. The one who is driving all these fancy cars. What's he doing in a new car every week anyway?

"Those ain't his cars Grandma. They're rental cars," Tasha said.

"If he's driving, he's too old for you. You are only sixteen. How old is he?"

"He's sixteen too!"

"So what's he doing driving, Tasha?"

"I don't know."

"Where's his mama at? She knows he drives them cars around here?"

"She's home. But he doesn't live with her," Tasha said.

"Why doesn't he live with his mother?"

"I don't know Grandma," Tasha said, lying. She knew Prince had his own apartment.

"Yeah right. You know where he lives. Don't lie to me Heifer."

"I'm not a Heifer, Grandma."

"Well, don't act like one. You are always chasing these hoodlums. I see them guys standing on the corners. They dress just like him."

"No, he doesn't Grandma. He plays basketball and he's gonna be a rapper," Tasha said.

"Rapper my ass girl. What about school? I didn't hear you mention nothing about school. Listen Tasha, I wasn't born yesterday, okay?"

"I know that's right," Tasha said under her breath and giggled.

"I heard that. I don't want him around this house when I ain't here. You understand me? I don't want no dope dealers around my damn house."

"He doesn't sell drugs Grandma," Tasha said angrily.

"Yes He Does!" Tasha's cousin said, interjecting the conversation. She had been in the hallway eavesdropping the entire time. "He sells over there on Foch and 142nd Street."

"I knew I seen that long-headed nigga somewhere. He always stands out there in front of that supermarket. Don't he?" Grandma said.

"Yep," the cousin said.

"No, he doesn't," Tasha declared.

"That's ENOUGH! I don't want him in this house, calling this phone and you better stay your fast ass away from him. You understand me?"

Tasha remained silent.

"I Said Do You Understand Me?"

"Yes Grandma. I understand," Tasha said rolling her eyes at her cousin who was enjoying every minute of it

◆ ◆ ◆

Tasha laid in the bed naked with Prince, with her breast exposed and her bottom half covered with the olive colored sheets.

She thought about everything her grandma had said, but she would not listen. She was indeed in love with Prince and nothing would ever change that.

"What's the matter Tasha?" Prince asked while he was rolling his weed in a Dutch Master cigar.

"Nothing! You about to smoke that thing?" Tasha said, frowning up her face.

"Yeah, why?"

"I hate the smell of that stuff," Tasha said.

"Shut up girl."

"No, you shut up. You shouldn't smoke."

"I don't smoke. I smoke weed," Prince said.

"Nigga, weed, cigarettes, it's still smoking," Tasha said.

"Is that what's wrong with you?" Prince asked.

"Nothing is wrong with me."

"So why are you lying there like your dog died?"

"It's my grandmother. She hates you."

"I know," Prince said laughing and lighting the blunt.

"She doesn't want me around you," Tasha said.

"And?" Prince asked.

"What do you mean, And? I'm only 15. I don't have anywhere to go. What if she kicks me out?"

"She ain't kicking you out and if she does, don't worry. You'll be alright," Prince said.

"Yeah uh huh. All that shit sound good nigga."

"Tash, if I said you going to be alright; I mean that," Prince said and took another pull of his blunt and placed it in the ashtray. He began to run his fingers lightly across her firm breast, making her tingle between her legs. She removed the olive sheet and he removed his boxers.

◆ ◆ ◆

Prince walked around in the Associated Supermarket swiftly and with precision. This was his regular Saturday morning routine. He knew exactly what he wanted and he knew exactly where it was, He grabbed a box of Fruity Pebbles cereal, a box of Entenmann's chocolate donuts and a half-gallon of milk. He asked himself if he needed anything else. He didn't. He then proceeded to the express line. He wasn't surprised that the supermarket was crowded on a Saturday morning. He looked briefly towards the magazine section at the latest tabloids and moved up in the express line as the next customer left. He looked to his left and his heart skipped a beat. He had seen her. She was beautiful, definitely older, but beautiful. She stood in the regular line with a shopping cart filled with groceries. Her hair was wrapped held by bobby pins; her grey sweats hung loosely but yet showed her curved body. Her face had been without a doubt the prettiest face he had ever seen in his entire life. Prince stared at the woman as if they were the only ones in the room. He being 16 years old, he knew that she had to be at least eight or ten years older than him. It didn't matter; he had been with older women before. Prince backed out of the line he was standing in, put his items down and went next door to Miss Margie's Flower store. Miss Margie hated Prince because he and his crew hung out in front of her establishment, but she would not turn down money.

Miss. Margie, I need some flowers," Prince said.

"What type of flowers? She said with an attitude.

"Here, hook me up something for a beautiful lady," Prince said, handing her drug money. Business was business. She began to make an arrangement of roses and to his surprise. Miss Margie had really hooked him up.

"Miss Margie, I ain't rushin you but I gotta go," Prince said, rushing her. She handed him the arrangement of flowers and he rushed back next door to the supermarket. When he stepped through the automatic doors he saw her at the cashier getting her items rung up.

"Excuse me Miss?" Prince said with confidence.

"Yes?" she answered.

"I don't do this type of stuff, but I saw you standing in line and you are the prettiest woman I've ever seen in my entire life."

"Awe, thank you! That was really sweet," the woman said smiling.

"Do you mind if I ask your name?" Prince asked.

"I don't mind. My name is Silky," she said as every syllable slid off her tongue beautifully. "And yours?"

"P.I., my peeps call me P.I. My name is Prince though."

"How are you Mr. P.I., nice to meet you."

"Nah the pleasure is all mine, Silky. If you don't mind, I'd like to give you these," Prince said holding the arrangement of assorted long-stemmed roses in front of him

"Awe, these are beautiful. Thank you so much," she blushed.

"It's nothing Ma. You deserve way more than flowers. If I could I would buy you the world," Prince said.

"Um, excuse me Mr. P.I. How old are you?"

"I'm seventeen. I'll be eighteen in two weeks.

"Well at least you're legal," she said rolling her tongue.

"You from around here?" Prince asked, picking up her southern accent.

"No, actually I'm from Maryland. I'm up here visiting my mom. She lives around the corner. She's sick, so I am doing some things for her. How about you, you live around here?" she asked.

"Yeah, I don't live too far from here. I'm just buying some breakfast."

"Oh you live with your mom?" Silky asked, being funny, getting a chuckle from him.

"Nah Ma. I don't live with my mom. I live by myself," Prince said proudly.

It seemed as if all the shoppers had stopped what they were doing and watched the two converse. A young handsome man was trying to court an older woman. A beautiful princess suited for a Prince and he was doing it the old fashion way with flowers and good conversation.

"Girl give him a shot," an older gray haired woman whispered to her from another line.

"Do you have a way I can get in touch with you?" Silky asked.

"Of course, 917-222-1212," Prince said, spitting his number out and to his surprise the cashier had written it down for him. All his cards were going his way. The shoppers were on his side.

"I'll call you later handsome," Silky said, getting smiles from her onlookers. They both were embarrassed, but she gave Prince points for being so bold. Silky finished shopping and headed outside to her car. Prince paid for his groceries and rushed behind her. She was loading her groceries with the help of a young supermarket hustler, who asked if he could help her with her bags. They loaded the trunk of her black BMW 323i convertible and Silky headed to the driver's seat. Prince opened his door to his brand new rental car and placed his bag in the front seat. She looked back over her shoulder and noticed the young Prince and gave him a quick smile and pulled off.

"I'ma see you later cutie," Silky said to herself as she drove off.

Prince didn't know if he scored a point but he definitely put up a hell of an effort. He was about to drive off when one of his homies from Baisley Projects pulled up next to him.

"Yo P.I., what's good boy?"

"Oh shit, Darren, what's up with you?"

"Same shit. Yo check it. They got some Harlem niggas comin' through tonight at IS 8. This nigga they picked up is supposed to be the truth. I heard he dropped 50 points on Boys and Girls High School the other night.

"Oh yeah? Dem Harlem niggas get their heads right. What's his name?

"I think some shit like Sin," Darren said.

"Sin?"

"Yeah, like Cardinal Sin," Darren explained.

"Oh yeah. I think I heard about him when I was getting a haircut at Tim's barbershop."

"So what up?" Billy Medley told me to see if you were playing with us tonight."

"My nig, have you ever seen me back down from competition"? Prince said.

"Now that's what the fuck I'm talkin about," Darren said.

"What time is game time?"

"It starts at seven, but Billy want us there at six"

"I'll be there. We're going to crack their ass," Prince said.

"You already know," Darren said, giving Prince a smirk and pulling off. Prince pulled behind Darren's' Q45 and headed home. Darren was Prince's comrade. They played the point and shooting guard positions very well together. Some say they were the best backcourt in Queens. Prince knew that IS 8 would be crowded to capacity. He and Darren would give them the show they are looking for. He heard some things about Sin and now it was time to see for himself on the court. Prince knew what he was capable of doing on the basketball court. It was second nature to him. It was up to Sin to prove himself.

"Not against me," Prince said, pulling in front of his apartment.

"Yo Ma?"

"Yes Dennis?"

"Can you come in here for a second," Dennis said as he was lacing his sneakers.

"What's the matter Dennis?" Janice asked, standing in the doorway of her son's room.

"Oh it's nothing serious. I just wanted to remind you that my chain is gonna be ready today," Dennis said.

"I know. The jeweler called me this morning. We'll go by and pick it up on your way to your basketball game.

"Oh yeah Ma, I forgot to tell you. Mike is picking us up. We have a team meeting before we go to Queens tonight."

"Okay, so I'll pick it up and it will be here when you get home."

"Thanks Ma, I love you," Dennis said.

"I love you too Dee. You don't have to thank me. Just keep getting those good grades and most importantly, enjoy your birthday," Janice said walking over to where Dennis sat and gave him a kiss on the top of his head.

"Dag Ma. I can't believe I'm seventeen years old. I'm going to get my driver's permit, then you won't have to drive me around."

"That'll be nice."

"Yep, now I can drive Dad's Benz," Dennis said laughing.

"I don't know about that," Janice said leaving the room.

"I will Ma," Dennis said as he finished getting dressed. He unplugged his Motorola phone, put it in his pants pocket, grabbed some money and headed out the door to meet his teammates. Today was his birthday and he had gotten what he wanted. At first his dad was against buying the twenty thousand dollar necklace. It wasn't the money because they were wealthy. With Marvin's great investments and Janice's inheritance, Dennis was set for life. Janice's family didn't agree with her current family arrangements. They hated the fact that she married a black man and worse adopted a black child. It was her life and to her it didn't matter what her family thought. In fact, they weren't her family. Her family consisted of Marvin and Dennis. However, Dennis getting a twenty thousand dollar necklace would draw concern for his safety. Dennis convinced them that the average person wouldn't be able to tell how much the necklace was worth. However, in reality he knew that the necklace would put him in two categories, drug dealer or rapper. He was neither, just a fortunate kid who was adopted by two people who sincerely loved him.

Dennis went down stairs and saw Mike parked out front. Yo-Nitty was sitting in the passenger seat. Yo-Nitty, aka, The Yo-Yo, was a Harlem basketball All Star at the point guard position. Dennis and Yo-Yo paired up, was called the best backcourt in Harlem. Everybody they faced, they destroyed and both of them, being sixteen years old were definitely worth a watch, especially by college scouts. The only problem was Dennis went to high school and Yo-Nitty did not. Yo-Nitty sold drugs on 8th Avenue and lived with his girlfriend. Basketball was his first love, but the streets were his life.

"Yo-Nitty, like, what's good," Dennis said sliding in the back seat.

"Ain't shit. What's good with you Sin?" Yo-Nitty said, extending his hand.

"Nothin man. I'm chillin. Today, a nigga turned seventeen," Dennis said.

"Happy birthday My Dude," Mike said, extending his hand.

"Thanks y'all," Dennis said as Mike pulled off.

"Yo check it, we in Queens tonight. You never been there Sin. The spot is gonna be real live. IS 8 gym is the basketball mecca of NYC. They got these two young niggas, one named Darren and one named P.I. They are the truth for real," Mike said.

"Yeah, them two niggas tough," Yo-Nitty said.

"Word? So we gotta play extra hard huh?"

"Hell yeah. It's gonna be hostile. We gotta bring our A-game tonight," Mike said.

"That ain't a problem. You know how we do," Dennis

said.

"Yo, I ain't playin with them niggas. From the tip-off, I'm breakin somebody's ankles," Yo-Nitty said. Both men knew he was talking about his signature crossover dribble that twisted many opponents' ankles.

"I'm gonna shoot the lights out. I'm looking for my shot early. You feel me Yo-Nitty?"

"I got you Sin. Just spot up and I'll break them niggas down and hit you if you're open. You do the rest. Swish!," Yo-Nitty said referring to Dennis' jump shot that was usually on target.

Dennis sat back as Mike drove uptown to 155th street, Ruckers playground. He had become a young legend at the Ruckers Park. From day one, he knew that this is where he wanted to shine. On the first day, he played a pick up game, hit eleven three- pointers in a row and the last one with his eyes closed. Mike watched closely at the thirteen year old and couldn't believe his eyes. He walked up to the young kid and asked him his name.

"Hey Lil Homie, what's your name?"

"My name is Dennis, but I say it backwards."

"You say it backwards?" Mike said, confused.

"Yeah, Sinned. That's what my peeps call me."

"Okay, okay," Mike said, looking at the medium build teenager. He had the build of an athlete and yet he was only thirteen years old.

Dennis remembered his first tournament game. He walked into the park and was greeted as if Michael Jordan had entered the park. That night, Sin King had made his mark by scoring forty points. A few nights ago he scored fifty in Brooklyn. Tonight, he would claim his fame in the place which brought him so much trauma; South Jamaica Queens.

"Beep! Beep! Beep!" Prince looked down at his hip and saw a too familiar number displayed across his pager; 718-529-9404. It was the pay phone from the block where he hustled. He knew it couldn't be of any importance because there was no code such as "9-1-1" behind the number and it was peculiar to see "718" in front of the number. "Who is this?" he thought to himself.

"Hello,".

"Hey sexy, what are you up to?"

"Who is this?" Prince asked.

"Excuse me! How many ladies do you give flowers to while they are food shopping?"

"Ooh Snap! What's good beautiful?"

"Nothing, Just seeing what's up with you," Silky said.

"What are you doing on my block?" Prince asked.

"This is your block? I thought this was a public pay phone?" Silky said in a sexy tone.

"Nah, not like that Ma. You're on the phone in front of the supermarket, right?"

"Yeah and?"

"It's nothing. It's just that is where I am ninety percent of the time, that's all," Prince said and continued. "I would be right there now, but I'm getting ready for a basketball game tonight."

"Are you going to a game?" Silky asked.

"Yeah, something like that. I play ball. Tonight I have a big game. We're playing some dudes from Harlem."

"I should've known you were an athlete with your sexy self."

"Thanks Ma. You ain't too bad yourself," Prince said blushing. "What's up with tonight, what are you doing?"

"Well my mom is all taken care of. My uncle is there with her. Maybe we could meet up after?" Silky asked.

"Meet up?" Prince said mimicking her southern accent.

"You know what I mean; talk," she said in her beautiful southern accent. "Yall make fun of us and y'all the ones who talk funny," she said smiling.

"Oh yeah? You're funny. But check it, I don't want you on that corner too long. It's dangerous around there. I got a game at 7 o'clock. I gotta meet my team at six. If you feel up to it, you can roll with me. You can watch your boy do his thing. You're more than welcome to come. That's if you ain't busy. Do you know where IS 8 is at?" he asked.

"Excuse me Mr. Prince, I told you I was from Maryland and before Maryland my family lived in the Philippines."

"Oh yeah, my bad beautiful. Look, I'm on my way out the door right now. Get in your car and wait there. I'll be back there before the next song comes on. We'll go get something to eat real quick and I'll show you how to get to IS 8. Only if it's okay with you?"

"Yeah that's fine with me. I love basketball. I go to all the Wizards games in D.C. and I go to Dome games in Baltimore."

"Dome games?" Prince asked.

"Never mind, I still don't see your car," Silky said in a sexy childish tone.

"I'm on my way," Prince said, hanging up his phone. He rushed out the door. He looked down at his pager and saw Tasha's number with a "9-1-1" code behind it. He thought about calling her. "Fuck it. I'll call later. I can't fuck this up. I gotta go meet Shorty," he thought to himself and jumped in his car. Seconds later, Prince was pulling up alongside Silky's BMW. He gave her a head nod to follow him. He pulled off and she followed behind him. Silky drove behind the Ford Taurus and thought she was following a man she didn't know; a younger man at that.

Damn P.I., this fish is good as shit," Silky said taking a big bite out of her sandwich smothered in hot sauce on wheat bread.

"I told you Ma. This is the spot. Not a lot of people are hip to this joint. My mom loves this spot. I like to eat this before I play ball because it ain't too heavy."

"You need to come to Maryland, the seafood capital by the Harbor. You like Alaskan crab legs?" Silky asked.

"I don't think I've had those. They are the ones they sell

in the Chinese restaurant?"

"Nooo silly!" Silky said laughing. "They're humongous crab legs and you eat them with butter sauce."

"They sound good. I gotta check them out and see," Prince said, taking a bite from his sandwich.

"P.I., you know what's crazy?"

"What's that beautiful?"

"I can't believe I'm sitting here eating in front of you. I usually don't eat in front of a man when we first meet."

"Well I'm P.I. and I ain't your average man. I'm the Prince of all Princes."

"I guess you are. I don't know P.I., I just feel comfortable with you," she smiled.

"I feel the same way. I feel like I've known you more than just a few hours (Beep! Beep! Beep!)," Prince said as his pager went off.

"Well?"

"Well what?" he smirked.

"You ain't gonna call her back?" she said.

"Call who back?" Prince said smiling.

"Your girlfriend. The one who keeps paging you?"

"Nah Ma, that ain't my girlfriend. It's my man Darren. It's 6 o'clock and they wanna know where I'm at," Prince said.

"Uh huh. So do you have a girl?" she asked, raising her eyebrows.

"I wouldn't say yea and I wouldn't lie and say no. I talk to a few people," he said honestly.

"You talk to a few people? Do you mean before or after they take their panties off?" she asked as Prince almost spit his ice tea out of his mouth.

'You funny Silky. Nah, I'm saying talk, like it's nothing serious. I don't have a significant lady in my life. I ain't got time. I gotta get bread, I have a lifestyle I gotta pay for. I pay my own bills. I take care of myself," Prince said proudly.

"So, what if I said I gotta get bread and I don't play games or "talk" and I too take care of myself," Silky said looking at

Prince.

"Then it is what it is. I can't lie. For you Ma, I'll change the game up for you. I'll do anything to be a part of your circle. I wanna give you flowers everyday for the rest of your life," Prince said looking directly into her eyes.

"Even if I wasn't beautiful," she said.

"I can't imagine you not being beautiful. It's genetically impossible. Thank God for your mammy and your pappy," Prince said smiling as he twirled his finger in her silky hair.

"Boy shut up," Silky said pushing against his strong shoulders.

"Ooh shit!" Prince said looking at the clock on his dashboard, startling Silky. "It's ten to seven. I was supposed to meet them niggas at the gym at six o'clock. Yo, you still wanna roll with me?"

"Of course I wanna come," Silky said seductively.

"Okay good," Price said as if he didn't catch on to her sexual invitation. He knew that he was close to fucking one of the prettiest chicks he had ever seen. Silky sat next to him and her caramel complexion glowed under the car light. Her facial features showed no flaws as the half Filipino, half black beauty sipped on her ice tea through a straw. She looked better than Kimora Lee Simmons, but you could tell they were from the same tribe.

"So you want me to follow you right?" she asked.

"Yeah. Follow me," Prince said as he got an unsuspected kiss on the cheek.

"Thanks for a nice first date," she said and got out of his car.

"Damn, I think I scored. Big Time!"

It was Saturday night, July 1st and IS 8 Junior High School gymnasium was packed. Harlem was definitely in the building. They arrived twenty cars deep to cheer on their Harlem

All Stars; Sin and Yo-Nitty. Prince arrived a few minutes after seven with Silky behind him and all eyes were on her. Even the women were staring at Silky's beauty. Prince and Silky headed over to where his team sat and showed her where to sit behind his team's bench. Prince took off his diamond and white gold necklace that was weighed down with a diamond studded key. He walked over to Silky and placed his chain over her head. He began to get dressed in his basketball shorts and warm up with his team. Silky watched on in anticipation as the energy in the gym was about to blow off the roof. Harlem made hella noise as they watched Yo-Yo do tricks while on the lay-up line. Sin, then grabbed a pass and pulled up behind the three point line and "Swoosh!" nothing but the bottom of the net. Prince looked in their direction while he stretched his legs on his end of the court.

"Yo P.I., you late my nig. You ready?" Darren said slapping him five and helping him off the floor.

"You already know. I'm always ready. I'm watching Son. I see he got a jump shot; huh? He knocks them shits down from everywhere."

"Yeah, that's the nigga Sin. I'ma guard him. I ain't givin' Son no room to get shit off. Hopefully he doesn't click them shits like he's doing on the lay-up line," Darren said.

"Don't worry about that . We're gonna crack their asses. Yo, them Harlem niggas is here deep as a motherfucker. They got that whole side," Prince said looking into the bleaches.

"Yeah, they are in the building. Fuck em yo. Yo, who the fuck is that you walked in here with? I thought that was Kimora Lee. That bitch is baddd, Son," Darren said looking in Silky's direction.

"Oh, that's something new. She is from outta town," Prince said modestly.

"Yeah, she looks like she ain't from this planet. I ain't never see a bitch that bad. She got sisters?"

"Dee, we're gonna holla later. Let's get focused. We gotta get on this lay-up line and warm up," Prince said grabbing the basketball from one of his teammates. His team lined up and began to lay the ball in the rim. Prince's first warm up shot was a hard dribble with his left hand to the rim where he completed a reverse dunk that awakened the South Jamaica, Queens fans. Darren followed behind him and pulled up behind the three point line and shot a left handed three pointer and "swoosh" nothing but the net; oohing the crowd because they all knew he was right handed.

The whistle blew. Playtime was over. It was time for Harlem and Queens to get busy. The referees summoned both teams to their benches so the game could begin. Both starting fives headed to half court for the jump ball. Each player greeted each other with handshakes. Darren and Sin greeted each other and Prince greeted Yo-Nitty whom he knew already from prior games.

"Yo P.I., this my son Sin," Nitty said, introducing Sin to Prince.

"Okay. What's good Sin. I heard some things about you."

"Same stuff. I heard some things about you too," Sin said.

"Yo where are you from? You live in Harlem too?" Prince asked.

"Yeah, I'm from uptown," Sin answered.

The referee threw the ball in the air and the game was on. Prince's center Slim won the tap and passed the ball to Darren. He dribbled the ball up the court and waited for his team to set up.

"Two, two, two," Darren said referring to Prince as the two guard. Slim set the back door screen for Prince. Prince rolled off the screen and elevated to meet an awaiting alley-oop, thrown by Darren and dunked the ball viciously on Harlem's big man head while drawing the foul.

"Yeah nigga. And one," the crowd yelled as Harlem sat there shocked while Prince shot his free throw. Silky sat there in amazement as she watched Prince set the tone of the game. After Prince made the extra point, Harlem's big man grabbed the ball out the net and passed the ball to Yo-Yo. Prince knew not to play him up close or he would become a spectacle of Yo-Nitty's tricks. Nitty dribbled the ball as he skipped up the court with his yo-yo in his hand. He reached half court where Slim and Prince double-teamed him and this is exactly what Yo-Yo wanted. He took a quick mental picture of the court, threw the ball behind his back catching it with his opposite hand and swiftly spinning the ball through Prince's legs and around Slim's back. He continued to dribble as the Harlem crowd went crazy as he had just made a fool out of Prince. He broke down another defender who headed towards him and saw a wide-open Sin cutting quickly towards the basket. He hit Sin with a no look pass. Sin caught the pass and could have easily scored two points. Instead he waited for Darren to catch up and play defense. Once Darren was back in Sin's face, Sin dribbled behind his back and backed towards the three-point line. Sin rose and shot the ball, turned to the Harlem crowd and put up "three fingers" without watching the ball go through the rim.

"Three up," Sin yelled loudly as the Harlem crowd went crazy. The game went on with oohs and aahs giving the crowd exactly what they came to see. After three quarters, the score was tied at seventy-five. The fourth quarter would begin in seconds.

"Yo check it, we gotta play some defense in this quarter. Don't let that nigga Sin touch the ball. He ain't missin. Try to put a hand in his face," Billy said.

"My hand is in that nigga's face. That nigga won't miss," Darren said with exhaustion. Sin had made ten three pointers. He only missed one shot at the end of half time and that was from half court.

"Yo P.I., you keep attacking. They can't hold you," Billy said. Prince had forty points already and the fourth quarter was still under way.

"Good luck P.I.," Silky yelled from her seat as she knew it was a very close game. She was enjoying the show that P.I. and Sin had put on thus far.

"Yo, this is our quarter. We gotta put them away," Yo-Nitty said.

"Yeah, we got these niggas. I ain't playing no games this quarter," Sin said.

"Listen, just play yall game. Don't do anything different. Yall is playing excellent. Have fun and let's go back to Harlem with the win. Come on, let's put it in. Make money on three. One-Two-Three, MAKE MONEY." The team yelled in unison revving up the Harlem crowd.

"Yo, this is it yall; Southside on three. One-Two-Three; SOUTHSIDE!" The Queens team yelled, getting the crowd hype.

"Tasha, who is that bitch wearing P.I.'s chain?" Tasha's friend asked.

"Girl paleeze! Ain't nobody stressin him. You see all these niggas here stressin us?" Tasha said looking over at Silky with a jealous smile. She was visibly upset, however, she was liking all the attention she was receiving.

"Girl you see number fourteen on Harlem's team?"

"Yeah, why?" Tasha asked.

"That nigga keep staring at you."

"Nikky, shut up bitch," Tasha said smiling.

"Tasha, I'm serious. Just watch him. He's a damn cutie. He kind of reminds me of P.I. They both got big heads," Nikki said laughing.

"Girl you are so crazy," Tasha said smiling while looking in P.I.'s direction. She was upset, but in her eyes it was Prince's loss. She had seen him parked by the fish spot while she was riding with her grandmother. She saw his new friend sitting in his car. When she paged him and he didn't answer, she began to cry. He had used her. He had sexed her and threw her to the curb. She should have listened to her grandmother who warned her. She wanted to walk up to him and let him know that she hadn't gotten her monthly period, but he would only embarrass her. Plus, it was impossible that she could be pregnant. Tasha continued to sit there and look sexy when a young hustler from Harlem sat next to her. Prince came on Harlem's end of the court and saw her talking with the young hustler. He smirked and continued to play knowing what he had parked behind his bench. He had A Top Model waiting for him.

It was thirty seconds left in the game and Harlem was winning by two points with the ball. Sin brought the ball across half court and P.I. had Yo-Nitty on lockdown denying him the ball. Sin dribbled around Darren and saw his big man cutting towards the rim. Sin threw the no-look pass to the big man who was not ready for the ball. The ball went through his hands and out of bounds.

"Time out!" Darren yelled with seven second left in the game. The ball was advanced to half court and Queens would have a chance to win the game or tie it up.

"Yo look, they're gonna be on you P.I.. I want the ball in Darren's hands. Stack it up at half court. Yo Slim, you slide off and set the pick for Darren. P.I. you cut straight to the basket. Dee you pop out to the corner behind the three-point line. We're going to live or die by this," Billy said sternly.

"Yo, P.I. if you open, I'ma hit you with the extra pass," Darren said.

"Just put it in the air by the rim and its two points." Prince said with confidence.

The whistle blew and the South Jamaica team executed the play as if the great Phil Jackson designed it. Darren caught the ball in the corner and saw surprisingly an open Prince cutting towards the basket. Prince elevated and dunked the ball viciously over Harlem's big man drawing two points and the foul with the chance to win the game.

"Yeah motherfuckers. SOUTHSIDE! SOUTHSIDE! The crowd yelled and chanted as Prince banged on his chest like a silverback gorilla. With three seconds left Prince went to the line and made the free throw, putting his team ahead by one point. Harlem had one chance to win the game, but that chance was taken away by a steal from Darren. Sin walked up to Prince and shook his hand.

"Yo, good game son. You the truth," Sin said, giving him a firm handshake.

"Nah son, you the real deal. I ain't never seen a nigga shoot like you," P.I. said.

"Thanks man. I'll see you next week when yall come to our house right?"

"You already know. We'll be there," Prince said.

"Okay. Be easy," Sin said.

"You too. Both men parted and went back to their benches.

"That was a really nice game P.I.," Silky said, giving Prince his props. He walked over to her and kissed her on her cheek. He didn't even notice Tasha walking behind him and slapping him all over his head. Prince raised his hand trying to block her hits.

"Tasha, what's wrong with you girl?"

"Nothin. Fuck you nigga. You bitch," she said and walked away with tears in her eyes.

"I guess you should have called her back," Silky said.

"Now you see why I didn't call her back," Prince said shaking his head while getting dressed.

"Is she someone you "talk" to?"

"Shit, not anymore. I don't need the headache."

"Oh here," Silky said, passing him his chain.

"Nah, hold it. So what's on the agenda for later?" Prince asked.

"You tell me," Silky said seductively.

"Come on, let's get out of here," Prince grabbed her hand and they left the gym.

CHAPTER FIVE

"1997"

The Park Central Hotel located on the Union Turnpike was two minutes off the Grand Central Parkway.

Prince decided to take Silky there because he felt it was somewhat of a decent spot that wasn't too far. Plus at 17 years old, he hadn't been to too many places in his lifetime. Prince went in and checked for vacancies. When he found out there were, he paid $250 and went back outside to get Silky. He looked at her through her window; she was dozing off. He admired her beauty. He had scored. Silky was more than a catch of the day. She was the catch of the century. Prince saw how all the other ballers' eyes were glued to Silky when they walked through the gym together. She had her own car, her own crib and from the looks of her appearance, she had her own profession back home in Maryland. He wondered for a moment how this could have happened. How could a young hustler get so lucky with a woman of such caliber? He popped his collar and smiled to himself. "I'm the shit, that's why." Prince used the key to open the door of room #142. Silky immediately went to the bathroom and Prince couldn't barely hide his excitement. He looked at himself in the overhead mirror and saw the dried sweat on his forehead from the basketball game. He began to undress in route to the shower when Silky stepped out of the bathroom wearing a pink Victoria Secret set that consisted of boy shorts and matching bra. Prince stood in amazement at her beauty while she wrapped her Silky hair around her head.

"What are you staring at?" she asked looking at his erection through his boxers.

"Damn my bad Ma. I can't help it," he said.

"Awe baby, you sure know how to make a woman feel good," Silky said, turning towards him and walking up to him. She stuck her tongue in his mouth giving him his first taste.

"Go take a shower. I'll be here waiting for you," she said, releasing the back of his head and letting him go to the shower. Prince rushed in the bathroom and took a two-minute shower and was back where they left off, standing in front of Silky. She began to massage his muscular body with her soft hands moving down to his dick. She pulled his dick through his boxers and stroked it as she kissed lightly on his neck, shoulders and chest. She slowly kissed around his ripped stomach and now she had the shaft of his dick in her hand and the head in her mouth.

"Damn Ma. That shit feels good," Prince said as her hot tongue circled the head of his dick, making his body shake as if a cold chill ran through it. She began to suck hard on the head of his dick while she lightly massaged his balls.

"Ooh daddy, you taste good," she said as she began to take more of him in her mouth. She began to gather as much spit as she could and lather his dick so that it felt like it was in her pussy. She began to bob back and forth slipping and slobbering, taking him as a whole, which felt like his dick was past her tonsils. She sucked and sucked causing him to grab the back of her head.

"Go ahead Daddy, hold me on you. Cum in my mouth I want to swallow every bit of you, okay, Daddy?" she mumbled in between sucks.

"Yeah, do you," he said, shaking his head in disbelief.

"Fuck my mouth P.I.," she said as Prince began to stroke back and forth until he felt the best feeling in his entire life. Every bit of cream that he possessed at that time, shot to the tip of his dick as he came uncontrollably in Silky's mouth. She sucked and jerked his dick at the same time, at times backing away so he could see his cum in her mouth.

"Yeah Ma, swallow that," he ordered.

"Yes Daddy, I'm swallowing it all," she said as she sucked

the last drop out of his erect dick. "Kiss me baby", she instructed. He began to kiss Silky on the back of her neck.

"Your lips are so soft," she moaned. He kissed her lightly on her forehead and her face and said; "Fuck it", sticking his tongue in her mouth, sucking her tongue real hard. He made his way down to her chest area and kissed on her perfectly erect nipples.

"No baby, not yet. Can I teach you how to kiss me?" she asked.

"You can teach me anything," Prince said, kissing her on her beautiful face.

"Kiss me around my titties first. Try to stay away from my nipples." He did as she instructed and she began to rub her dripping pussy. "Okay baby, now lightly lick each nipple as if it was the most gentle thing in your world. Nobody else's world, your world. Yeah just like that," she moaned as Prince lightly licked her nipples causing her to moan.

"Now baby, slide down and stick your tongue in my belly button." He did just that and she began to remove her boy shorts and now Prince was face to face with her perfectly trimmed pussy.

"Okay baby, this is where I want you to put all the love, hate, envy, lust, energy and expertise," she said. She did not know that Prince had never been in this area with his tongue.

"Here taste it," she said as she stuck her cum dripped finger in his mouth.

"You like?"

"I love!" he said and began to kiss on her pussy.

"Baby you see this right here?"

"Yeah."

"This is the key to every woman's body and this is your key," Silky said, massaging her clitorous, making it jump.

"Now take your tongue and lick it as if it was your favorite candy."

"Cherry balls," he smiled to himself.

"Ooooooooh my goodness baby. Yes! Yes! Yes! Yes! Just like

that," Silky moaned and she had no reason to instruct any further to the young student. It was evident that he was a natural. Prince sucked and licked all the right spots as she squirmed trying to get away from the killer tongue. Prince held tightly on her ass cheeks as he ate her pussy like it was his last supper before an execution. He licked the wetness between her legs making her shake as if she were having a seizure.

"Ooooh Babbby, P.I., I'm, I'm, I'm about to cccuuummm."

"Cum for me Ma. I wanna taste it," Prince said not realizing that his middle finger danced around the rim of her asshole driving her crazy.

"Ooh my God, right there. Keep your finger right there baby. I'm about toooo." To his surprise, Silky squirted her cum all over his face. In his entire sexual life, he had never seen such an act. She squirted so much cum, it looked as if she was spraying milk out of a garden hose that she had between her legs. He opened his mouth and tried to catch every bit of her like a kid in front of a sprinkler.

"I'm sorry baby. I should've warned you," Silky said looking down and saw his face covered in white cream. She began to lick her cum off his face.

"Baby, you okay?" she asked.

"Yeah, I'm good."

"Well," she said, turning her back to him and bending over the bed. "Fuck me. Fuck me real hard and fast. We got all night to make love. Get your nut off in me. I don't care if you cum quick. Do what you want with me, any hole," Silky said with her ass positioned so he could stick her with ease. Prince entered her juicy pussy and stroked slowly at first then picking up his pace. While he fucked her pussy, Silky fucked herself with her middle finger in her ass.

"Yeah, I like it. I love it Daddy. Just like that," she moaned with pleasure.

"You like that?"

"Yessss I love it!" she tried to say as Prince slid in and out with a rhythm hitting her every spot. He remembered what an

O.G. had told him about fucking. "You gotta hit her with at least one thousand strokes before you even think about cumming. Concentrate on not cumming. Think about anything else besides pussy." Prince thought about those magic words as Silky looked back at him in amazement as he stroked her hard and fast.

"Ooh baby, you fucking the shit out of me. I'm about to cum again, ooohhh."

"Me too," he said as sweat dripped from their bodies. He felt a spraying sensation hitting his shaft as he stroked faster and exploded deeply inside her.

"I'm cummin too Ma. I'm cummin too."

"It's okay. Cum daddy. I said do what you want," Silky said wiggling her ass shaking his excess cum out of his dick with her pussy. She put his soft dick in her mouth and sucked the last of him. They both took another shower, went to the bed and Silky taught him some beautiful things. She taught him the art of eating, fucking and finally, the art of making love to a beautiful woman. It was final. A match was made. Prince laid and stared at the woman he would come to spend the rest of his life with. They would become unbreakable....almost.

CHAPTER SIX

"1997"

Yo Pop, where Kah at?" P.I. asked.

"P.I., what's good? That nigger just pulled off. He said he'd be right back," Pop said as Prince walked up on his team that was hustling in front of an old abandoned house.

"Yo, T.N.T is setting up down the block. Tell Sha to chill for a little while," Prince said referring to one of the workers who sold crack and cocaine for him.

"Nigga you late. You didn't see all them customers standing around waiting for us to open back up?

"Yeah, I thought they were waiting for Sha to come out the hole."

"Nah, I told Sha to step off. That's them parked right there in that cable truck. Them stupid motherfuckers don't think we see them."

"Damn, I didn't see them Yo, let's go to Ajax Park and play some ball. Leave this block for a little. Feel me?"

"That sounds like a plan to me. I got the block money in the car," Pop said as he saw his stepfather walking up the block.

"Damn that's my mom's husband. He's looking for coke," Pop said.

"Well, we're closed. He better go up the block to Rockaway Blvd, because we ain't workin," Prince said as the cable van drove by.

"Nah they left. The other van went toward Van Wyck," Sha said as he rode up on his pedal bike,

"You sure Sha?" Pop asked.

"Yeah, they gone. I'm positive. What your Pops want?"

Sha said smiling at Pop.

"Nigga you see he got two fingers up. He wants two dimes of coke," Pop said.

"I got that on me. I got these last two dimes cheeked," Sha said digging in his ass and pulling out two glass vials of coke that was stashed between his butt cheeks.

"Eeww nigga. The tops are supposed to be white. They are brown now. They got shit on them," Pop said with his face turned up and Prince shook his head smiling at Pops comments.

"Yo here. Put these in your mouth. It's wild hot out here. T.N.T. is everywhere." Without thinking Pop's stepfather dropped the twenty-dollar bill on the ground and placed the two shitty vials in his mouth.

"Yo what the fu…" Pop's stepfather began to say as he saw Pop and Prince burst into laughter as they walked away. Sha rode on his bike.

"That nigga Sha is a foul nigga," Prince said as he and Pop continued to laugh and head towards Pop's rental car.

After the game with Harlem and Queens at I.S 8, where Tasha and Sin had first met, they had been spending a lot of time together. Sin traveled to Queens to visit Tasha at her grandma's house. She met him in Harlem once but he didn't take her to his house. He liked Tasha and he wanted her to like him for who he was and not for what he had. Luckily for Sin, Tasha's grandmother liked him also, so he was able to chill at her house without any problems. They sat on the steps in front of Tasha's house with her family.

"Sin, you play basketball for your school," Tasha's aunt Tracey asked, trying to look sexy.

"Yes ma'am," Sin answered.

"Yes ma'am? Um, where the hell was your type when I was coming up? The only time I heard ma'am was when a nigga wanted some pussy," Tracy said laughing; making Sin blush and embarrassing Tasha.

"Nah, that's how I was taught, to respect women. I can't help it," Sin said.

"Ooh noo baby! It ain't nothing wrong with it. You need to teach some of these nasty motherfuckers around here some manners."

"Tracey!" Tasha yelled getting tired of her.

"Okay heifer. I'ma go get a 40 ounce of beer from the store. Yall want something," Tracey said, getting up intentionally putting her big ass in Sin's face.

"Yo, your aunt is crazy,' Sin said shaking his head.

"I know. They all get me sick. I hate this house. I gotta get outta here, I swear!" she said, shaking her head.

"And go where? You got money?"

"No, but I'm leaving, watch me. I'ma get me a job and I'm leaving. I just don't wanna leave my grandma here by herself with all my cousins. I graduate next year and after that I'm leaving."

"I graduate too, and I'm going away to college. You gonna be here waiting for me when I get back?" Sin asked, rubbing her thigh.

"I ain't gonna be here waiting. But I'll be somewhere waiting for you," Tasha said.

"Yo Tash?

"Huh?"

"I gotta tell you somethin. I've never told a girl this," Sin said turning directly towards her looking in her eyes.

"Ooh my goodness. This is the part when you leave me?"

"Shut up girl. Let me finish," Sin said smiling.

"Well, what is it Sin?"

"Yo Tash. I'm not sure what it's supposed to feel like, but think I'm in love with you.

"You think?" Tasha asked.

"Yeah, I think. I mean, I don't know what it's supposed to feel like but I gotta feeling in my stomach when I'm around you. I've never loved a girl before and it's not because we had sex. I mean, I used to get groupies all the time.

"Excuse me?"

"Girl cut it out. You know what I mean. I play ball. Everybody thinks I'm their meal ticket out the hood," Sin said.

"I know Sin, and that scares me. I'm in love with you too. I feel like God has sent you to me," Tasha said looking into his glassy eyes. She knew that her next statement would make or break their relationship; as a tear fell freely from her eyes.

"Yo, why are you cryin Tash?

"Because," Tasha sobbed.

"Because what?" he asked, looking at her worried.

"I'm pregnant, Sin."

"What?"

"You heard me. I'm pregnant," Tasha said, wiping her nose with her hand.

"Damn. We used condoms Tash," Sin said.

"I know you did Sin. It ain't yours."

"What da fuck!" he yelled.

"No baby. You don't understand. I was pregnant before we met."

"And you knew?" he asked.

"Yeah I knew. I was getting rid of it. I didn't know how to tell you."

"You *was* getting rid of it?"

"Yeah I was. I don't know now. I'm scared. I went to the doctor and I'm thirteen weeks.

"4, 8, 12, damn, that's three months," Sin said, doing the math.

"I know Sin. I'm really scared. The doctors said the baby's heart beats at three months."

"Wow."

"I'm sorry Sin. If you wanna go, you can leave. I'm going inside," Tasha said getting up off the steps."

"No Tash, wait. It's not your fault. There is someone else involved. Where's the father?"

"He doesn't know. You're the first person I told."

Damn," Sin said rubbing his head. His world had crashed down on him.

"I told you, you could leave. It's not your problem Sin".

"Listen Tash. I just told you how I felt about you. Whatever decision you make, I'ma try my best to support you. I'm just shocked to hear this, that's all."

"I know Sin. How do you think I feel? You see, I have no mother, no father, no sisters or brothers. I live with my grandma and I'm three months pregnant. How do you think I feel?"

"I can only imagine Tash. I can only imagine. So who's the father? If you tell him, will he help you out?"

"I don't know what he'll say. He's such an asshole. He got his little girlfriend and he won't answer my calls. He thinks I'm calling to get back at him and I'm not. I don't want nothing to do with him; I swear," Tasha said, shaking her head. "You know him Sin, at least you know of him," Tasha said.

"I know him? Who is he?"

"They call him P.I. He's the one you played against that night," Tasha said.

"Ooh shit!! That's why you slapped him up?" Sin said, smiling.

"Shut up silly," she said pushing his forehead.

"Damn. Son seems like an aight dude," Sin said.

"Yeah, that's what I thought, but lately he's been acting like an asshole. I don't know how he's gonna react to this," Tasha said.

"Well, you're gonna have to let him know Tash."

" I know Sin. I know," Tasha said and sat back down between his legs.

"Until then, we gotta prepare for the little Tasha to enter the world. I ain't leaving you for nothing. This is gonna be my reason to go extra hard with this basketball shit. I'm gonna give you the life you deserve. Trust me, I know what it feels like to be alone; to be without a mother and without a father," Sin said as he began to tell Tasha the truth about his past life and now his new life as an adopted son of rich parents.

"Hey Boo, where are you?"

"Hey, what's up Silk? I'm on the block. I got a game uptown tonight. Why, what up?"

"Oh nothing, just calling to tell you I love you and I miss you. That's all."

"I love you and miss you too Ma. You rollin 'with me tonight or what?" Prince asked.

"No. I can't baby. I promised mommy I would make shrimp fried rice and watch Godfather's I, II, and III with her," Silky said laughing.

"Yo, put a plate aside for me babe. Give you mom a kiss for me. I'll be there to get you after the game."

"Okay. Call me when you get to Harlem."

"Of course. That's a must. I gotta hear my baby's voice before I crack Harlem's ass," Prince said smiling.

"Oh yeah baby, one more thing."

"What up?"

"Get the car washed. The inside is filthy. I know you noticed it when you got in," Silky said.

"That's what I'm doing right now. Wilbur is vacuuming the inside as we speak. See, we think alike."

"Yeah, we're on the same page. I love you. I'll speak to you later. Okay?"

"Okay, Ma, later," P.I. said, ending the call. He looked down and saw Tasha's number across his pager, He shook his head.

"I wish this girl would leave me alone," he said to himself as he sat back and watched Wilbur clean his car for a few vials of crack.

CHAPTER SEVEN

"1997"

Harlem 155th 8th Avenue

It was a beautiful summer day in Harlem, New York.

The sun was shining; the children were playing in the water that shot from the fire hydrants. Young mothers sat in front of their apartment buildings with their children on display who wore the latest fashions. Hustlers were hitting licks, elderly men sat around card tables and drank whatever they preferred. The police car sirens roared up and down 8th Avenue without a target, with the intent of disrupting a beautiful summer day in Harlem. Nothing would stop the show that would be held in Ruckers Park on 155th and 8th avenue. Sophisticated women and hood rats held their positions as exotic cars pulled up. An NBA player pulled in front of the park in a brand new Bentley convertible, getting attention drawn to him and his passenger. Prince and Darren had circled the block a few times looking for a parking spot for the black 1997 BMW convertible; to no avail. They had to settle for parking on 8th avenue in front of a building that had five beautiful women sitting in front of it. Prince closed the electric hard top, putting on a show for the on-lookers. He grabbed his gym bag and headed down 8th avenue, but not before they hollered at the women. The women gave both men compliments on their dress and jewelry. Darren vowed to holla back at a specific one after the game. When he reached the park, police were turning people away from entering. It was too crowded. Prince had gotten the attention of their coach Billy, who was waiting at the entrance for his star player. After getting escorted through the barriers without hassle, Prince and Darren couldn't believe what they saw. It was Tasha and Sin getting out of the back of a 1997 Mercedes Benz S600. All eyes were on Tasha and Sin as the crowd roared at the sight of the Harlem All-Star, Sin. It was to Prince's surprise to see how Tasha had matured physically in such a short time. She was extremely thicker and every curve showed through her summer dress. She waited for Sin to get his gym bag as the driver of the Benz parked on the sidewalk without any hassles. Tasha stepped lively with her man as he headed through the police barriers heading to Sin's bench. Marvelous Marvin King got out of the Benz and followed behind them.

"Yo, ain't that Marvelous Marvin King?" Darren asked.

"Yeah, I think so."

"Yo, what is Sin and Tasha doin with that nigga?" Darren asked out loud.

"That's Sin's pops nigga, everybody knows that," a nosey bystander said answering Darren' question.

"Oh thanks, Oprah. You stupid motherfucker; who asked you?" Darren said laughing.

"Your mama," the nosey man said and hurried through the busy crowd; eliciting laughter from both Darren and Prince.

"Now I see where son got his jump shot from. His pop was a beast on the Knicks," Prince said as he and Darren joined their team at the bench. Prince sat down and began to change into his basketball gear when Tasha walked up on him.

"Hey P.I."

"Oh, what up Tash. What are you doing here?" Prince said acting as if he didn't see her.

"Nigga, I know you got my pages. I beeped you a million times, P.I."

"What are you beeping me for? I see you got your hands full already," Prince said looking in Sin's direction.

"Yeah, but what does that have to do with you callin me back? I really need to talk to you."

"Listen Tash, now is not the time. I gotta stretch for this game. I'll talk after the game or I'll give you a call at home."

"I guess I'll talk to you later then. You can't call me at home. I don't live there," Tasha said as she spun off putting an extra twitch in her switch as every curve her body sashayed back and forth. Prince couldn't help but to look at her new shapely fat ass. Just as he went into a trance, his mobile phone went off ; it was his dime piece. Tasha was nice looking, but she was nothing compared to Silky. Prince said to himself and opened his Motorola flip phone.

"You, what up Ma?"

"Hey baby, you ok?"

"Yeah I'm good. I'm about to stretch and warm up. What are you doin?"

"I just came back from the fish market. I picked some fresh fish and shrimp, I'm about to clean these shrimp and start frying them, Baby these shrimp are big as hell. You should see em," Silky said.

"Yo remember what I said. Put mine to the side."

"I got you Boo. I told you, I'm gonna take care of you Baby. That's for life," Silky said.

"So far so good. Look, I gotta go Ma. I'll call you when I'm on my way."

"Okay Babe," Silky said.

"Okay Ma."

P.I.?"

"Yeah Silky?"

"I love you daddy."

"I love you too Silk," Prince said, smiling and ending his call.

The whistle blew and all players were ordered to their benches. Sin and his team danced around in a circle formation as the rowdy Harlem crowd cheered them on. Prince and his team sat on the bench and listened carefully to their coach's instructions. The whistle blew again and the starting five players were ordered to half court. The game was set to begin and Harlem was out for revenge and blood.

"Yo, y'all already know. We do the same shit we did on

our court. South Side on three. One, Two, Three, South Side," the team yelled in unison and walked to half court. Harlem fans booed the South Jamaica team and were ready for Harlem's superstars to step on court.

"Listen, they stole one in Queens. This is our house; we go out and smash them from the start. Harlem World on three. One, Two, Three, Harlem World," they yelled along with the fans making the sound travel to 8th Avenue. "Yo-Nitty and Sin lead their team to half court and now both teams were faced-off on one of the most famous playgrounds in the country. Sin and Prince greeted each other but both men knew that after today their relationship would change.

The basketball was tossed in the air and just as expected South Jamaica Queens and the Harlem USA All-stars had definitely entertained the fans. The park was jammed packed and Yo-Nitty (Yo-Yo) entertained the crowd with his Globetrotter dribbling. There was one play in which he brought the ball up the court on his knees. Prince stepped up to play defense and then Yo-Yo put the ball through the back of Prince's jersey. Prince turned to see where the ball had gone and was called for traveling with the ball. The crowd went crazy but Sin stole the show. After Prince came down and caught a thunderous dunk, Harlem's center grabbed the ball out of the net, took it out of bounds and passed it to Sin. Sin from the opposite end of their basket, launched a three pointer. Before the ball sunk through the net, Sin raised three fingers and hollered "Harlem", making the crowd go bananas. Play after play the crowd oohed and aahed. Tasha and Mr. King sat and watched Sin make shot after shot; he couldn't miss. At half time Harlem was winning by ten points. When the game ended, Harlem celebrated a twenty-five-point victory.

Prince and Darren left the park upset and headed back to the BMW and back to Queens. Tasha searched through the crowd in hopes of telling Prince about her pregnancy, but to no avail. He was gone. Sin saw the look on Tasha's face, grabbed her from behind and whispered "Don't worry Tash, we'll be okay. Trust me, we will be okay."

"I sure hope so," Tasha said holding on to his hand as she stared into the crowd of many people.

"You trust me don't you?' Sin asked softly.

"Of course I trust you," Tasha said holding onto his hand.

"So when I say don't worry, you'll be okay. I mean what I say," Sin said. Tasha had heard those exact words before from her baby's father the last time they were together and he had just up and left her alone to have a baby at fifteen years old. It was hard for her to trust. But what would she do? What could she do? She said a prayer to herself something that her grandmother had taught her when her mother died and turned to face Sin.

"I trust you Sin."

For some reason, Silky's mother had taken a liking to Prince. She adored him. Prince always said that Silky's mother's foreign accent was cool. She was born and raised in the Philippines and her accent had not changed. Prince could see where Silky got her beauty. She was fifty-four and she looked as if she was twenty-five. Her and Silky could pass for sisters. Her and Silky's father had broken up after Silky's birth. He moved to Baltimore, MD and she stayed in Queens. She had many successful establishments but her wealth was not exposed and she lived and average middle class Filipino-American life. Prince entered the kitchen and smelled fresh fruits and vegetables on the table. He stuck his hand in the fruit basket and grabbed a handful of grapes and headed for the living room where Silky and her mom watched the Godfather Part III.

"Hey Ladies."

"Hey Baby," Silky said excitedly.

"Hey Prince," Silky's mom said. "See this movie right here Prince? This movie is based on greed. There is enough money for everybody but yet everybody still has to die. Who's going to spend the money? What happens to the money and power when everybody is dead?' She asked.

"It gets passed on, I guess," Prince said.

"Exactly, there's always someone waiting in line for your position. So don't be greedy. If there's anything I've learned from Silky's sorry ass dad, is don't be greedy. See, he's a great dad financially but he's got a problem with keeping his dick in his pants. You see Silky's cousin that runs my salon on Hillside Avenue?" she asked.

"Yeah," Prince said.

"Well, she might be Silky's sister."

"Ma," Silky yelled.

"Don't Ma me baby. That whore of a sister of mine was fucking around with your daddy and his sorry ass thinks I didn't know. Luckily the bitch ain't with us no more because I would have beaten it out of her," Silky's mom said as she laughed and headed to the kitchen. "Prince, I got your plate made already. You want fresh salad?" Silky's mom asked.

"Yes please," Prince answered and sat down.

"Yo, your mom is crazy," Prince said smiling and placing a soft kiss on Silky's lips.

"EEELL, you're all salty. You got some boxers and white tees in the room. You want to take a quick shower?"

"Nah, I'm starving. I'm washing my hands and that's it."

"You nasty."

"Yeah, I'm hungry too,"

"Did y'all win?" Silky asked.

"Nah, we lost by twenty-five points," Prince said shaking his head.

"Nah baby, you didn't lose, you win.

"How is that Silk?"

"Because you're here with me," Silky said, placing her tongue in his mouth.

"Get a room," Silky's mom said smiling as she walked into the living room with his plate. He quickly rose, headed to the bathroom to wash his hand and face leaving the two women to talk.

"Ma, I love that boy," Silky said.

"I see that Silky."

"I mean he's younger but he's so mature," Silky said.

"Girl, age doesn't mean a thing. Your hearts are on the same page. He's a young man, a young good man and that's all I see.

"Me too Ma, me too," Silk said as Prince entered the room and a tear of joy fell from her eye.

CHAPTER EIGHT

"**B**et five or betta for fitty."

"Nigga you trippin. You know you ain't got no five in you," Pop said as Prince shook two red and one green dice.

"Nigga, you gonna bet the half-man or what?"

"Bet Nigga!" Pop said as Prince rolled the dice smoothly out of his hand onto the sidewalk in front of an abandoned house.

"Cee-Lo bitches, now pay up!" Prince yelled as 4,5,6 hit the ground.

"Damn man, you lucky mother-fucker. I swear to God," Pop said as he had lost again. Prince stood there counting his winnings, close to four g's as he saw Silky driving up.

"Well Homies, yall see wifey pulling up. Hate to win yall shorts and bounce, but it is what it is. I'll holla," Prince said and walked to the passenger's side of Silky's car.

"Hey Ma, what are you doing out this early?" Prince asked, looking at his watch. He looked over at Silky's face and saw seriousness about her. She was not the same giddy person he was used to seeing. Something was wrong. "You ok Silky?"

"I'm leaving Prince. I'm going back to Maryland. My mom is going back to the Philippines. She has to take care of some important business. We had death in the family."

"Damn Ma, just like that. You gonna up and leave?" Prince said and began to become overwhelmed with emotions. He really loved this woman and he felt as if her last statement had torn a piece of his heart.

"No, Baby, that's why I'm here. I can't go without you. Please Daddy; come to Maryland with me. I have a beautiful life set up for us. You have to trust me."

"Damn Ma, I can't just up and leave this block. This is my bread,butter and meat. This is the only way I eat.

"I know Baby, but if you really wanna eat, let me feed you," Silky said.

"What about my crib, my clothes?"

"What about it? I told you I got you. We'll get you a whole new wardrobe."

"And what if I say no?" Prince asked and Silky's heart began to slow down. Then she saw his signature smile.

"So it's yes Daddy?" she asked.

"Yeah, why not. I'll go with you."

"Thank you Baby. Believe me, I won't let you down. I'm gonna share my entire world with you. Listen, how much money is that in your hand?"

"About four g's."

"Okay. Hey Pop!" she yelled and saw Pop motion towards the car.

"Hey, what's good Silk?" Pop said.

"Listen, me and my Daddy are going away for awhile. He wants you to manage the block."

"What?" Pop said, confused.

"Here, this is my cousin's phone number. Her name is Lu-Lu. She'll be expecting your call. She has something for you. It's a gift from us. Um Pop?"
"Yeah Silky?"

"Don't play games, keep it business with her and you're gonna be on top quicker than you know it. Prince how much money you got in your pockets?"

"I don't know why?" Prince was confused. He had never seen this side of Silky. Her confidence when she spoke, her leadership ways began to flourish. Silky had done this before.

"Give Pop all the money you have on you Daddy," Silky said seriously.

"What?"

"Please, just give him the money," Prince gave Pop his

money.

"Give him the keys to the apartment and the combination to the safes."

"Yo Silk, you buggin out," Prince said.

"Baby do me a favor. Open that duffel bag. The red one with the Nike sign."

"He opened it and was shocked to see stacks of crispy hundred dollar bills.

"Oh shit Silk. How much bread is that?" Prince asked.

"That's only 50 grand. That's your traveling money. If your ass would've said you were not coming, I would have used it to get you whacked," Silky said and they both laughed. Silky got out of the driver's seat, her pants showed every curve in her flawless body. Her tight fitting pink wife beater explained the rest. She got in the passenger's seat and Prince walked off to talk to Pop. He had just transferred his entire life savings to Pop along with his power. He gave brief instructions and recommended that he should add Kah, Big Boi and Darren to his team. Prince got behind the driver's seat. Silky kissed his cheek and smiled.

"Where to?" he asked.

"Your moms. We got a surprise for her too," Silky said as Prince pulled off.

Prince and Silky arrived at his mother's home and to his luck, all his brothers and sisters were there. He had almost forgotten that it was his younger brother, Laron's birthday. Everyday was a good day when Prince came over. His energy towards his family was always positive. He had been living on his own for three years and he regularly stopped by to check on his mother and his grandmother, Lily Bird. He and Silky walked through the front door and cheers came as if a celebrity had walked in. His sisters hugged and kissed him and his brothers attacked him playfully.

"Hey, what's good?" Prince said. He hadn't seen everybody in the same room in a while and it felt good to see them all.

"Hey Nigga!" Lily Bird said from her seat. She began to stand and sat back down quickly under the influence of Smirnoff Vodka.

"Hey grandma, how are you? I bought you something for us." Prince said, pulling a half pint of Absolute out of his back pocket.

"Nigga, that ain't for us, that's for you," she said slurring her words. "I don't drink Absolute. I drink Smirnoff S-M-I-R-N-O-F-F," Lily Bird said eliciting laughter from everyone.

"I know grandma," Prince said laughing as he pulled out a half pint of Smirnoff.

"Now that's my baby. I knew you wouldn't forget grandma."

"You ain't nothing like your dope-fiend-ass daddy."

"Ma," Ms. Ronnie yelled, cutting Lily Bird off.

"You heard me. Fuck his daddy. He ain't neva did nothing for none of yall. Where yall went when he killed himself, huh? Lily Bird's house, nowhere else. Y'all came to my damn house. All of yall. Loddy. Doddy and Every Goddamn-Body," Lily Bird yelled from her seat.

"Don't get yourself worked up Grandma."

"Oh I ain't. Go in the kitchen and get some ice. Put it in a clean glass, my throat is getting dry," Lily Bird said. Prince hurried in the kitchen and everybody greeted Silky with smiles. They had met her before and the boys were all admiring her looks.

"Hey Sooky, Sooky," Lilly Bird said.

"It's Silky Grandma," Jeannie, Prince' sister said.

"Sooky, Silky, same shit. Come on over here and give me a kiss girl." Silky smiled and walked to give Lily Bird a kiss.

"Girl you a beautiful lil' thing. I see why that boy is strung out over you. You are just as pretty as a button. How are you doing sweetie?" Lily Bird asked.

"I'm fine Ms. Lily and you?"

"I'm okay baby. I'll be even better once this Nigga bring my damn ice. Where did he go to get the ice, Alaska?" Lily Bird said and everyone laughed.

"Yo, everybody listen-up. I got something to tell y'all," Prince said returning from the kitchen.

"What's wrong baby?" Ms. Prince said.

"Oh nothing Ma. It's what's right, that's the question. I came to let yall know I'm moving down south. Me and Silk is moving to Maryland."

"You what?" Lily Bird asked.

"I'm moving Grandma. I'll only be 4 ½ hours away. I'll come back and check on y'all, I promise."

"You got a job and stuff down there?" His sister asked.

"Yep. I got everything I need. I just came here to let yall know. It just so happens that everybody I love is here,"

"Wow, so sudden?" Ms. Ronnie asked and sat down.

"I know Ma, but I've been thinking about this for a while. I need this change of scenery," Prince said.

"Who got your crib?" His older brother asked.

"My lease is up," Prince said, lying.

"Oh well, best of luck Dennis," his other sister said, surprising him by calling him Dennis.

"Watch your mouth Mimi," Prince said smiling.

"You know we love you no matter what," MiMi said and they all grabbed him and hugged him. Silky walked over to Ronnie and asked if they could speak in private. They exited the living room and headed into the back bedroom.

"You taking my baby, huh?" Ronnie said.

"Yeah, I guess so. He's my baby too," Silky said smiling.

"Yeah, I can see that boy really loves you. I haven't ever seen him talk about a girl like he talks about you. He told me how y'all met. Shit, that surprised me. He damn sure ain't get that romance side from his daddy. That nigga walked up on me and asked me to paint my house for a date," Ms. Ronnie said laughing.

"Aww, that was sweet," Silky said.

"Girl please. The nigga charged me an arm and a leg,' Ms. Ronnie said smiling.

"Ms. Ronnie, I wanna give you something that my mother gave to Prince."

"Oh yeah, what is it?" Ronnie asked. Silky opened her coach bag and handed Ms. Ronnie an envelope with documents in it.

"What is this Silky"? Ronnie asked, confused. She knew exactly what it was, but she was confused as to why she was holding a deed to a house.

'It's a deed Ms. Ronnie. Prince told my mother how he had wanted to buy you a house. My mom loves her Prince," Silky said laughing and continued. "She has a beautiful two story house in Bayside Queens. It is newly renovated and it is for you and your family. Everybody can live there comfortably. And this," Silky said, passing her a cashier's check. "This is a check for fifty thousand. You can get all your furniture and things you need. I'll let your son buy you a car when he gets ready."

"Girl, I can't accept this."

"Please Ms. Ronnie, my mother has cancer. This was her only wish. She left and went back to the Philippines. She didn't want Prince to know she was sick," Silky siad. Ronnie looked at the check in awe and couldn't believe her eyes. She had never seen that much money before. Not to mention a 800 thousand dollar house that awaited her and her family.

"Baby, I don't know what to say. I don't know why God sent you to my son, but thank you Baby," Ms. Ronnie said as she and Silky began to cry. "Please promise that you'll take good care of my baby, Silky."

"With my very last breath," Silky said as they both headed to the bathroom to wash their salty faces.
Meanwhile, back in the living room, Prince had given all of his siblings, and his grandmother, Lily Bird some money from the duffle in the trunk.. Everyone hugged and kissed one more time. Prince went and spoke with his mom in private. She gave him her blessing and he and Silky were off to their new lives.

. Ronnie watched from the doorway, as her son had finally become a man. Tears freely flowed from her face as they all waved as Silky and Prince pulled off in their black B.M.W convertible.

"Yo what the hell did you do to that lady?" Prince asked.

"I just kept my word, that's all," Silky said as she thought about her mother, who had just a few months to live. She wanted to be with her mother, but her mother refused to let her daughter watch her deteriorate into nothing. Her tears flowed freely as Prince shifted gears and headed to the highway.

"I'm just glad we made everybody happy," Prince said as Mary J. Blige's voice filled the airwaves and Silky swayed to her lyrics.

"Me too Baby, me too." Silky said as she put her hand behind Prince's neck and massaged it relaxing him. Life would change for Prince drastically. He dreamed about being the next Frank White, the King of New York. Little did he know, his dreams would soon be a reality.

CHAPTER NINE

The King's residence had been turned into a nursery.

Ever since Tasha moved in with them, Mrs. King had been spending every second preparing for the new bundle of joy to arrive. Janice and Marvin had turned the guest room into the most extravagant nursery money could buy. There were enough toys, clothes and accessories to last for a girl or boy until he or she was eighteen years old. Mrs. King held a huge baby shower for Tasha and invited all of Tasha's family from Queens. Her grandmother, still upset, came along with the rest of the family and enjoyed the shower. After the baby shower was over, Tasha and Mrs. King put the gifts away and began to clean up the apartment.

"Thank you for everything Mrs. King," Tasha said while folding some new baby's clothing.

"Oooh you are so welcome Tasha. I'm just glad to be a part of all of this. I mean, what would you expect for us to do for our son?" Mrs. King said proudly.

"I know, I'm just so grateful; especially since this is not Sin's, I mean Dennis' baby."

"When did that ever matter, young lady? Dennis loves you, he loves your baby, we love Dennis and we love our grandbaby," Mrs. King said wiping off the table.

"I guess it never mattered. When I told him, I thought he would leave me. I would have never imagined it would be like this," Tasha said as she gathered up the last of paper cups and headed to the kitchen.

"Just know that God is good, baby. God is good"

"Amen to that," Tasha said as she smiled and walked

away. Marvin and Sin sat on the balcony overlooking Manhattan's skyline. Marvin sipped on Absolut Vodka while Sin sipped on a chocolate milkshake. Both men were staring into the night.

"It was a nice shower, huh?" Marvin asked.

"Yeah Dad, Mom outdid herself," Sin said smiling.

"You know how your Mom is. She's gonna go broke for her son."

"Yeah I know. She loves Tasha too."

"Yeah man, I like Tasha too. She's a very nice girl. I hope you guys can make a nice life for that baby. I don't want you to worry about nothing! I got you. Just get that diploma and if you decide to go to the next level, it's your decision. No pressure on you at all!" Marvin said.

"Dad, I'm going to the next level. You see all those letters on the table already? They are all Division One schools. I was thinking about going to Duke but I'm not sure yet. Tasha wants me to go to St. John's because it is in Queens.

"Ha ha hah, yeah I know she wants you close to home. Like I said, you can only make the decision where you feel is most comfortable. I can give you this advice though; if you do pick one of those schools, take advantage of the education. Shit, we could spend money and send you to Yale or Harvard. It's the love of basketball that drives you and I gotta respect that," Marvin said.

"Dad?"

"Yeah son?" Marvin said, refilling his cup with vodka.

"Can I ask you a serious question?"

"Go ahead, ask me anything."

"Okay, why mom?"

"Do you mean because she is white?"

"Uh, yeah, I guess so." Sin said.

"Well, I'd be lying if I said that when I was growing up that white women was my taste. I mean, on every television, billboard, everywhere you looked, you saw beautiful white women. So when I got older, I couldn't wait to fuck one," Marvin said as they both laughed. He was feeling the effects of the vodka.

"So that's why you married Ma; because of what you saw on T.V.?"

"Oh son. That's not why. Seriously, your mom is the best. She's the best thing that ever happened to me. She chose me. Before I became a NBA star, your mom was a successful woman. She went through hell with her family and chose me over them and their so-called values. She looked beyond this," Marvin said pointing at the skin on his hand. "Color was an issue, I can't lie. That's how society made it. But to us, we were too young people in love and nobody outside our Cocoon mattered. I can honestly say that she gave me the strength I have today. When I blew my knee, I was depressed, man. Basketball was all I knew. Your mom coached me back to life. She showed me purpose out-side of basketball. We've had our issues. We found out that we couldn't have children. Her family was happy about that. Then God brought you to us. Now he has bought Tasha and the baby. Son, our life is complete with yall in it, Marvin said sipping his drink.

"Whoa Dad, I'm speechless," Sin said.

"Well go in there and talk to your woman. I know yall got a lot to talk about. I'm gonna sit out here with my good friend, Absolute, watch the beautiful New York Skyline and count my blessings. I love you Son," Marvin said, taking another sip.

"I love you too Dad. I'll holla at you in the morning."

"Okay, in the morning Son," Marvin said, extending his hand to his son, grabbing him and hugging him.

Tasha and Sin lay in their bed while Sin rubbed Cocoa butter on her stomach to prevent stretch marks.

"We gotta keep that stomach sexy," Sin said as he rubbed her with his warm hands.

"Why, you gonna leave me because of some lousy stretch marks?" Tasha asked in her sexiest voice.

"Nah Ma, I can't see myself without you."

"Sin?"

"What up Tash?

"Are we gonna have kids of our own?"

"Tasha, first of all, this is our kid! I don't know what the future brings but I know what it feels like to be a little boy without parents. I promise you that I won't allow this to happen with our baby that you're carrying. I mean, I know I didn't conceive it, but I ain't going nowhere. Second of all, hell yeah, we're gonna have kids of our own. We're gonna have a basketball team and football team. We're gonna have so many kids that we may have to buy our own country," Sin said laughing.

"Boy Paleeze, I ain't even having all them damn kids. I can see three or four, but you talkin about a whole country's worth?"

"I'm sayin Tasha!"

"What you sayin Sin?"

"We're gonna be rich. I'm going to the Pro's, you'll see."

"Yeah and? What does that have to do with stretching my body out? You already rubbing Cocoa butter on me worried about a few stretch marks. Imagine how my stomach is gonna look after 50 kids."

"Aight, maybe not fifty, but is ten okay?" Sin asked, smiling.

"Whatever Boy!" Tasha said, turning her backside to him. Sin looked at her thick round ass and immediately began to rise to the occasion. He let his dick drop from the opening of his boxers and eased up on Tasha's panty covered butt. He began to kiss her neck softly and she pushed back against him. Sin tried desperately to ease her panties off while not being overly aggressive. Tasha lifted up, helping him at his task. Sin removed her Victoria Secret panties and continued to kiss lightly on her neck and both of their breathing began to speed up. He guided his dick towards her soaking wet pregnant pussy. Tasha reached behind her and grabbed his erect dick and guided him into her heated pussy. Sin slowly stroked back and forth as Tasha followed his lead by moving her body back and forth meeting his dick with her pussy maximizing the pleasure for both of them.

"Ooooo Sin, this feels so good Daddy."

"You like it?" He asked.

"I love it baby. I love it. Go faster," she begged.

"Turn around and kiss me."

Tasha kept her back to him while awkwardly turning her head to kiss him. Their lips met passionately as he continued to speed up his temp stroking her and eliciting pleasure.

"I'm not hurting you, am I?"

"No Baby. Lay on your back," she instructed him and he laid on his back as Tasha straddled him and rode him until they both were about to explode in ecstasy. Tasha began to breathe even harder as her body began to shake.

"Ooooh my goodness Sin, I'm about to; oh my God," Tasha said as white cream seeped from her inner body. The look on her face and her reaction had taken Sin to a point of no return as he exploded holding her still on his dick as he shot his semen into the depths of her body.

"Sin?"

"Yeah Ma?" Sin said breathing fast and heavy.

"You okay?" she asked.

"Yeah, you?'

"I'm good," she said as she laid on his muscular frame and fell quietly asleep with his soft manhood still inside of her.

"Marvin! Marvin!"

"What Janice?"

"Come on Baby, let's do it."

"Okay, let's do it," Marvin said and went back into a drunken sleep.

"Oh well. Thanks again Mr. Absolut Vodka." Janice said laughing looking over at the finished bottle of Absolut Vodka. Janice knew that Marvin had a wonderful day. All the latest festivities overwhelmed him and he hadn't enjoyed himself like this in a long time. She removed his size 19 sneakers and tucked him under the covers. She put her arms around him and watched him sleep.

"I'll catch your behind in the morning," she whispered and closed her eyes.

CHAPTER TEN

Prince and Silky arrived in Baltimore, Maryland safe and sound.

Unfortunately, State Troopers on the New Jersey Turnpike pulled over the BMW they were driving twice, for DWB (Driving While Black). Both times, the State Troopers were upset with Prince because he refused to slide his window down less than a half-inch; just enough to pass his license and registration through the window.

"Sir, can I see your license and registration?"

"For What? What are you pulling us over for?" Prince asked through the thin crack of his window.

"Why don't you roll down your window so I can hear you sir?" The arrogant trooper asked.

"Nah, there's no need. I can hear you loud and clear Mr officer. My license and registration fits through there perfectly," Prince said getting a slight giggle from Silky. They both knew they were legit and refused to go out like Rodney King. The State Trooper took Prince's license and ran his name for warrants. When it came back clear. The trooper walked back and tossed Prince's paperwork through the crack of the window.

"Drive safely and yall have a nice evening," the trooper said while Prince fetched his paperwork off the floor.

"Fuck you and your mother, officer," Prince said and rolled up his window.

"What?" the trooper said, looking at the BMW pull off. "Fucking stupid niggers," he said and headed back to his patrol car just as he sat behind the wheel, he saw a burgundy Mercedes Benz shoot pass him. He noticed the two young black men look in his direction.

"We got two more Bret," he said and pursued the two black men in the Benz.

"Well, welcome to Baltimore, Baby."

"This is it, huh? This shit looks like New York. Niggas is huggin the blocks like a motherfucker.

"Shit, that ain't nothing. You gotta come out early in the morning to see the show," Silky said, shaking her head.

"What do you mean? What show?"

"Don't worry Prince, you'll see. Let's go to the mall and get you some clothes."

"Yeah, that sounds good. I ain't got shit. I can't believe I let you talk me into leaving all my shit behind. You know how much shit I had?"

"Yeah, I know Baby. But you're about to get ten times as much. I promise every piece you had, I'll get you ten of them," Silky said. Prince let Silky navigate him to different stores and he bought a whole new wardrobe. He knew that she had money to blow, especially after explaining to him who she really was and what she was a part of. At first, he couldn't believe it, but after a long talk, he had come to the conclusion that his girl was kin to a heroin empire. "One key of raw dope would set him straight. Two keys of dope would do even better, but two hundred keys would set him for life," Prince thought to himself as he tried on some jeans. The two finally made it to Silky's plush apartment in downtown Baltimore, looking at the Baltimore Harbor. Prince looked around the oversized condo-like crib, which was now his new home. Silky removed her Nike Air Max sneakers and ran to the bathroom. Prince looked out the living room window at the lighted boats that sailed peacefully in the Harbor.

"Yo, this is an aight crib, Ma."

"Thanks. I'm glad you like it Babe. Do me a favor? Put

those new sheets on our bed. It's a brand new bed. I had it de-livered before I left for New York."

"Yeah, where are the sheets at?" Prince asked.

"I don't know. They are in one of those thousands of bags," Silky said heading towards the kitchen. "You want some-thing to drink P.I.?"

"Yeah, anything is cool." Silky bought him a cold glass of Pepsi and they both sat on the couch in the living room flooded with shopping bags.

"Yo Ma, I feel like I'm dreaming."

"Nah, it ain't a dream Boo. After all you're the one who made a fool outta yourself in that supermarket," Silky said laughing.

"Oh shit, that's cold. I did look crazy; right?"

"Hell yeah. I couldn't believe you did that shit. But you were sooo cute and you went hard."

"Yo I can't front, I didn't know what to do. I had to try the flowers."

"Well, that crazy shit worked. I fell in love with you at Hello!"

"Word?"

"Word!" Silky said, placing a kiss on his lips.

"I should smack Miss Margie for making up that bullshit arrangement of flowers."

"Shut up boy. The flowers were nice. My mother loved the whole idea of it."

"Yo, I like your moms. I can't believe she left without say-ing bye," Prince said. Silky fell silent.

"What's the matter Silk?"

"Nothin. I'm good. I just miss her, that's all."

"Yeah, me too," Prince said.

"Prince?"

"Yeah, what up?"

"What's the only thing in this world you haven't done?"
Prince wasn't quiet for a second before he came up with an an-swer. Un-expectantly to himself, he said 'cry; I can't remember

crying."

"Cry? You mean like boo-hoo? You've never cried before?"

"Well my mother said I cried after the doctor slapped my ass twice," Prince chuckled. "But after that first time, nope."

"Not even as a kid? Not even at your father's funeral?"

"Not even at the funeral."

"Damn Baby, you never cease to amaze me. I guess that's why I fell in love with you. I never know what to expect. I hope that this is the one thing you never get to do on my account, unless they are happy tears. Now, name something else you haven't done," she demanded.

"Let's see. Oh, I never skydived," Prince said playfully.

"Okay, then that's what we'll do. This weekend we'll go skydiving in Virginia."

"Woman, are you nutz? You pick one. I ain't white. The only thing I'm jumpin off is a basketball rim. That's ten feet high. I ain't jumpin off nobody's cliff or out nobody's plane, unless somebody's hijacking that shit."

"Yeah whatever scaredy-cat," Silky laughed.

"Call it whatever you wanna. I call it staying alive," Prince said and they both laughed. Silky hit the power button to the widescreen television and turned to a basketball special. Prince diverted his attention towards the T.V. screen. Silky grabbed the loose bags and began to put their stuff away.

"Damn. My baby has never cried," she said.

"What up Ma?" he said.

"Oh nothing, I was talking to myself. I'ma put this stuff in your closet, okay?"

"Yeah, I'll be in there to help you. Aight?"

"No, go ahead and watch the game. I got this."

"I love this girl. Thank you God," Prince said to himself, took a sip of Pepsi and watched the basketball game.

◆ ◆ ◆

CHAPTER ELEVEN

In Sin's first year of college, he did better than he expected.

His peers were no match for him. He averaged twenty-seven points and eight assists per game in his freshman season. His grades were just as good as his on-court performances. He was focused. He had a lot of support and people who truly believed in him. Sin enjoyed his celebrity status. The groupies were all over him looking for a meal ticket. He dibbled and dabbled with many of them but his heart was back in New York with Tasha and his stepson. He was not overjoyed by the fact that she named his stepson after him, but it was her decision. He promised them both that no matter what, if he stayed in college or went to the NBA, he would always be there for his family.

Meanwhile, back in Manhattan, Tasha raised her son. She was a great mom. With the help of Janice and Marvin, she was able to move into her own condo in the same building. Tasha decorated the condo to her and Sin's liking and played the loyal role of "wifey" while Sin was away at college. She was happy about the fact that she was in contact with Prince. She finally told him about the baby. He agreed to a maternity test. When the results were in, he and Silky promised to be in the baby's life. She at first thought it would be drama. It wasn't. In fact, Prince became very active in his son's life. When he visited his mother in Queens, he would call first and stop to see his son. He seemed very happy with his new life in Baltimore with Silky, Tasha thought. When she told Sin about contacting Prince, he was happy too. All too unusual to her, but she prayed for this outcome and God was definitely good. She had finally gotten her diploma and was taking classes at a local community college online. She decided to major in sports management so she could help Sin with his promising career.

Prince didn't expect life to be so good. It's been two years since he moved to Maryland and already he had made a substantial amount of money. He had become an instant millionaire. He rode shotgun in a brand new Jaguar with his partner-in-crime, Ralo, they went from spot to spot-checking their investments. Ralo was the first person he met and trusted when he stepped foot in the town. From that point, they broke a lot of bread together.

Silky's father, Amir, was actually the one who taught him the dope game in Baltimore. Prince admired Silky's father. He was overprotective of his daughter but he respected her space. Together, Silky and Amir flooded the streets of Baltimore with the best dope the city had ever seen. Prince remembered the first day he met Amir and sat back as Ralo drove and reflected.

"Daddy, this is Prince," Silky said.

"Oh, this is the royal one I've been hearing so much about?"

"I don't know about the royal part." Prince said smiling.

"Yeah, once you enter this family, you're royalty."

"Oh yeah?"

"Well Dad, I'ma leave you two alone to get acquainted. Prince I'ma go back to the house and fry these shrimp."

"Okay ma, I'll be there in a little while," Prince said as he kissed her lips softly. Both men watched her pull off and began to walk and talk.

"So young blood, what's up?"

"Nothing much. Same shit."

"You ain't lyin. It's the same thing daily. So how's everything with you and Silk?" Amir asked.

"Aw ma, it's crazy. I can't lie, it feels like I'm dreaming."

"I don't know how yall found each other, but I can tell you, you're a lucky man. Did she hip you to the family business?" Amir asked.

"Yeah she put me on, somewhat."

"Well, I'll hip you to the rest. You see the city in front of you?' Amir said, referring to Baltimore City. "Well, we own it. I supply every major hitter in town. I pay politicians and anybody else who needs to be on my payroll. Now I'm hanging up my jersey and handing the torch to you."

"But why me? You don't even know me?" Prince said seriously.

"Ha ha ha," Amir laughed and continued. "I know you very well. Well enough. I know our entire family. I know enough to pass the torch and most of all; my daughter loves you more than she loves herself. She admires your loyalty to your team back in New York. See Lil Bro, it's almost like hustling in New York but the flow is a little different. In New York you have certain areas that supply heroin addicts. Out here," Amir said pointing at his city. "Everywhere there's heroin addicts from the rich to the poor neighborhoods. You will see more money than you can spend. All you have to do is stay true to the law of the streets. Now, I could supply you with an entire team, but I'll let you feel your way around. Find your own team. They're some good dudes out there who will be loyal. Then you're going to have your share of haters, who will hate you just because you're from New York. Man fuck that, they'll hate you just because you ain't from here. You can be from New Orleans and they'll still hate you. Plus your girl is probably the prettiest woman in B-more. You're gonna face some adversity," Amir said laughing.

"I know, but it ain't nothin to me. I can handle it though. Som what do they sell around here?" Prince asked.

"Same shit nickels and dimes. The only difference is a lot of it is called scramble."

"Scramble?"

"Yeah scramble. It's cut dope. It's mixed with Bonita and Quinone; especially our product. It's too potent to sell raw. Now, don't get it misunderstood. You can chop up a few bricks and sell raw, but the majority of the city sells these," Amir said showing him a plastic gel cap that looked like a casing for medication. "They sell these instead of the pyramid bags you're used to seeing."

"Oh word?" Prince said surprised.

"Yeah, but this is not your concern. You're gonna supply the dealers with wholesale prices."

Both men talked a little bit more. Amir spoke immaculate numbers and Prince agreed. A deal was made.

Now a few years later Prince rode with Ralo and enjoyed the atmosphere.

"Yo, where are we going today?" Ralo asked.

"Yo, go by Caroline and Preston. Let me see if Son got that bread for us.

"How much do we owe anyway?"

"He gave me a buck Tuesday. He still owes another 50 stacks."

"Yeah, Son, is definitely good for it. I heard the pigs been harassing him lately."

"Yeah I heard the same thing. I still want my bread though," Prince said smiling.

"Nigga you already know. If he ain't got the bread, he gonna get what the last nigga got."

"All day; everyday," Prince said, inhaling the purple haze. They pulled up on Caroline and Preston to a group of men in a circle.

"Yo, they rollin dice?" Prince asked excitedly.

"I don't know, it looks like dem niggas is rapping i a cypher."

"Let's get out and see what they gotta say,"

Ralo pulled over and exited the Buick and walked up to the cipher where a young local rapper, Ish was spitting bar after bar. He turned towards Prince and Ralo's direction and immediately switched his flow and started disrespecting New Yorkers calling them rats (snitches) and any other disrespect he could think of. After all, he had a valid excuse. Alpo, from Harlem, had snitched on Washington D.C.'s and Baltimore's most prominent figures in the drug game. Baltimore and D.C had a bad taste in their mouth for New Yorkers, especially hustlers. Prince carefully listened to Ish strategically hit his punch lines soliciting props from his natives.

"Son, he gotta point there. Alpo fucked the game up." Ralo said, shaking his head.

"Yeah, I know. But I gotta rep NYC," Prince said and stepped to the front of the cipher. Everybody knew that he wanted to go next. Ralo was the only one who knew that Prince could hold his own in the rap game. He was better than Ish and his rap would embarrass the young rapper.

"Yall niggas is losers like the New York Knicks and yall New York niggas could suck my dick," Ish said as he finished his lethal rap.

"Oooh," the crowd roared as Ish looked over at Prince. Prince stepped to the front of the cipher and began to go mayhem!

"On Caroline and Preston/I splatter minds with Wessons/ Got battle rhymes to stretch him/with asinine suggestions/ Like I'm supposed to be Po/C'mon this joker needs flow/Plus he's mad I'm getting cash, meanwhile he's broke and needs dough/ For real, this cat works in a bakery, he broke and kneads dough/ House nigga, I'm in the field where the Cocoa leaves grow/You don't wanna hear this heat roar at you/So you better take a page from Shannon Holmes's book and Be More More Careful/ See if I ain't got the drop, I'ma dump the mac stupid/Leave you wrapped in/black plastic/In the trunk of that Black Buick/ Cause drama with cats. I handle it the "rest in peace" way/ Straight swap em'/ Then I'd dump em'/In the Chesapeake Bay/

and whenever Prince steps on the block, lames worry/Rep New York but gotta gun game like Wayne Perry/and the last cat that invited his privates/this 40 cal left his brain on fire, by the side of the hydrant/Easy!

Watch your mouth Homie, you see the 40 cal bulging on my hip/Ask Ralo what happened to the last nigga who told me to suck his dick...." Prince stepped out the cipher and he and Ralo walked to the liquor store. The entire group stood in awe, as they couldn't believe what they just saw. It was as a prophet had spoken.

CHAPTER TWELVE

Prince, Ralo and Amir sat in Moe's Seafood restaurant and munched on snow crabs dipped in hot butter sauce. The three men sat and talked.

"Yo, you saw that dunk last night by Kobe? Yo, son the truth. He almost looks like me," Prince said smiling.

"Yeah I saw it. I respect Kobe. But did you see North Carolina's highlights last night? That boy Sin King had 80 points last night. He set a college record."

"Word?" Prince said surprised.

"Hell yeah. I couldn't believe it myself," Amir said.

"I know him. I used to play against him when I was in New York. Son is the truth," Prince said.

"Yeah, that boy going number one in the NBA draft. I'm surprised he didn't go straight to the pros. He was averaging 40 points in high school."

"No need to leave school. His family got bread. He doesn't need money. His parents are rich," Prince said.

"Yeah, I'm hip and so are we," Amir said, lifting his shot of Hennessy.

"Yes sirrr!," Ralo said, raising his glass. Prince looked up and saw a beautiful woman carrying a dozen white roses. It was Silky.

"Silk, what are you doing here?" Prince asked, surprised. "I thought you were going out with friends."

"Yeah, I was but something I gotta ask you first."

"Aw man. What you done heard Silk?" Prince said smiling.

"First of all, these roses are for you," Silky said, passing him the white long stemmed roses.

"For what?" Prince asked, confused. Silky's eyes became watery and she got down on one knee.

"Prince, ever since that first day you approached me, you had my heart. Your honesty, your loyalty, your compassion for others are just some of the qualities I can mention. When I am feeling lonely, you appear. When I am sad, you make me smile. I love you and the ground you walk on. I promise if you give me a chance, I will be your companion until I stop breathing. Please, Prince you are my soulmate. Will you marry me?" Silky asked as tears flowed from her eyes. Prince stood in shock as the most beautiful woman he had ever seen kneeled in front of him with a platinum diamond studded ring in her hand awaiting an answer. Prince stood from his seat.

"Yo, this is crazy. But what's even more crazy is how we are always on the same page. It's almost unreal," Prince said reaching inside his pocket and pulling at a green velvet box.

"See, when you told me you were going out with your friends, I had fifty dozen roses delivered to the crib for you. I had an entire night planned for us. Me, your pops and Ralo were sittin here celebrating. Your pops gave me his blessing to go give you this," Prince said, opening the velvet box exposing a 5-carat diamond that lit up the entire restaurant like a strobe light. "Yo, Silky, you already know how I feel about you. You make my life complete. I want to spend the rest of my life with you. Without you in my life, I don't know what I would do. You know about my son, but I want to start a family with you. Before I answer your question, please answer mine. Will you marry me Silky?" Prince asked as he kneeled in front of her.

"Yes Baby! Yes I will marry you," Silky said as he slid the diamond on her finger and she slid a diamond studded band on him. They hugged and kissed passionately. All of her friends appeared in the restaurant. She had secretly rented Moe's for the evening and the pre-reception party began. To Prince's surprise, the singer Case appeared with a cordless mic and began to sing his hit "Happily Ever After". Prince watched in awe as Silky

cried as Case sung to them live

Prince and Silky arrived back at the apartment. When Prince opened the door it looked as if the entire floral store was in the living room. White roses throughout the apartment and there were two trails of rose petals; one to the bathroom and one to the bedroom. Prince lifted Silky off her feet and with her stilettos waving in the air, he carried her into the rose filled apartment.

"Awe Baby, this is beautiful," Silky whispered in his ear.

"I'm glad you like it," Prince said as he lowered her onto their bed. He began to remove his shirt exposing his muscular frame. Silky quickly removed her dress showing lace boy shorts and matching bra. Prince kissed her lightly on her lips and said, "wait here," as he went into the attached bathroom and ran the water in the Jacuzzi. He quickly entered the room and removed his pants and boxers. Silky removed hers too. Prince lifted her again and carried her into the awaiting Jacuzzi. He sat her down and gently grabbed a sponge and began to bathe his future wife. He squeezed cucumber smelling body wash down her back giving her a tingling sensation.

"Oooh baby, this water feels so good," she said.

"I know, I'm about to get in with you.

"Please hurry up," she said seductively. Prince stepped into the perfectly temperature water and sat as the jets shot the massaging waters against his back. Silky grabbed the sponge and began to wash her man. She rubbed his chest, his back, and his dick as it began to rise to the occasion.

"I see you're ready to leave this water," she said.

"No not yet. Sit on it," Prince said holding his dick in his hand. Looking at her.

"You want me to put my back to you or face you?" she asked.

"I want you to look at me when you ride me," Prince said

as Silky rose from where she was and straddled him. She slid up and down as the water shot out the jet hitting her ass. Prince put his head back and bit his lip as Silky, began to lose control as she began to ride faster, moaning and wrapping her arms around his neck and she began to cum uncontrollably on him. Silky collapsed in his chest and Prince used his leg strength to lift her and carry her into the bedroom. Once they entered the bedroom, Prince laid her down on her back. As they both dripped soaking wet, smelling like cucumbers. Cum seeped from Silky's pussy and Prince began to kiss her neck. He kissed her eyes, her nose, both cheeks and finally her warm mouth.

Silky sucked on his tongue not wanting to let loose. Prince pulled back and began kissing her lightly on her neck. He kissed her shoulders, down to her firm perky breasts. He began to kiss lightly around each breast without coming into contact with her ½ inch erect nipples. Silky squirmed as his kisses covered her flaming body. He grabbed her left breast and took her left nipple into his mouth, lightly biting it making her moan. He repeated this task on her right nipple and proceeded down to her belly button. He began to suck hard on her belly button causing her body to shake. He moved lower kissing just above her pussy. He licked the top of her and began to suck softly on her clit. She moaned while she held his head, telling him that he had done everything right so far. He kissed between her thighs, her knees and down to her pretty toes. He sucked every one of her pedicured toes and raced back to her pussy. He opened her up with his tongue and began to suck and eat as if it was the last supper. Silky screamed as he locked into her and sucked her hard on her swollen clit.

"Oooh baby, you know I'm about to..." Before she could finish her sentence, a white creamy substance squirted from her middle section with as much pressure as the jets in the Jacuzzi. Prince continued to eat and suck as she sprayed his face with her pleasure juices. He grabbed her waist and turned her on her stomach.

"Ooh shit," Prince said, as he was surprised to see his

name tattooed across her lower back.

"You like it?" she asked.

"Yeah, that shit is really nice," Prince, said looking at his name. He kissed her lightly on her ass cheeks and she tried to hold it in but she couldn't. She farted.

"Ewe Ma. What the fuck was that," Prince asked, breaking out of his sexual trance and they both laughed until tears fell from their eyes.

"That's my bad Daddy. I ain't never fart in front of anybody before. You got me excited."

"Well you stink too," he said smiling as he stared down at her fat ass.

"I'm sorry Baby. Please Baby, fuck me," she begged. He guided his dick inside her pussy and began to stroke slowly with a little stir as if he was stirring a cup of his morning coffee. Silky met his movement with her own movements and he began to viciously pump deep into her pussy. Sweat poured from his face while his strokes sped up. Silky threw her back towards him as he dug deep into her soul.

"Oooh shit Prince, this feels sooo gooood. Please cum inside me, please," Silky begged as he sped up on the verge of explosion.

"Yo, I'm about to cum too. Don't move," he said as his entire body shook as he exploded inside of her. She instructed him to pull out and place it in her mouth. He followed her instruction word for word as he laid flat on their bed. She placed his cum drenched dick in her mouth and began sucking wet, hard and slow as Prince moaned with pleading cries. After 20 minutes of wet sucking, Prince was again ready to explode.

"I'm about to cum Ma," Prince said as she sped up, pushing him to the limit until he came uncontrollably. Silky swallowed the first shot, pulled his dick out and jerked the rest all over her face. She put him back in her mouth to make sure he was empty and went to the bathroom to get a hot wet rag. She wiped her face, his dick and jumped back into the bed. She noticed he was still big but soft and quickly put it in her mouth.

He was hard again and laid on his back as she straddled him with her back facing him and rode him until they both came again. She laid next to him with her ass against his dick. He slid into her again, stroked a few more times until they both fell into a comatose and much needed rest.

CHAPTER THIRTEEN

Zuri and her boss Marco spoke exclusively Tagalog, a language native to their village in the Philippines.

Marco's men stood guard outside the room while his top man stood behind him with an A-K 47. Marco Chen was born in Taiwan and just like Zuri had migrated to the Philippines with her parents after World War II. The son of a rebel, he had gained notoriety when he and a few men denounced the government for the harsh treatments and inequalities of the Filipino people. His army grew stronger in the late seventies as he took control of the opium trade with Japan, China and Taiwan. He had been in love with the much younger Zuri, who was a low-level heroin dealer, who bought kilos wholesale from his men. He admired her ambition and her strong ties with the United States. After their "Talk" and Zuri riding him until his eyes rolled, she became the underboss and controlled all drug trades between the Philippines and the United States. When Zuri came to report one day, Marco noticed she was pregnant. He was excited until she told him that her baby's father was a young American hustler named Amir, who was a black man. Marco disowned her; she built her own team and became just as powerful as he was.

"Zuri, what graces myself with your presence today?" Marco asked, twirling his cigar in his hand.

"I've come to give you a proposition Marco."

"You've come to proposition me, Marco Chen, your boss?"

That's my former boss. I don't work for you any more Marc," Zuri said sternly.

"What's with all the hostility my dear? I hope you're not

upset with me?" he smiled.

"Oh no, never. I don't harbor feelings. Listen, I want you to stop sending product the way you are sending it. I told you before, my ways are foolproof but you're being reckless. If one shipment gets caught, the US government will be all over us. The UN will get involved and we'll have sanctions up the ass."

"All over us? Don't you mean Marco?"

"Marco, please. Don't flatter yourself. You know you're too scared to stand at the scratch line. I have a way we can make tons of money without taking risks," Zuri said.

"And which ways are that? By dealing with the niggers?"

"Whatever you wanna call it. It's the best way," Zuri said.

"I'm sorry Zuri, but I can't accept your proposition. Maybe if you would give in like the ole times, I would think about it," Marco said rubbing his dick. Zuri walked closer to him and seductively licked his face.

"Just maybe if you act right," she said. Just then Marco gave his guard the sign to leave. He hesitated as if he were not sure.

"LEAVE!" Marco yelled and the guard hurried out of the room, "Now pull that dress up and come over here woman," he said, unzipping his pants. Zuri raised her dress over her head exposing her flawless body. Marco began to lower his pants while he watched her position herself to sit on his lap/ He leaned back and closed his eyes while Zuri grabbed the sword that hung above his head.

"Are you ready for the ride of your life Zuri?"

"Oh I sure am," Zuri said as she stood in front of him with the sword in her hand.

"What the fuck? Guard!" he tried to yell as she swung the sword hitting him clearly in his neck, decapitating him instantly. Marco's lifeless body sat in the chair with his pants around his ankles. Zuri placed the bloody sword back on the rack and went to retrieve his severed head. She left the room and saw two dead guards with blood seeping from their foreheads as Marco's main guard smiled at her looking at her naked body.

"Where to next boss?" the guard asked.

"Call a meeting in an hour," Zuri commanded.

"Will do," the guard replied and left.

"What the fuck is going on here?" one man yelled. "Is it true what they said about the boss?" another man yelled.

"I don't know. A meeting was called and you're gonna wait and see. Now shut the fuck up and sit down." Another guard said sternly. Just as he made the statement, she walked in. She was beautiful. Her hair pinned into a Japanese bun, her tight fitting dress showed all of her curves. Her skin was flawless. Zuri, surrounded by her security detail, looked around at everyone as they stared in cold silence. Zuri walked to the front of the room where one of her men placed a huge black duffle bag in front of her.

"I know you are all anxious as to why you are at this meeting. You're also wondering why Chan-Ho is standing behind me." No one said anything but their expressions said it all. She continued.

"There's gonna be some changes today. Marco is no longer with us. He's dead."

"What do you mean Bitch? Chan-Ho, where is the Boss?" he asked nervously. Chan-Ho gave his man a head nod and just like that a dead man was sitting in the room amongst them.

"Now anymore outburst?" Zuri asked and continued.

"Like I was saying, your former boss is dead!!!" Zuri motioned to Chan-Ho to open the duffle bag. She reached in and lifted the severed head.

"You see, this is where greed, dishonesty, hate and lack of loyalty gets you. This organization will not be based on those characteristics. From now on, this organization will be based on trust, honesty, love and most of all loyalty." She nodded to Chan-Ho and he dumped twelve million dollars in US cash on the table. Each man's eyes lit up.

"This is twelve million dollars. I found this in Marco's office. We haven't searched his house yet. This is more money than you'll see in your entire lives. This is what he kept from all of you. You're the ones...." She pointed at all of them. "You're the ones who earned this money, not Marco. You were loyal to him in hopes of promises he never kept. Now, this money is only a fraction of what you will earn as long as you stay true to your-selves and loyal to this organization. We will build our country. We will feed the poor and impoverished. We will help the sickly and we will do these things swiftly and strategically. Our busi-ness will go on as usual but the way we operate will be different. No man in this room will make more money than the other. No man will denounce the other. We are a family and we will move and act as such. Do I make myself clear?" Zuri asked. Each man looked in her direction, looking at the bloodied 12 million.

"DO I MAKE MYSELF CLEAR?"

"Yes Boss!" one man yelled.

"Yes Boss!" another yelled.

"Hail to the Queen," they chanted together.

"Okay, now Chan-Ho will fill you all in with your new roles in this organization. We are proud members of the nation of the Philippines and we will act as such," Zuri said and exited the room flanked by her security detail.

Zuri laid in her hospital bed and reflected back on the day when she overtook the organization. She loved her position. She had lived two lives; one as a solid respectable upper middle class filipino-American and one as the underground Queen of the Philippines. She fed the poor, helped the sick and protected the weak. Now she lay in her hospital bed surrounded by her most trusted men while she suffered from cervical cancer. She had become a wealthy and powerful woman as well as her fam-ily, including Silky, her daughter. Zuri was happy to hear about the engagement to Prince. She wished that she could be there for the wedding but she would not spoil the moment with her sickly appearance. Chan-Ho had been with her everyday and brushed her long silky hair. He loved Zuri. She made him the man he had become. She loved him also. However, she would not mix business with pleasure, which would distort his job and jeopardize the organization. Zuri looked around the countless balloons and flowers that were sent by villagers, politicians and world leaders . Even as a so-called Filipino gangster, her image had been plastered on the news as the "Savior of the Filipino People".

"Chan?" she whispered.

"Yes Zuri?"

"Do you know what has to be done?" she asked.

"Yes Zuri, I know."

"Protect this organization with your life."

"I will. I promise."

"Chan-Ho?"

"Yes Zuri?"

"Get a wife, a nice woman who will deserve you. Have some kids, live your life."

"I will, but who will protect you?" Chan-Ho said as a tear fell from his eyes. Zuri smiled at his last statement and continued.

"Even as I die, you still try to protect me, huh?"

"Boss, I promised that I would protect you with my life."

"And that you did Chan-Ho. That you did, but I will not live much longer."

"Don't say that. We have the best doctors in the world working on you."

"I know, but I certainly don't feel that way. Shit, it feels as if they're the worst," Zuri said.

"You'll have surgery this week. After surgery you will be fine, I promise," Chan-Ho said.

"Yes, I will be fine. I have made peace with God. Chan-Ho, I don't want to suffer anymore. My body aches."

"I know Boss, but I've seen worse cases."

"Oh yeah? Where, on T.V?" she smiled.

"You know I don't watch television, I watch you Boss," Chan-Ho said smiling.

"I know Chan-Ho. I know and you've done a wonderful job," she said beginning to cough.

"Boss, you okay?'

"Yes, I'm fine. Chan-Ho, do me a favor."

"Anything Boss."

"Make sure my baby is all right. You have your men in the States look after her."

"Will do Boss. I promise. I'll do it myself."

"That's my boy," she smiled.

"Boss! Boss!" he called out. She kept the same smile on her face. The doctors had told him that she only had moments left. He had made up the surgery to make her feel better. In fact, she was dying. The only thing recognizable was her Silky black hair. Her body was at rest. He called her again; no answer. Zuri lay there with the most peaceful smile on her face. She had finally met her maker. He could tell she was enjoying the other side already. Enjoying heaven. Zuri had died.

"Hello?" Silky said on the other end of the phone.

"Hey Silky, it's Chan."

"Please! God no!" she cried.

"I'm so sorry Silky," Chan-Ho couldn't hold back his tears. "I will grant her last wishes Silky. I promise."

"I know you will Chan-Ho. I'll see you soon, she said softly and ended the call.

CHAPTER FOURTEEN

"Come on Sin, hurry up!"

"I'm running as fast as I can."

"Come on, we gotta get away."

"No! I must stay with Daddy. You go!"

"No, Daddy's gonna die if we leave him here."

"So let him and your mom die. They don't love us."

"Yes they do. Why would you say that?"

"Look at us. We're poor. We haven't eaten in one hundred days."

"Yeah but when Daddy finishes his job, we'll eat."

"No, we're never gonna eat again. We're gonna starve. We gotta run away from here. We can buy a zillion cherry balls, ice cream and chicken where we are going."

"Well where are we going?"

"We're going to Scooter's house."

"Scooter? Who is Scooter?"

"He has food. He'll feed us."

"No, you go. I gotta watch Daddy. He's gonna die!"

"No he's not. He's gonna shoot drugs with your mom."

"They don't want us, they want drugs."

"Are you sure?"

"Yeah, I'm sure."

"They told you that?"

"Yes, they told me, now come on."

"Sin! Sin! Wake up," Tasha said, shaking Sin and awakening him.

"No, don't leave Dennis, don't leave," Sin yelled.

"Sin, wake-up. You're having another nightmare."

"Oh shit, Tash. I saw him. I saw him, clear as day; my brother. He's out there somewhere. I know he is. We were running away," Sin said with sweat dripping from his face.

"What if he had to go through what I've been through? What if he's in trouble?" Sin said.

"Baby, what are you talking about?" Tasha asked.

"I gotta find my brother Tash. I know we are doing good. The draft is tomorrow, but my brother will complete my life. Let me show you something," Sin said and went into the closet where he pulled out a Spider-Man book bag. "He gave me this Tash."

"What's that?"

"It's the book bag he gave me. It had hot food, which I ate. The clothes are still in here and nine single dollar bills. The nine single bills are right here in the small part. I promised myself when I make it to the pros, I'm gonna give him one million for each dollar he gave me. It was his only money. He snuck food and clothes from his mom. He was the only person that ever gave me anything before I was adopted. He is what I live for."

"Wow Baby. I heard you talk about him, but never in this much detail. You have to trust in God. If God wants you to find him, you will. Just trust in God. Just like tomorrow, you must trust in God that you'll be drafted as the number one pick," Tasha smiled.

"Yeah God willing," Sin said looking up at the ceiling.

"Yes Baby, God willing," Tasha said, zipping the backpack.

"Maybe you could fit your practice gear in here," she said laughing.

"Girl, shut up. One of my sneakers can't fit in this small ass bag. I'ma hold on to this bag for the rest of my life. The contents in that bag are priceless. They define the generosity of my brother; his heart, his love for me," Sin said and laid back in the bed with his hands intertwined and his head staring up at the ceiling.

❖ ❖ ❖

"Dennis Mack, you've been bailed out," the court officer said.

"Yeah Motherfuckers! I know yall want me to stay but I'm getting the fuck out of here," Prince said happily as he stepped to the gate. He had gotten arrested for possessing an open bottle of Absolut Vodka while he drove. He had been in the holding pens for twelve hours, but it felt like twelve years. His bail was $1,000. He tried to bail himself out, but the magistrate denied his requests. He called Silky who paid his bail eleven hours prior, but the process to get him released had taken forever.

'Yo, yall be easy," Prince said to the others who were waiting to make bail.

"You too, New York. Be easy. We're gonna see you on the other side."

"Okay, do that," Prince said and left. "Damn, I missed the fucking NBA draft," Prince said.

"Naw, you didn't miss too much, it just started. New York took Sin King," a young African-American officer said.

"Word? Sin went number one?" Prince said.

"Yep. He's a New York Knick now," the officer said as he signed Prince's release papers. Prince stepped out the front door and saw Silky, Amir and Ralo.

"Hi Baby! You okay?"

"Yeah, I'm good Ma. What took y'all so long?" Prince said, smiling as he kissed his wife.

"Shit. I paid the bail ten minutes after you called. You know how slow these people are," Silky said.

"Come on Son, let's get away from here. This place gives me the creeps. I ain't ever hate a place as much as I hate the precinct," Amir said.

"You good P.I.?" Ralo asked, slapping his hand.

"You already know. I'm always good. I gotta go home and take a bath," Prince said.

"Okay, let's get out of here then," Silky said, grabbing his hand and leading him away. "Baby you scared me."

"I know. I'm sorry Ma. I shouldn't have had that bottle in my lap," Prince said as they walked up to a 2001 platinum Range Rover.

"This shit is all right," he commented.

"Yeah, I know. It's yours Daddy. Happy Birthday."

"Ooh shit," Prince said looking at his watch. "It is my birthday, huh?"

"Yeah nigga, it is. You started celebrating without me," she said and they both laughed.

"Nah, never that Ma," he said as he jumped in his new truck. "Never that!"

Prince and Ralo rode around Baltimore City in the 4.6 Range Rover, collecting money. Almost all accounts were clear. However, there was one odd ball who liked to live on the edge; or die on the edge. Their dope had been moving faster than it arrived and both men were able to stack a substantial amount of money. Prince and Silky invested in real estate in Maryland and New York, while Ralo invested in local hot spots. Amir had everything he needed, money, cars, homes and with that, his share of women.

"Yo, what up with Scrams who owe that forty cent?' Prince asked, referring to forty thousand that was owed to him.

"Who, son from Lafayette?" Ralo asked.

"Yeah, he got forty stacks for me."

"Come to think of it, I haven't seen him in a while. I drove through yesterday and the Trap was jumpin. The corner man was yelling out his stamp but he was nowhere in sight," Ralo said.

"See, it's dudes like him that need to be made an example of. We gettin soft Ralo," Prince said, shaking his head.

"Nah we ain't getting soft. He duckin us, that's all," Ralo

said.

"Well, make sure the next time he sticks his head up, you don't miss," Prince said as he inhaled on the blunt.

"Say no more," Ralo said and raised the volume on the radio.

◆ ◆ ◆

"Sin! Wake up," Tasha said, shaking him.

"Huh?"

"Wake up Sin. You're gonna be late for practice."

"Damn, what time is it?"

"It's after six. You're supposed to be at the practice facility at 6:30."

"Don't worry, I'll make it. I'll drive the Ferrari. I'll be there in ten minutes."

"Boy you know I don't like when you drive fast," she said.

"Don't worry Ma. I'm Dale Earnhardt King," Sin said, rising out of bed.

"Who?"

"He's a race car driver. The best ever and so am I."

"Just get there safe."

"I will Ma. Yo, where's the baby?"

"Oh, he went with your parents. They took him to FAO Schwarz."

"Again?"

"Yep, that boy is spoiled."

"Yo, that lil nigga was here before. I swear to God. He does shit that grown folks do and he catches on fast. I was in the bathroom peeing yesterday and this lil nigga stood beside me with no pamper on and tried to piss in the toilet. His aim was a little off because he peed all over me," Sin said and they both laughed hysterically.

"Yeah, he is something else. Sin?"

"Yeah!" Sin yelled while he was getting dressed.

"His dad is coming to get him next week."

"Oh, that's good. Why did you say it like that?" Sin asked.

"Because that is the same day as my first doctor's appointment."

"Doctor's appointment? For what?"

"Take a guess," she smiled.

"Nah, no guesses," Sin said.

"I'm pregnant, Sin. I'm having another baby."

"Ooh shit," he yelled and ran towards her. "You serious Tash?'

"Yeah, I found out this morning. That was them who called."

"Wow Ma. I should miss practice for this, right?'

"Nah, go to practice. We'll celebrate later," she said handing him his Ferrari keys.

"Aight, I'll see you later. I love you."

"I love you too," she said as she saw him running out the door, the happiest man alive.

CHAPTER FIFTEEN

Prince sat in his plush living room sipping Absolut Vodka without ice.

The television watched him as he was zoned into serious thoughts. He reflected on his past and his current life and was proud of what he had accomplished. He had a beautiful wife, cars, jewelry, property and lots of money. He even had what was rare; loyal comrades. One thing missing in his life was his brother Dennis. He had other brothers and sisters by his mom, but Dennis was on his mind every single day. He could remember clearly when they were kids and Dennis had stood up and pissed in a forty ounce beer bottle. He thought about all the nights his brother went without the bare necessities like food, clothing and hot water. He had been fortunate to have his mother and Lily Bird who cared for him. However, he was never at ease being "okay" when he knew that Dennis was somewhere in a foster home with parents who probably didn't love him. Prince drove by the old house where their father overdosed. It had been completely renovated, but he still saw the old beat down shack where he and his brother played basketball with a crate nailed to a tree. With all the money Prince had, it seemed as if his brother had dropped off the face of the earth. All he knew was, he was in foster care. He hired private investigators to find his brother. The only Dennis Mack that came back was himself and their deceased father. Prince didn't know if his brother was dead or alive, hungry or full. He prayed every night for God to give him the strength. He knew in his heart that Dennis was a lot stronger than him just by the way he adapted to poverty so easily. No matter how hard it was, Dennis always smiled as if everything was alright; it wasn't. Dennis had lived worse than or just as bad as those kids in a third world country. His mother didn't send him to school, but yet he knew how to read and count. He was special in many ways, but yet he was left alone in a heroin shooting gallery with a dead father to suffer. He wished that when his mother picked him up that day, that Dennis could have joined them. Unfortunately, Dennis was placed in the custody of social services and just like that, he was gone.

"I hope you're okay, Dennis," Prince said to himself and took another sip of his Absolut.

Later on, Silky, Prince and Amir sat at the oval shaped glass table. Prince smoked his weed, Amir pulled on his Cuban cigar and Silky sipped her cognac. This was a nucleus that supplied seventy-five percent of Baltimore and ninety percent of South Jamaica, Queens with heroin. They made it a mandatory rule to meet and discuss business.

"Okay gents, our first order of business; we got two hundred kilos coming this week. I already sent Chan-Ho the money. Pickup is at 8:30 down at the harbor," Silky said.

"Good, I'll put Ralo on it," Prince said.

"Next, my salons are doing well. Better than I expected. Our quarterly numbers were very impressive. I guess a bitch gotta get her hair done, huh?"

"Yeah, I knew that was gonna be a great investment, especially since we expanded to Atlanta," Amir said.

"Yo speaking of Atlanta, I heard that one of the salons was featured in that movie," Prince said.

"Yeah, our Atlanta spot is number one in the country. Beyonce gets her hair done there. Well at least she used to. Now, one of my stylists is on tour with her. It reminds me; I must send her a bill," Silky said and continued. "Um, Dad, Chan-Ho said that mom got her wish. He donated her money to poverty stricken families in the Philippines."

"Okay, that's good. I miss that crazy lady," Amir said shaking his head smiling.

"Yeah me too," Prince said smiling. "Yo Pop, she used to go hard on you," Prince said.

"Yeah, I know. She told you I had sex with her sister right? I never fucked her."

"Dad!"

"My bad Silky."

"Next order of business. There is a lot of questions being asked about James' murder."

"Yeah, I heard about it. Fuck him though. He gave his life for forty gees. It wasn't about the money, it was principle," Prince said.

"That's right son. You give a nigga an inch and he take the neighborhood. Nip that shit in the bud early, but make sure all tracks are covered. It was a bad idea to leave him in an abandoned house. Who else owes us," Amir asked.

"Nobody. Shit, now niggas us paying early. They don't want the same fate as James," Prince said.

"Oh well. He got what he asked for," Silky said and continued. "Dad, I put your money in your accounts and Baby our money is safe too. I was thinking about investing in this clothing line. Its called T.L.C. ; The Linen Closet. We'll sell different pastel colored linen suits for the spring and summer. You, dad and a few others will be my models."

"Excuse me? I ain't no model. You better call Tyson Beckford," Prince said smiling.

"I don't need him. You're beautiful," she said leaning over and kissing him.

"You're a handsome motherfucker, Amir said laughing. "But it definitely sounds like another good investment."

"It is. We'll get all the designers to run with us. We'll have T.L.C. by Heal-Thy, T.L.C. by Sean Jean, T.L.C. by Polo and whoever wants to invest. I really think this is gonna work," Silky said.

"It sounds like a go to me. I'm in," Prince said.

"I'm in too," Amir said.

"Well it's a done deal. I'll get on it ASAP. We gotta leave this game soon. I promised mommy this. I mean, I love this game, I was born into it, but I don't wanna lose everything by being greedy.

"You're right Silk. We can quit now," Amir said.

"Nah, not yet Dad. We got two hundred keys to sell. No time for quitting, just time for getting," she said.

"That's my girl," Prince said inhaling his weed.

"Well, I guess that's it. The meeting is over," the boss said, raising her glass. Each of them sat at the table silently. They were rich. The game had driven them to measures of no return. They all loved power and this was something they didn't wanna give up. Money ruled the world. Anything and anyone could be bought and they knew it. With this knowledge, there would be no stopping.

CHAPTER SIXTEEN

Prince was driving in his Range Rover making a few pit stops while he talked to his wife on the phone.

He made a stop at Ralo's house to get the remainder of the money he was owed, $250,000. Ralo's count was clear, Prince pulled up to a red light and continued to talk to Silky. He shook his head from side to side and smiled at a few comments that were made sexually towards him. He didn't even notice two beautiful women also stopped at the red light, who were desperately trying to get his attention. He pulled through the green traffic light only to get caught at another red light. He looked to his left and saw the two women who had been chasing him for the last two traffic lights. He glanced over at them and saw them making gestures towards him, He paid them little attention and continued to talk to his wife.

"Hello? Hello?" Silky yelled out.

"Yeah, my bad. Something caught my attention," He said.

"Who?" Silky said smiling on the other end.

"I don't know. Two chicks in a Jaguar coupe."

"Well what do they want?" she asked.

"The hell if I know. I'm on the phone talkin to you ," he said.

"Well find out what they want Daddy," Silky said.

"Man, I ain't got time for them bitches," he said.

"Nigga, every man wants to see if he still got it. You know, it's a swag check. Don't tell me you don't wanna keep your game tight. I'm giving you a pass," Silky said.

"A pass?" Prince asked curiously.

"Yeah, a pass. Tell them bitches to pull over. See what

happens next," Silky said now beginning to enjoy herself.

Prince pulled into a nearby shopping center ignoring Silky's request or set up for that matter. As soon as he cut his engine off the two women pulled in front of his Range Rover, blocking him in.

"Yo, these hoes are following me," he laughed.

"Where are you now?" she asked.

"I'm at the shopping center. I'm picking up some shit for the crib."

"Prince, let's see what dem bitches want. Keep me on the speaker so I can hear em when they holla at you," Silky said as Prince jumped out of his truck and walked towards the store, heading in the Jaguar's direction.

"Excuse us Mr. How you doin cutie?"

"I'm good and you, Prince said. Silky smiled enjoying every second.

"You a sexy motherfucker. I swear to God," the driver said, rolling her tongue.

"Tell her that she ain't too bad herself," Silly said across the sound waves.

"Shut up Silk," Prince said laughing.

"Excuse me?" the driver asked.

"Nah, not you. I'm just buggin that's all."

"Damn, I see that shiny ass wedding band on your finger. You married, huh?"

"Tell them no!" Silky yelled.

"Yeah, I'm married," Prince smiled.

"So why are you talkin to us? You must not be happy," the passenger asked.

"I'm not the one who blocked you off. Yall stopped in front of me," Prince said smiling. He thought about Ralo. He would have been all over them.

"Well I guess you're right," the driver said and continued. "Shit, we're married too. It doesn't make any difference. We're still trying to holla at you, ain't that right girl?" the driver said turning to the passenger and kissing her passionately.

"Oh word? Well, I'm trying to holla at both of yall at the same time," Prince said, eliciting laughter from Silky and getting applause as well.

"Oh you want both of us huh? The driver asked.

"Yeah, I wanna fuck both of yall and I want my wife to join us. Yall with it or what? It can't be nothing else. I mean, we're all married right?'

"I know that's right," the passenger said.

"Well here's my number. Give me, I mean give us a call and we definitely can make something real freaky happen."

"Nigga what you doin right now? Let me suck your dick right here in the parking lot," the driver said.

"Nah, I'm on a business run at the moment, but I'll take you up on that later," he said smiling.

"Yeah, you do that. Please!"

"Daddy, give them our house number," Silky said.

"Nah, okay ladies y'all be easy. I'ma holla at y'all later, okay?"

"Okay and tell that wife of yours that she is a lucky bitch and I can't wait to eat her pussy," the driver said.

"You ain't gotta tell me shit Hooker, I know what I got," Silky yelled as loud as she could. Prince smiled, exited his truck and walked towards the store.

"Excuse me, what is your name?" the passenger yelled out.

"Lucky," Prince said and kept walking.

"Daddy, hurry up and come home so I can do what they wanted to do to you but better. I'll be here butt naked and wet with my face down, ass up and you can fuck me any way you wanna fuck," Silky said rubbing her pussy through her panties.

"I'll be there in five minutes."

"I'm wet Daddy," Silky said, licking her fingers.

"Two minutes," Prince said, turning away from the store and jogging back to his truck.

CHAPTER SEVENTEEN

"Uncle Steve"

Prince and Silky laid under the air conditioner, both exhausted after hot and steamy sex.

No matter how many times they had sex, they always got maximum satisfaction. It was something to both of them that was unexplainable. No matter what, Silky always had a squirting orgasm and Prince came enough to fill a cream pie. Their sex had become more than sex. They had become mentally, physically and most of all, spiritually connected. They were soul mates.

"Yo Silk, I'm going up top tomorrow."

"I know, I'ma miss you Daddy. I don't know what I'm doing while you're away," Silky said sadly.

"I asked you if you wanted to come," he said.

"Cum?" Silky said seductively.

"Stop playing. You know what I mean," he said.

"Nah, I gotta stay here and take care of a few things. I'm meeting with this new clothing designer. Her name is Debra Norwood. Have you ever heard of her?"

"Yeah, ain't she the one that sponsored the last ski trip?"

"Yeah, that's her, but she came out with a new line of dresses for women. We spoke about (T.L.C.) The Linen Closet and she's coming by this weekend."

"That's good Ma. I'm proud of you."

"Thank you Baby. I'm proud of us. We are doing so good," Silky said leaning over and kissing him. Prince began to rise below the belt, and again, they began to connect.

◆ ◆ ◆

Prince rented a car. He decided to leave his truck parked in the underground parking lot. Instead he settled for the Cadillac CTS and hit the highway heading towards New York. Three and half hours later, he was crossing the Verrazano Bridge, heading back towards his old neighborhood. He missed his old neighborhood, but it was nothing compared to the life he became accustomed to. He was rich. He couldn't believe it, but he was a respected millionaire. He put his family in a very comfortable position and looked out for his team that he left behind. He stopped at a few of his comrades' spots and went to get a haircut from his old friend Tim; who owned Mr. Rooney's Barbershop on Merrick Blvd. After he had gotten his haircut, he headed to see his team who were stationed on 142nd and Foch Blvd. Things didn't change much. The block was still making money. He noticed his friends posted up in front of Associated Supermarket. He drove past in the burgundy Cadillac and no one noticed him. He made a quick right and parked on the corner of 143rd street. He walked in his friends' direction and he saw the smiles on their faces as he approached them.

"Oh shit! P.I., what's good my Nigga?" Kah yelled out as he approached.

"Same shit," Prince said, extending his hand. Kah bear hugged his close friend and tried to lift a now heavier Prince.

"Damn Nigga, you been eatin good, huh?" Kah said.

"Yeah somethin like that. I see y'all ain't doin too bad either," Prince said looking across the street at the exotic cars.

"Yeah, the Bentley coupe is Darren's the Mazi (Maserati) is Big Boi's and the Range is mine," Kah said.

"Yo, what's good PI?" Darren said, giving him a hug.

"You already know. Same shit," Prince said.

"P.I., niggas miss your presence in the hood Son," Big Boi said smiling.

"I miss yall too."

"Yo, we got yours put away in the safe," Darren said.

"Mines?" Prince said confused.

"Yeah, your money. You started this shit. Loyalty first, remember?" Kah said.

"Yeah. Yeah. I remember, but I'm good. Yall split that bread. Split it three ways," Prince said.

"Yo, you sure Prince?"

"Positive!" Prince said as he began to walk and they followed him up the block.

"Put these on." They put the surgical masks on and Prince began to unwrap the brick of heroin. The four men sifted and mixed Bonita Block with Quinone, a perfect mixture that would be used to cut the grade "A" heroin.

"Yo," Prince said through his mask. "When yall bust the next ones, make sure you always got your mask on." They all shook their heads and did their parts cutting and bagging the heroin for the next few hours. They spoke on numbers that were agreed upon by all of them and then Prince left.

"Yo, we rich," Darren said, locking the door behind Prince with a smile.

Prince drove down Rockaway Blvd. He passed a man that looked very familiar. He quickly made a U-turn and looked closely at the tired old man pushing a shopping cart filled with his life's belongings.

"Yo?" Prince called out. The man kept pushing his cart, not paying Prince any mind.

"Yo, you with the cart," Prince called out, pulling up following the man now determined to get his attention.

"Yo, what's up man," the man yelled with a scraggy voice aggravated because his route was being disturbed.

"Um, do you know my pops?" Prince asked.

"I might, who is he?"

"His name is Dennis. I mean his name was Dennis. He's dead now," Prince said.

"Dennis?" the old man said lifting his slumped body to an erect position.

"Yeah, Dennis Mack," Prince said.

"Why you ask me that? Who are you?"

"I'm his son, Prince."

"Lil Prince. Dennis Jr., that you?"

"Yeah, who are you? Why do I feel like I've seen you before?'

"It's me, your uncle Steve. You don't remember me? You're still eating all those cherry balls?" the old man asked. Prince couldn't believe it. He wanted to reach for his gun and blow this old man's head off. He had been responsible for his father's death. At least, that's what his mother had told him. Prince grew up hating this man. But after learning the streets, he knew that his father would have met the same fate with or without Steve's help.

"Oh shit. It is you ain't it?" I got a question for you," Prince said.

"What's that," Steve said scratching his face.

"The little boy I used to play with while y'all shot dope, where is he?"

"You talkin about Dennis?"

"Yeah, my brother Dennis. Where is he and what happened that day my pops died? I was there and I heard the stories, but what really happened?" Prince asked.

"What happened? I'll tell you what happened. What happened was what usually happens. Your father was a selfish bastard. That's what happened. He didn't want to share shit. I couldn't use his car' he wouldn't give me shit. He was just pure selfish. He had a wife at home and he had to come and take mine too?"

"Yours too?"

"Yeah, you heard me. He stole my woman. Sarah and I were in love way before that pretty-boy motherfucker of a father of yours came along. I had the bitch first. We used to go on dates to the movies, Coney Island, everywhere. But he had to come along and fuck with mine. I wouldn't do that to him. You ain't gonna never hear about me pushing up on Ronnie, your mama."

"Yo, keep my mother's name out your mouth," Prince said sternly.

"Anyway," Steve said, brushing off his threat and continuing. "The day we decided to go all the way. He gave me some money to buy the dope and I bought some coke too. When we went back to Sarah's, I tried to split everything equally. But your selfish daddy wanted it all and that was his downfall. His greediness led to his dumping all the coke and his entire dime of dope. I warned the motherfucker, but he wouldn't listen to me," Steve said shaking his head.

"So his greed led to his death, huh? Not the fact that you volunteered to buy coke that he didn't ask you to buy?"

"Listen, that nigga was thirty years old. He was grown. He didn't have to speedball. He knew the consequences. Just like he knew what he was doing when he fucked my woman," Steve yelled.

"So this is what this is all about huh? A dope-fiend bitch? You killed our pops so you and your Aids infected bitch could be together, you coward?"

"Hey, you watch your mouth. I'm still your uncle."

"Nigga, fuck you. You ain't shit to me. You're lucky I don't blow your head off. Now tell me about my brother.

"I ain't tellin you shit!" uncle Steve said, raising his finger. "Give me two dollars." Prince shook his head in disgust and reached in his pocket and pulled out a wad of hundred dollar bills.

"Now tell me about my brother."

"Man, you don't know about Sin?'

"He's Mr. Harlem USA. He played for North Carolina. He

on the Knicks now. I even heard about you. Why aren't you in the pros with him?" Steve asked.

"Sin? What Sin?"

"His name is Dennis King. He was adopted by Marvin King of the New York Knicks. He calls himself Sinned; that's your name backwards.

"You tryna tell me that the little boy from the house is Sin from Harlem and he's my brother?"

"Yep, that's him."

"He sure doesn't look the same," Prince said.

"Shit you don't either. The last time I saw you, was when……"

"Yeah, when you killed my pops Bitch?" Prince said as he ripped the hundred dollar bill into pieces and threw it at Steve. Steve pushed his cart aside and dove to the ground grabbing the ripped pieces to a puzzle that would get him high for the rest of the day.

Prince drove off thinking about what he had heard. He couldn't believe that all this time, the kid he had been searching for his entire life, had been right in front of him and he hadn't even known. He was his son's stepfather.

"Damn," Prince said and smiled as he called Silky.

"Hey Baby! What are you doin?" Silky asked, excited to hear from her husband.

"Nothin! I'm good. I just saw a ghost, that's all."

"A ghost? You saw the boogeyman? Well make sure you bring some of that shit you just smoked," Silky said laughing.

"Nah, I'll explain to you later. Yo, lemme call you back. I gotta take care of something," he said.

"Okay Baby. I love you. Call me later."

"I love you too Ma. Bye."

"Be safe!" she yelled.

"I will," Prince said, ending the call.

He made a U-turn and headed back towards the hideout. He saw Steve leaning against a dumpster, taping his hundred dollar bill together.

"Yo Steve!"

"What now man? This some foul shit you did to this money. What, you want your money back now?" Steve asked.

"Nah, come on, get in. I shouldn't have done that. I've got something for you. Yo leave that cart and take a ride with me," Prince opened the passenger door and Steve got in.

"Damn, you stink!" Prince said holding his nose.

"Nah nigga, dat ain't me. That's you. I washed up at the park this morning," Steve said.

"Nigga you smell like seaweed."

"Whatever. Where we going anyway?"

"Man, be easy. I got you." Prince pulled two doors away from the hideout and ran towards the spot.
Knock! Knock! A nervous Big Boi looked through the peephole and saw Prince.

"Yo, " Prince said, entering the house. "I need like a gram of that shit uncut."

"A gram. For what?" Darren asked.

"I want somebody to test it out."

"Yo, I thought you said earlier...."

"Yeah, exactly. This is gonna be this niggas last test," Prince said smiling and also hurrying to get away from the fumes that filled the air. Kah broke a chunk off and handed him a nice piece.

"Yo, I'm out. Holla at me in the morning. Oh yeah give me some of that coke too," Prince said. Big Boi handed him an ounce of coke.

"Nah, not this much. Give me a gram of that too," Prince said.

"Yo Prince, whatever you are about to do, be safe," Kah said.

"Yeah, yeah, always. This shit right here is personal. I gotta do this. This is personal," Prince said.

"Aight Son. Be safe."

"You already know," Prince said, shaking their hands and leaving. He jumped back in the car with Steve. He drove to a hotel right off the highway. Steve went in and paid for a room. They both went in. Prince emptied the contents on the dresser and Steve's eyes widened. He began to dig into his pocket for his used needle so he could get high. Prince watched Steve prepare his fate. He smiled and left the room.

"Now you can rest in peace Dad. Fuck you Uncle Steve," Prince said and pulled off.

◆ ◆ ◆

"Hello Tash?"

"Yeah," Tash said, answering her phone.

"How's everything?" Prince asked.

"Fine. What's up with you? You in New York yet?" Tasha asked, trying to hide her nervousness. She felt uneasy talking to Prince now that they had both moved on.

"Yeah, I'm on the highway now. I'll be uptown in ten minutes. You got his things ready?"

"Um, I live downtown Prince. And what things do he need?" Tasha said playfully.

"Oh my bad. I call all of Manhattan "Uptown", but just make sure he got a change of clothes. I'ma take him to Dave and Busters, and then we'll go shopping and shit. If it gets too late, I'll stay at my mother's house and bring him back in the morning."

"Oh, okay. He'll be ready. That's all he's been talking about since I told him you were coming," Tasha said.

"Yeah, I took him to the toy store last time."

"Okay. I'll see you when you get here," she said.

"Yo Tash, Sin there?"

"No. He went overseas with the team for exhibition games. He won't be back for two weeks. Why?"

"Oh nothing. I need to holla at him about something, that's all."

"Holla at him?" Tasha said mimicking him.

"Yeah, I just heard some crazy shit. I'll talk to both of yall when the time is right. "Tell him to call me when he gets back."

"Okay. Is everything okay?" Tasha said nervously. She knew that Prince and Sin were totally different people and the only thing they had in common was basketball.

Prince pulled into the visitor's parking lot, parked the Cadillac and headed to the elevator. When he entered, he saw a white couple headed in his direction. They were walking fast to catch the elevator. He held the button until they reached and got on.

"Oh thanks," the man said without looking at Prince. Once they saw that he was black and over six feet tall, the man quickly grabbed the door before it closed.

"Oh honey, I forgot something in the car," the white man said.

"Okay, you go ahead. I'll meet you upstairs," his wife said. She was immediately attracted to Prince. He smiled at the nervousness and jealousy of her husband.

"Honey!" the man said louder, holding the door. She followed him off the elevator. Prince smiled and pressed "Penthouse" and went to get his son. Once he reached the penthouse, his son was waiting for him

"Daddy!" he said, running into his father's arms.

"What's up lil me? How have you been?" Prince said looking at his son who began to look exactly like him.

"Can I bring my toys?"

"Yeah. You can bring whatever you want."

"No. Don't tell him that Prince," Tasha screamed from her bedroom. "He'll try to bring every toy he has. Just take two toys boy," Tasha yelled.

"Okay Ma," Lil Prince said.

Tasha walked out of the room and she was as beautiful as ever. Her clear skin complimented her sexy curvaceous body and her long black silky hair. She had become a woman; a beautiful woman that had all the qualities that any man would want. Prince blushed at the sight of her as she walked in his direction.

"What's good Tash?"

"Nothing. Dennis get your bag out of the closet," Tasha said.

"Okay Ma, I'm getting my toys."

Prince noticed she had gained a few pounds in all the right places.

"You gained some weight," he commented.

"What, I'm fat?" she flirted.

"Nah. It looks nice on you," Prince said.

"Thank you Prince. But I'm gonna get bigger than this. I'm pregnant," she said.

"Oh word? That's nice Tash. I'm happy for you. Shit, you may as well start a family. From the looks of around here, y'all doing real good for yourselves," Princes said sincerely.

"Yeah, I've been blessed. Excuse me, we've been blessed," Tasha said as they both watched Lil Prince lug his toy collection into the living room.

"Boy, I said two toys. One, two," Tasha said counting on her fingers as Prince laughed. "How's Silky Prince?" she asked.

"Oh, she's good Tash. I think she's meeting with a clothing designer today. She is about to start a clothing line of men and women linen suits. It's called T.L.C. , The Linen Closet."

"That sounds like something. Tell her I wish her the best of luck," Tasha said sincerely.

"I will Tash," Prince said as his son walked in carrying his book bag.

"Boy, not that bag," Tasha, said. Prince looked at the bag his son had lugged. He had spotted it. It was the Spider-Man book bag. The bag he had given Sin almost twenty years ago. He couldn't believe it, but it was reality. Uncle Steve was right. Sin was his brother. Prince stood there and stared at his son lugging his toys with the bag around his shoulders.

"Tasha?"

"Yeah?"

Lemme see that book bag?'

"That's Sin's book bag. He had it ever since he was a little boy. He said his brother gave it to him."

"Can I see it, Tasha?"

"Come here boy. Give your father that bag," she said as their son walked towards them and handed him the bag. Prince looked at it, opened up and looked at the inside information. He looked down at the contents and saw a brand new pair of underwear and some single dollar bills. He grabbed the money. He knew it. It was nine-dollar bills. He counted them to be sure. It was in fact the same nine dollars he had given to his best friend in the whole wide world; his brother. He handed Tasha the bag and showed her the name on the tag that was sewn in by his grandmother, Lily Bird.

Prince Dennis Mapp

131-21 Rockaway Blvd

6 years old Phone #: 555-4122

Tasha couldn't believe it. A tear dropped from her eyes as she realized that her husband and her son's father were brothers. She had been awakened many nights because of Sin's nightmares. She didn't know how to feel. The only two men that she had ever loved were brothers.

"Oh my God Prince. Oh my God."

"This shit is crazy, right?" he asked.

"You knew the whole time didn't you? That's why you wanted to talk to Sin?"

"Nah, actually, I just found out on my way here. I ran into my uncle. I heard some things but I wasn't sure. Now this bag confirms everything."

"I gotta call Sin."

"Nah let him focus on basketball. Just let me know when he gets back. Me and Silky will come back to New York and we'll tell him together."

"Daddy, you ready?" Lil Prince asked, getting restless.

"Yeah, I'm ready Lil homie. Let's go," Prince said, grabbing his son and the right book bag; heading towards the elevator.

"Yo Tash, I'll see you in the morning. You okay?' he said as he noticed her facial expression. "Listen, don't worry. Just take care of that baby. It's not bad. Actually, today is one of the best days of my life. You couldn't have been married to a better man. I can sleep better at night because I know for sure that my son is good. Me and my brother got a lot of things to discuss. I've been waiting my whole life for this," Prince said as he kissed her cheek. Lil Prince kissed her too and they left.

"Oh my God," Tasha said as she watched the elevator close.

CHAPTER EIGHTEEN

Silky and Debra Norwood talked while they drove to the airport.

The meeting went very well and Deb's ideas would definitely be considered. Silky swerved her new Mercedes Benz in and out of traffic trying to avoid the five o'clock rush hour. The two women enjoyed each other's company. They had seen eye to eye and they both shared a T.L.C. vision. While Debra continued to shoot out ideas, Silky drove and listened. She glanced at her left and noticed a familiar face two cars over from her. She wasn't sure so she switched one lane to make sure it was the face she knew. When she was close enough to the Audi A8, she had seen him. It was her ex-boyfriend and ex-business partner; Black. She hadn't seen him in years since they split. It was rumored that Black had moved out of town. It didn't matter. Black was no competition for her. She was his connection and no supplier could compare to her. Black hadn't only disrespected their relationship by getting arrested for raping a minor, but he had also stolen money and product. Her father, Amir wanted to kill Black. He didn't trust him and most of all he lacked loyalty. Silky had convinced Amir not to kill Black and Black disappeared until now. "But why is he back?" she thought to herself. She glanced over and noticed he had a passenger who had his seat adjusted all the way back. The passenger's jewelry lit up the car and his oversized fitted hat laid low on his face. The passenger had looked familiar also. Debra continued to talk not knowing what ran across Silky's mind. She had no idea who she was riding with and Debra would never know. Silky saw the exit to the airport, got in the right lane and the red Audi sped by them. She could only get a glimpse of the passenger but for some reason, she thought it was Ralo. "That chain", she said to herself and shook it off. "He would never be in the car with Black," she thought to herself. She thought wrong. Silky dropped Debra off at her terminal and headed home.

"Yeah , I got you. You don't gotta play the backseat to nobody, especially a New York Nigga. You know dem New York Niggas ain't no good. You see what that Nigga, Alpo did to the homies," Black said over the low music while he drove.

"Yeah, I'm definitely feeling you ."

"I know you are. Who wouldn't feel Black. It's because of me, Silky is in the game. I made that Bitch," Black said. He knew he was lying. Silky had given him his identity.

"I'm the one who had the connections, not her. I showed that bitch how to cut dope. Me. The legendary Black, and now I'm back in my city! I got a new connect. I got these Africans that will give me anything I ask for as long as I can move the weight in an ample amount of time. You feel me?"

"Yeah, I feel you," Ralo said, inhaling his blunt.

"See Lo, it's like this. Y'all got Baltimore on smash right now. But for what? You ain't seen no real dough. I mean, what's a few hundred geez when you gotta pass off millions to that Nigga Prince? Are you a millionaire yet?"

"I got a couple of dollars," Ralo said modestly.

"Well, I'ma make you a multi before you die like B.I.G. said, We're gonna be partners. I don't need no fuck-boys who run my errands. I need a business partner who likes to move keys and stack bread", Black said as he too inhaled on the potent weed.

"Yeah, I'm feelin that," Ralo said.

"See, we can do it like this. I put up two million and try to get as close to the number as possible. From there we go see the

Africans and it's on and poppin," Black said and continued.

"This shit I got is fire. We can put a two on in and flip bricks real fast. The ball is in your hands. Just think about it. You don't need no bitch for no boss and that Nigga Amir, fuck him too. We can leave them all where they stay."

Ralo sat back as his weed kicked in and listened to Black babble on as if he were a little nigga. He wanted to burst out laughing in Black's face when he called off two million. Ralo had way more money than that. However, Ralo was jealous of Prince. He wanted Silky. He felt he had been around way before Prince and she went to New York and met this Nigga. He wanted Prince out of the picture. He wished it was he that Silky had proposed to at Mo's restaurant, but it wasn't. Ralo had everything he wanted but his obsession for Silky was his weakness. Prince was the total opposite. He loved his wife but he was not obsessed. Yet Silky was obsessed with him, Ralo couldn't see what she had seen in Prince. What did he have that Ralo didn't? This was a question that boiled inside of him and this is why he tolerated Black's babbling. Ralo would never do business with a broke snake. Black thought because he was older, that he was smarter than Ralo. However, he was being used as a critical pawn to eliminate extra pieces on the board. When the coast was clear Silky would need Ralo's shoulder to lean on. She would turn to him for comfort and forget all about Prince. He would be with her and she would be all over him the way she is with Prince. Then, the money would roll in thick and he would not only have the baddest bitch, but he would be in control of Baltimore City.

"Yo, drop me to my car. I'll call you in a few days."

"Yeah, Lil Homie, take all the time you need. It ain't no rush," Black said.

"I got this dumb ass nigga," Black smiled to himself as he drove.

CHAPTER NINETEEN

Prince arrived in Baltimore after a long surprising weekend.

He still couldn't believe what he had learned about his brother. He never expected to kill his uncle either, but it was all in a weekend's work. It had been confirmed that Uncle Steve was dead after he saw it on the local news while he and little Prince stayed at his mother's house. Steve had died from an overdose of cocaine and heroin, the same way the senior Dennis had met his demise. Prince entered his condo; he heard movement in the back room. He knew it was his wife. He didn't call to let her know he was in town. He decided to surprise his wife with gifts he picked up for her while he stopped on 5th Avenue. Silky would love her new Gucci bag and matching sandals that Prince had bought her. Silky had her head tilted to the side as she combed her long silky hair and noticed Prince standing in the doorway through the wall-sized mirror.

Hey Baby, you're back. Why didn't you call?" she said running to him kissing and jumping in his arms.

"What's up Ma? I wanted to surprise you. You miss me?"

"Hell yeah I missed you," she said as she kissed his forehead.

"I miss you too Boo," Prince said shaking his head.

"What's the matter Baby? You look exhausted."

"I am, to be honest with you. It's been a long weekend," Prince sighed.

"Oh yeah? What's been so long about this weekend? You and Tash got into an argument?"

"Nah. Actually we were fine. Tash is good. I picked up Lil Prince. Yo that LiL Nigga is smart as hell. Oh yeah, Tash is pregnant too."

"Ooh, that's nice. Is she fat yet?"

"Nah not yet, but she's getting there," Prince laughed.

"So, if all that went good, what's wrong Baby?"

"I found my brother."

"Oh yeah? That's wonderful. Where is he? Is he all right? When can we meet with him? Wait a minute. Why are you not happy? Is he okay?" Silky asked.

"Oh, I'm happy as hell and he's doing real good. Shit he's doing better than me. He plays for the New York Knicks."

"Yeah and?"

"It's Sin, Silky. Sin is my brother. Tasha's husband is my brother," Prince said shaking his head.

"Get the fuck outta here? Sin-Sin is your brother, Prince?"

"Yeah, Sin King, the number one draft pick of the Knicks is the long lost brother I've been looking for."

"Wow Prince. How did you find that out?" Silky asked.

"I was coming back from meeting with Kah. So I'm driving up Rockaway Blvd and whom do I see? I see my Uncle Steve, my Dad's brother. This nigga was pushing a shopping cart and I stopped and hollered at him. I also found out how he let my pops die because my pops took his bitch."

"Get the fuck out of here Prince? Are you serious?"

"That's my word to my son. My uncle Steve was found dead in a hotel the next day."

""Um," Silky said, turning her face to Prince's last comment.

"I ain't get to speak to Sin yet, he's overseas. I told Tash we'll go up there together and holla at him. She promised that she wouldn't mention it," Prince said.

"So how did Tasha feel about this?" Silky asked.

"Shit, she was just as surprised as you and me. And you wanna know what's crazy?"

"What's that?"

"He still had the same book bag I told you about with the same nine dollar bills still inside of it. Lil Prince grabbed the wrong bag and I noticed it right away. I looked in it and my name was still in the motherfucker. He kept the bag Silk."

"Damn Baby. Well congratulations, I guess," she said with a confused face.

"Thanks. I just don't know what I'm going to say to him, but I can't wait."

"Baby?"

"Yeah?"

"Where is Ralo?"

"Ralo?" he said confused and continued. "He went out of town to meet a new client in North Carolina.

"Oh because I seen that nigga Black on the highway. I knew it was him for sure and his passenger had on a chain that resembled Ralo's, but I couldn't see him clearly. I was in the Benz, so he didn't notice my car. When I finally got closer, my exit came up and I couldn't get a clear look.

"Yeah, Lil Calvin told me that he saw him on Spring Street. That was Saturday. He called me while I was in New York. Calvin wanted to murk him right then and there. I said "for what?" We ain't got no problems. I can't be going around getting all your exes murked," Prince laughed, ducking a playful punch by Silky.

"Boy paleeze! You know damn well the world knows who my husband is."

"Yeah, I know babe. I know. I'm about to take a shower. I'm sticky as hell. When I get out you already know what time it is," Prince said.

"So why can't I get it while you're sticky? It's gonna get sticky anyway," Silky said rubbing his dick through his jeans.

"You know what, you're right," he said, removing his shirt.

"We'll take a bath together after we're all creamy and sticky.

"Shut up and turn around," Prince said, tugging her grey sweats.

CHAPTER TWENTY

"...... "Nah that wasn't Charlie Murphy, that was Clifton Powell. That was the same dude that played "Bitch-Ass Chauncey" in Menace II Society."

"No Prince, I'm telling you, Pinky was played by Charlie Murphy," Silky said as they entered the condo.

"Well, whoever that was, he was a funny nigga," Prince said and entered the condominium behind his wife. To his surprise he was shocked to see two beautiful women sitting in the living room watching "Friday After Next" and laughing hysterically.

"Yo who the fuck......" Prince began to say reaching for his weapon immediately.

"Baby, be easy. These are my two friends. This is Cherry and this is Coco. I let them in earlier," Silky said seductively.

"Oh yeah? For What? Since when have we started letting people in our crib when we ain't here?" Prince asked, confused.

"Since I decided to give you your personal party."

"Personal party?" he asked.

"Yeah, you never heard of Cherry and Coco? These are the two most famous porn stars in the industry and they're here just for you," Silky said.

"For me? Nah, I'm good. I got you," he said.

"Come on Baby. You think I didn't know you fantasize about fucking me with two women? Well, here we are. Say hello to your fantasy," Silky said as Cherry slipped out of her tight fitting jeans and Coco followed. Silky quickly began to undress, grabbing Prince's arm, leading him into the living room. Cherry went to the DVD player and placed one of her own DVDs featuring her and Coco. Now Prince knew exactly who they were. He watched the DVD for a few seconds and looked over at the real thing. Cherry had her back to him and was clapping her ass like thunder, while Coco rubbed on her own pussy and licked her fingers. Silky grabbed Prince's belt buckle, undid his pants, slipped his hard dick out of his pants and put the tip in her mouth. Prince watched Coco eat Cherry's pussy while Silky sucked his dick. Cherry and Coco joined in with them and Cherry began to eat Silky's pussy, while Coco ate hers and Silky sucked his. Prince warned Silky that he was about to explode and Cherry hurried and switched positions with Silky and deep throated Prince long and slow making his toes curl as he erupted deep down Cherry's throat.

"Um yes, cum in my mouth Prince," Cherry moaned. Coco hurried and switched positions with Cherry and caught the end of Prince's cum deep in her throat. Prince moaned with pleasure as he just had his dick sucked by three beautiful women, two of them porn stars. He quickly removed the remainder of his clothes and he watched Coco eat Silky's pussy. He smiled at the thought of knowing that she had done this just for him. Cherry pushed Prince on the couch and straddled him in reverse cowgirl position, while she rode his dick and he slapped her ass. Coco positioned her pussy in Prince's face and he began to taste her deep dark chocolate. She was liking it so much that she began to lose concentration while she ate Silky's pussy. Coco was the first to release her thick white cum all over Prince's face. Cherry began to moan faster and ride harder as she too was ready to explode all over Prince's dick.

"Oooh my God, I'm about too, too, cumm, cuuummm," Cherry screamed as Prince lifted his waist thrusting deep inside of her while she rode out of control.

"You like this Daddy?" Silky asked as she was getting her asshole eaten, by Cherry.

"Um huh," Prince moaned as Cherry clapped her ass uncontrollably as cream covered his still erect dick.

"Please, lemme get some dick," Coco begged. She positioned herself facing him holding his dick in her hand. She spit a glob of spit in her hand and rubbed her warm spit on Prince's dick. She lifted her body and guided him inside of her. She yelled with pain and pleasure. She began to ride him harder and faster. She grabbed Prince's hand and led his fingers to her dripping pussy. To his surprise, his dick did not occupy that hole. He was in her asshole. He hadn't even noticed the difference. It felt so soft and gushy that he'd swore he was in her pussy. Silky smiled and watched. Prince's dick grew a few more inches and he began to bust her ass wide open. He slammed her down and she yelled at the top of her lungs while he fingered her pussy. Silky rammed Cherry's ass with a ten-inch dildo. Cherry was in a zone. She hadn't felt this good ever. Silky kissed her softly on her neck and pounded her at a light speed pace. Everybody moaned with pleasure. Prince warned Coco that he was about to cum and she rode faster.

"Cum inside of me please, Prince! Please cum inside my ass," she moaned as a tear fell from her eye. She leaned over in his ear and whispered the unthinkable.

"I love you." Prince paid her statement no mind. He rammed harder and faster as he exploded deep inside of her.

"Oooh shit," Prince said as he slipped him deep inside her pussy. Silky and Cherry had switched positions and Silky was riding Cherry with the dildo deep inside of her. Silky yelled, "Ooh Prince." Coco yelled, "ooh Prince," and Cherry yelled, "ooh Prince," as he fingered her, massaging her oversized clit. Coco turned with her back towards Prince so that she could ride him harder and faster. Prince laid back and enjoyed the ride as Coco's cum drenched his dick.

"Yo Silky, get over here and get on this dick," Prince said commanding Silky to ride his still unbelievably hard dick. Coco lifted with a little resentment and Silky took her place. Cherry placed the dildo inside of Coco and began to fuck her doggy-style while Prince positioned Silky on his dick. She began to slide up and down and gave Prince the best feeling he had ever had. His entire body began to tingle with pleasure as she rode up and down, while planting soft kisses on his neck.

"Oooh my God. Daddy I'm about tooo cuummmm," Silky screamed.

"Yeah, show these bitches how you do. Who makes you cum?" he asked.

"Only you Daddddy. Only you," Silky said as ice cream plastered Prince's dick. She squirted so much that she had surprised both porn stars that entered the fun and lifted Silky from Prince's dick and licked her pussy as she again squirted onto both of their faces covering them with white cream. Coco again sat on top of Prince's dick and rode him until he was about to explode.

"Yo Silky, get back on it," he said as Silky made her way towards him and positioned herself face down on the sofa. Prince entered her from behind and pumped her slowly until he had gotten that ultimate feeling again. He held onto her shoulder and sped up his pace as he was again, about to explode.

"Ooooh my Goddd Ma," Prince whispered as he squeezed Silky, almost hurting her shoulder. His entire body shook as he released deep inside of his wife. After an hour and a half of sucking and fucking ,they all got dressed and the porn stars left. On the elevator leaving the building, Cherry noticed tears falling from Coco's face.

"Girl you okay?" she asked.

"I don't know Cherry. I just don't know. It's somethin about that man. I mean, I've fucked plenty of niggas, but it was something about his touch, the way he felt inside of me. It was like he fucked my soul. Cherry , bitch, think I'm in love with a customer," Coco said wiping her face.

"Well Bitch, you better snap out of it. This is a business we're in. We can't involve feelings with this shit. I mean, I can't lie either. That bitch Silky had me feeling a certain type of way, but I'm about this paper. Love can't buy these," Cherry said pointing at the diamonds that her and Coco wore.

"Yeah, you're right Cherry," Coco said and got in the

awaiting SUV.

◆ ◆ ◆

"Baby?" Silky said, laying on Prince.

"What up?" he answered.

"You okay?"

"Yeah, I'm good ma. That shit was bananas."

"Yeah, you deserve the best. I know you didn't expect that, but this is what this marriage is about; the unexpected. I want to give you the best of all worlds. I wanna satisfy all your fantasies. This will keep our marriage strong. Whenever you feel a need to go in, I'll call two more bitches and you do you."

"Damn Ma," was all Prince could say. He put on the DVD, "Friday After Next" and they enjoyed the rest of the afternoon together.

"Yo Silky?"

"Yes Daddy?"

"You know what that bitch Coco told me?"

"Nah, what?"

"She said she loved me."

"Yeah and, who wouldn't love you?" Silky said dozing off as the T.V. watched them.

CHAPTER
TWENTY-ONE

Saturday morning was a beautiful morning.

Prince was up bright and early. In fact, he had only slept a few hours. He was too excited, yet nervous. He had gotten up, taken a shower while Silky slept. He cooked breakfast; eggs, French toast and turkey bacon. Silky smelled the bacon and began to rise; it was finally going to happen. Life would be completely different after this day. His entire life he thought about his brother, his best friend. Even though he knew Sin played basketball against him and couldn't forget the fact that he was his son's stepfather, he hadn't dealt with him brother to brother. Many thoughts entered his mind; like how Sin would accept this fact. Life was crazy but who would have thought that the man he's been looking for his entire life was right in front of his face literally. To make matters better, his brother was a NBA superstar. Silky ate her breakfast, took a shower and was dressed and ready to go. She was more excited than Prince. They set their security alarm and left for their flight to New York City.

Silky and Prince arrived in New York at LaGuardia Airport at 10:00am. Tasha called and informed them that her, Sin, and Lil Prince would be there to meet them. When they stepped off the plane, they saw Lil' Prince waving at them. Silky commented on how beautiful Tasha looked while she was pregnant.

Prince hadn't realized that Silky began to have morning sickness after the threesome with Cherry and Coco. Silky planned on going to the doctor after their trip to New York. As they walked, Lil' Prince ran into his father's arms. Prince saw his brother and began to feel butterflies in his stomach. Sin was talking on his cell phone with his agent about some new endorsements.

"Hey y'all. What's good?" Tasha said happily.

"Hey Prego. What's good with you? You look beautiful. Look at you!" Silky said, smiling pointing to her stomach.

"Oh thank you Silky. You look beautiful too. You always look beautiful."

"Thanks girl. How's everything?" Silky asked.

"Oh everything is good. He doesn't know yet," Tasha whispered to Silky.

"Well this Nigga is a nervous wreck. I'm glad that they are getting their prayers answered," Silky smiled.

"Shoot, girl who you tellin? You know how many nightmares Sin has had?" Tasha said.

"Oh Sin too? Shoot Prince wakes up in deep sweats," Silky said. Prince and his son played fighting and they all walked towards Marvin King's Maybach Benz.

"Oh, I see y'all came in style," Silky said.

"Yeah, this is a special day. I figured we'd go straight over to Flushing Meadows Park ,so we can have a little picnic. Everything is in the car already; grill and all.

"That's nice Tasha. I'm down with that. I've been so busy, I've forgotten how to do the simple things in life. A picnic is just what I need," Silky said.

"Yep, life sure gets complicated, doesn't it?"

"Sure does," Silky said. Sin hung up his phone and walked back towards the car.

"Yo P.I., what's good Homie?" Yo Silky, how was the flight?" Sin asked, giving Prince a hug.

"Aw man, it was okay. That shit was quick as hell. We got

to New York in less than two hours," Prince said.

"Hey Sin. How are you," Silky asked.

"Oh I'm blessed. It's good to see yall."

"Yeah, likewise," Silky said.

"I brought my car too. That's my dad driving the Benz and the one behind it is mine. I don't know why Tash wanted to bring two cars. We can all fit in the Maybach." Silky looked at Tasha and smiled. Prince caught on quickly also.

"Yo, I gotta get the charcoal. Everything else is in the car. Yo P.I., you and Lil' Dennis can ride with me."

"Okay cool," Prince said, following him to his money green Maserati. Everybody got in their cars and pulled off. Sin sped up and pulled beside his dad. "We'll meet y'all there."
His dad shook his head and his mom waived at them and they pulled off. Lil Prince sat in the back seat and nodded his head to Drake's music and the two men began to talk.

"Yo Sin, what's good with you Homie?"

"Aw man, same shit. This N.B.A shit is crazy. 82 regular season games is easy, it's the traveling that's killing me," Sin said, shaking his head.

"Yeah, I can imagine."

"So what's up with you? You alright in B-More? I know you're being careful in those streets right Prince?"

"Yeah man. I'm stayin sucker free. I'm just being easy." Prince looked over at his brother and for the first time he began to see a slight resemblance.

"Yo man, It's me, Prince."

Sin looked at Prince with a confused face.

"Your brother. I just found out that we are brothers Sin. Yeah, I know." Prince glanced over as Sin drove in awe at the fact that he was hearing this news. " I can see it written all over your face. I feel the same way. I still can't believe it. The shit just smacked me in the face. I was driving in the hood and I saw our dad's brother, Steve. He told me a wild ass story. I wasn't even believing him But when I went to pick up Lil' D, he was carry-ing a Spider-Man book bag. That shit fucked me up Bro. I looked inside of it and my name and address was still stitched inside of it. My grandmother put my name in there. It's crazy because you still had the nine dollars in it that I gave you," Prince said as Sin was pulling his car to the curb. Sin jumped and ran around the passenger side opened the door, grabbed his brother and hugged him as tight as he could. Lil Prince watched and smiled from the back seat.

"Ooooh shit! It's been you the whole time? I prayed everyday of my life for this day," Sin said as tears flowed freely down his face. "I can't believe this shit man. This is the best day of my life. I didn't know what happened to you. Shit, now that I look at you closely, I can see the resemblance, we both got them football heads," Sin said and they both laughed.

"I was thinking the same thing," Prince said and for the first time he could remember, a tear had fallen from his eyes.

"Yo man, I promise you, I'm gonna make sure you and your family don't want for nothing. I got yall. I got a fund put away just for you. I promised to give you one million for every dollar in that Spider-Man bag. Nine million dollars is yours brother. I swear on my unborn child."

"Nah Sin. Be easy Bro. I'm rich. I'm good. I got my own dough. Plus me and Silk got a lot of legit businesses going on. You saw that billboard we just passed with T.L.C. ?" Prince asked.

"Yeah. You know something about that? My agent was just telling me about that. He said somebody wanted me to model for them," Sin said. Prince shook his head, thought about Silky and smiled.

"That's our shit Sin. We own it," Prince said smiling.

"So you already know what it is. I'm pushing T.L.C. hard and fast. My brother owns T.L.C. ," Sin yelled at the top of his lungs in excitement.

"Yo, let's get the charcoal and head to the park," Prince said, getting back in the car.

"Yeah you right. Tash just text me. Yo P.I., what the hell do we tell Lil P": Sin asked laughing.

"Man, leave it the way it is, He'll figure it out one way or another. Nothing has changed. You've been a great pop to him. Right Lil P?"

"Yup," Lil Prince said, not knowing what his father was talking about. They arrived at the park. Mr. King had the music playing and Sin and Prince went to set up the grill.

"Yo dad, that's my....

"I already know son. I just inherited another son. I knew when Tasha found out. We wanted to surprise you."

"Congrats Sin," Janice, his mom yelled over the music.

"Damn. This is the best day of my life," Prince said as everybody watched him and Sin walk off with their arms around each other. Just like they were six years old.

"Yo, you thinkin what I'm thinkin?"

"You ain't said a thing, I got two pairs of Jordans and shorts in the car,' Sin said.

"Well strap up Bro. You know you can't hold me," Prince said.

"Hold up. Let me get my camcorder. I gotta get this on tape,' Marvin said following behind them. The two brothers and Marvin went to the basketball court. They should have known that it would be packed with fans. Once Sin was spotted, cameras and fans were coming from everywhere. Now they were on the court and everybody surrounded to see the New York Knick superstar. Marvin had the tape rolling and his son stretched and Prince shot the ball.

"Check up," Sin said, passing his brother the ball. Just like old times, they put on a show for the huge crowd. Prince crossed Sin over and dunked the ball wowing the crowd. Sin crossed him back and with the free open shot, he refused it and stepped back to the half court line and shot the ball hitting nothing but net aahing the crowd also. It was nineteen to twenty and Sin had game point. Prince crossed him again and headed to the rim for the easy shot but to his surprise, Sin was waiting for him and pinned his ball to the backboard.

"Ooh, you didn't know I could jump huh?" Sin smiled

dribbling the ball.

"I guess that's why you went number one in the draft," Prince said out of breath trying to play defense.

"Well, I'm sorry Bro, but this game is over. Where do you want it at Babe?' Sin said to his wife as her, Silky, Marvin, Janice and Lil Prince looked on.

"From over here Baby, shoot it from here," Tasha yelled.

"Well you heard the lady Bro. I'm hungry," Sin said as he crossed his brother and went over to where his family stood and shot a three pointer. "Swoosh" nothing but net. The crowd went crazy. The two brothers hugged and went to eat grilled steaks.

"Damn Prince, why aren't you playing pro basketball?" Marvin asked.

"I hated school, Marv," he answered.

"Boy, you got a game. Damn a waste of talent," Marvin said to himself.

"You did good baby," Silky said with her arm around her husband walking back to the picnic area.

"Yeah but Sin is the truth," Prince said.

"He's supposed to be. He's your brother," Silky said.

"Yep. He is, isn't he? He's my brother."

CHAPTER TWENTY-TWO

Things were back to normal in the hood.

Prince had been occupied with so many other things, that he lost grip of his sole hustle; drug dealing. Even if he wanted to stop, he couldn't. It was an addictive life; a dangerous life. He could walk away today and still have enough money for his great-grand kids. He contemplated leaving the game especially after finding out that Silky was pregnant. She was two months and they were seriously considering retiring before the baby was born. But who would be "The Prince of Baltimore"? A title that came with money and best of all; power. He had just left meeting with Silky and Amir. Now him and Ralo cruised through the hood in his Maserati that Sin had given him. Life had been beautiful with him and his brother. Prince introduced Sin to his other brothers and sisters. They were all excited especially after getting season tickets to the New York Knicks games. They spoke on the phone everyday. They became best of friends all over again. Prince had flown to a few cities and watched his brother scorch other N.B.A. teams. However, with the launch of T.L.C. and the success of Silky's salons, he had neglected his bread winner, the heroin business. Prince gave Ralo a brand new X6 BMW for his birthday. He loved Ralo like a brother. Money was never an issue. He gave Ralo a fifty percent raise in salary and now he was making over a million dollars a month.

"Yo pull over to that liquor store so I can get a bottle,"

Ralo said. Prince pulled to the curb.

"Yeah get me a half pint of Absolut too, Prince said.

"A half? Nigga why you keep buying halves? Why don't you just buy a fifth and a plastic cup?" Ralo said laughing as he rose from the car.

"Because, first of all, a fifth can't fit in my back pocket. Second, I ain't no alcoholic. I only need a half."

"Oh yeah? But you drink four halves a day. You may as well buy a fifth."

"Nah, I'm good. Just get me a half. That's all I asked for and get two cigars so we can smoke a blunt with Raheem and Demi on the strip."

"Man, you wanna go to the block? Fuck dem niggas. Let's go find some hoes," Ralo said.

"Na na, not ya boy! I'm married my nig. I don't look for hoes. Plus the strip is where all this shit started at. We can't turn our backs on our bread and butter. The strip is where we pay homage. The generals must mingle with the soldiers or the soldiers will lose respect. Remember this; those on the front line are most important. Those who sit in the office are comfortable because of them. Look at us now," Prince said referring to the brand new Maserati.

"Yeah, you're right . You said a half and two cigars, right?"

"Yeah," Prince said. After Ralo returned,they made their way to the block and the trap was jumpin. Raheem stood at the corner and watched as his corner men directed dope fiends into the trap. Raheem smiled as he saw his lieutenant bringing another package to the workers. It was the fifth pack in two hours.

"Beep! Beep! The horn blew from the Maserati.
Raheem looked over not noticing the expensive car.

"Yo Rah, bring your little ass over here, Nigga," Prince yelled playfully.

"Ooh shit!" Raheem said, biting his finger. "That shit is tough," Raheem said looking at the car's design.

"Yo come smoke something with us Rah ," Prince said.

"Aight. Gimme a second. Lemme make sure that everything is straight in the Trap." Raheem called his lieutenant and gave him some brief instructions and headed to the Maserati.

"Raheem! Raheem!"

"Yo hold up!" Raheem yelled.

"Raheem Poppy Lee, I know you ain't talkin to your mother like that?" Rah's mother said as she stood in front of the Trap.

"Ma, I told you not to come down here.. If you need something all you have to do is call."

"Nigga, I'm sick as a dog. I called you a hundred times."

"No you di...." Raheem looked at his phone and his battery was dead. "Damn Ma, my bad. My battery is dead. Yo "E, go in there and get me two," Raheem ordered.

"Thank you Baby," his mother said.

"It's nothing Ma. Now please go wait in the car with the boys. Please Ma!"

"I'm going Baby. You coming home for dinner?"

"Yeah, always. I'll be there in a little while," Raheem said grabbing the drugs for his mother and walking her to the car.

"Hey Rah!" his brothers yelled in unison.

"What's good? Y'all aight?"

"Yeah," they both yelled.

"Yo, go get the game ready. I'll be home in an hour. I promise," Raheem said.

"Okay, but I'ma crack you. We've been practicing," Naheim said.

"Yeah, whatever. Just get the game ready. Get home safe Ma. I love yall," Raheem said.

"We love you too. Be careful out here," his mother said.

"I will Ma. Now go ahead," Raheem said, getting aggravated.

"Yo Last Call on Nikki Ménage'," the corner man yelled out the heroin stamp. Dope fiends from everywhere stormed the Trap knowing that Raheem's Trap would be closing until the next morning. Ralo finally made it over to Prince's Maserati. Prince was sitting on the hood rolling his weed

"Yo, my bad y'all. That was my mom."

"Yeah I know. She okay?" Prince asked.

"Yeah, now she is. She had the monkey on her back. I forgot to check on her earlier. The Trap was clicking so much I lost track of time.

"Yo Rah, how old are you?" Prince asked.

"I'm fifteen, I'll be sixteen on Sunday," Raheem said.

"Word? I thought you were older," Prince said.

"Nah, I'm fifteen."

"Yo, you a smooth fifteen though," Ralo said.

"Yeah, I know. My girl is twenty-one,' Raheem said.

'Man, you remind me of me. Real talk," Prince said.

"I'm just trying to look after my family. My pops held us down until he got killed. I'm holding us down now. Yo, your wife hooked me up with a crib downtown. I don't know if she told you, but her and my mom are good friends. In fact, she's like an aunt to me. My moms been fuckin up lately. I wish she could leave that dope alone. But who am I to judge her? I sell this shit.

"I know how you feel Rah. Trust me. Yo, maybe you could get her into a rehab," Prince said.

"Nah. I don't want her to leave the crib. She takes good care of us. The only thing is she sniffs dope and to be honest, she's calming down off the shit. I got faith in my moms. She's gonna pull through. My pop's death was really hard on her," Raheem said inhaling on the blunt.

"Yo if it's anything I can do, just let me know."

"Yeah will do. Yo,, I'm done too. I need some more product ASAP!" Raheem said.

"Word?" Ralo asked.

"Yeah, I got all the bread at the crib. I'll meet Ralo later with it. Y'all ready for me?" Prince looked at Ralo who was already making a phone call.

"... Yeah two of them. Take it to the Fish house, " Ralo said, giving his runner the code to drop bricks of dope off to Raheem's lieutenant.

"It's on the way. It'll be there in a half hour, " Ralo said.

"Aight bet," Raheem said, giving his men the signal to close shop.

"Yo, you run a tight ship, Lil bro . I like your style," Prince commented.

"Yeah, I gotta get my driver's license so I can get behind the wheels of one of these,' Raheem said touching the Maserati.

"Get your license and we'll talk. Just keep up the good work. You feel me soldier?"

"I feel you General. I definitely feel you," Raheem said and passed the blunt.

Lil' Raheem made it home to his family safe and sound. He gave Ralo $150,000 with no shorts. Raheem had a substantial amount of money himself. He paid for his girlfriend's college tuition and he and his family lived comfortably. He felt uneasy though. Ralo had propositioned him to sell for someone else's product that had nothing to do with Prince. He began to feel uncomfortable while he sat in Ralo's brand new BMW X6. He didn't know whether to call and tell Prince or just dismiss the whole thing. But for now he just answered "no" and that was that. Raheem would not sell any other dope besides "Nikki Ménage" in his Trap and he would not cross Prince. At fifteen years old he was old enough to recognize hate. He noticed the hate while he was talking to Prince. Ralo stood silent but his expressions told it all. He was jealous of Prince. When Ralo came through and crushed the hood in his brand new BMW X6, the next day Prince drove through in a mint green Maserati and "lights out" the show was over. Prince's car made Ralo's X6 look like a Honda Accord. Raheem noticed how Ralo began to duplicate Prince's swagger. He wanted to be Prince, Raheem thought to himself. Raheem went into his bedroom where his girlfriend slept peacefully in a pink wife-beater and panties. His mind was cluttered with so many thoughts. At fifteen years old his plate was full. "Fuck it, the next time I see Prince, I'm letting him know the deal about the backstabbing nigga," Raheem thought to himself. One thing his father taught him was to live and die for "Loyalty". Prince was the man that fed his family and Raheem would not cross him under any circumstances.

Prince laid in bed. He felt uneasy. He has seen an abrupt change in Ralo's attitude. He had been noticing the change since the trip to North Carolina. He hoped that everything was good on Ralo's end. He knew that Ralo was the breadwinner for his family and they all lived with him. It may have taken a toll on Ralo. Prince hoped that whatever it was, his partner would be okay. He was there for his people. Ralo was no different than Kah, Big Boi or Darren. They all ate from the same plate. They all were like brothers. His loyalty to his team was to make sure everything was okay.

Ralo sat in his crib and watched his daughter run around the house. He was glad that most of his family was out shopping so he could have peace with his daughter. He had a mini mansion in the suburbs of Maryland. His daughter's mother, LuLu was beautiful but she wasn't Silky. He was obsessed with Silky. His obsession made him hate Prince. Even when he had sex with LuLu, he called her Silky using the name as an excuse for the silk weaves she wore. He even made her get her hair done in a style that Silky wore. He wanted the real thing in his life, but he knew he would have to eliminate his boss. He could easily kill Prince but Silky would grieve and she probably would never deal with him. He had propositioned some of Prince's top workers and none were willing to cross their boss. He swore that Raheem would bite the bait since he was the youngest at fifteen years old. He didn't. Ralo met with Black a few more times and even took 10 keys on consignment. He sent them to North Carolina and Atlanta. However, Black wanted the dope sold in Baltimore, but with Prince still in the picture, Black's dope would not sell in the city. Ralo had someone test some of Black's dope straight off the brick and it tested well. He had some of Prince's dope straight off the brick and the tester died. Even if Prince put a ten cut on his dope it would still be better than Black's. Ralo had to come up with a plan and fast. He was tired of seeing Prince flourish, especially after finding out that his brother was a N.B.A. superstar. His envy for Prince was gaining momentum and life for him was beginning to be uneasy. He had once beaten LuLu almost unconscious after he saw her smiling at Prince. He threatened to kill her if he saw her smile at him again. Little did he know, There was a young hustler, who dug her back out while Ralo chased his fantasy of getting Silky, keeping LuLu's attention occupied.. When LuLu finally met the infamous Silky, it made her sick that Ralo wanted his best friend's wife. But as long as he continued to give her money, cars and clothes, she was good. She thought about telling Prince but what good would it do.That would end her run just as much as his. She brushed the thought off and continued to live a lie. Ralo watched his little girl play, while he fantasized about something he could never have.

CHAPTER TWENTY-THREE

"Washington, DC"

"Man, hurry up Cornbread. I gotta take a piss!"

"Nigga yo betta wait till I'm done. I told you I was taking a shit."

"Nigga you should've taken a shit at your raggedy-ass house."

"Flush!" Cornbread flushed the toilet and left the bathroom without washing his hands.

"Dirty ass nigga, ain't even wash his hands," Do-Dirty said while he took a piss in the fuming bathroom.

"Nigga, your mama don't mind me havin dirty hands; that old fat bitch."

"Yo mama a fat bitch." Do-Dirty said as he paced back and forth close to where Black and Cornbread sat at the table counting money.

"Yo, why y'all niggas always arguing?" Black asked laughing at the two bickering men.

"Man, this nigga always got something to say," Cornbread said.

"Nigga, if you wasn't my half-brother I'd clap your stupid ass."

"Nigga get to clappin then. I wish you would," Cornbread said laughing. They always had a good time with each other. They showed their love by arguing. They shared the same father who was a well known gangster; that ran the streets of Washington, DC. They both had their father's traits as gangsters and picked up their old school names in the tough streets of D.C.. Do-Dirty and Cornbread were considerably young, at least compared to Black who was thirty-five. Black recruited them a few years back and they have been getting money and dropping bodies ever since. It was rumored that the three men had over twenty homicides. Black finished wrapping the last 10 gee stack in preparation for his meeting with the Africans. Ralo's count had been correct but slower than Black expected. While Black passed through the hoods of Baltimore, he had seen the money flowing. He couldn't figure out why it took Ralo so long to get rid of a few bricks.

"Yo, everything is correct. I'm meeting with dem people tonight," Black said.

"Aight good. Yo what took that stupid nigga so long?" Do-Dirty asked.

"I don't know man. He said it was kinda slow, but shit picked up pace in the end," Black answered.

"Slow? It's hard to tell. I see that Lil Nigga Raheem's Trap getting it. He lookin like his dad more and more. The truth is, I don't think they like this dope we got. I heard about the shit Prince got. I heard that nigga is steppin all over his shit and it's still better than ours."

"Nah, his shit ain't better than ours," Black said angrily. "Nigga gotta get used to seeing our product again, that's all," Black said.

"Okay, if that's the case, then why don't we eliminate the competition?" Cornbread asked.

"Because Lil Bro," Black said pointing at his diamond studded Rolex. "Timing is everything. We don't eliminate the competition just yet. The competition is what's keeping the economy booming. We gradually slide our dope in the mix until it's spread throughout the entire city and then....," Black said, making a gun gesture with his finger. "Then we can eliminate the competition."

"And how long is that gonna take? Do-Dirty asked.

"As long as it takes . One thing yall must have is patience. See, this ain't like here in D.C. where we kill niggas and take blocks. We move in, body somethin' and the block is ours. We're taking over a major city. We're gonna control the drug trade in Maryland. We're gonna be filthy rich at the end of this, trust me. But patience is a virtue. See, Prince is not by himself. There are some powerful people behind him. He's making them a lot of money. Why do you think he's alive? He rides around in luxury cars and chills on blocks in the hood. Why? Because his money has turned into power, influencing respect. The powerful people who back him will eliminate his competition including us if they caught wind of what we're about to do. So, this is why we move with caution through Ralo. The product ain't a problem. We got tons of dope. We just gotta get in where we fit in. Trust, we'll have our time and all of Prince's power will be transferred to us. They don't care about the vehicle that makes the money; they just want the reliable vehicle. Pretty soon the vehicle that they have now will have too much mileage and they will be looking for a new vehicle; which will be us. Trust me," Black said, putting the money in a duffle bag.

"Man, I don't gotta clue to what the fuck you talkin bout, but it sounded good and I'm in," Cornbread said.

"Cause you a STUPID DUMB ASS nigga. Just relax and wait until it's our time to shine. What, you need it sung to you in a rap song." Said Do-Dirty

"Nah, I understand you ugly mother fucker. I gotta be patient just like I am with your mother right?" Cornbread said eliciting laughter from both men.

Let's Meet The Africans

Black sipped Grey Goose and listened to the music that

played softly over the low spoken guest who occupied the Prince Cartier Café; an after hour spot that suited most men and women of upper class. He waited patiently for the arrival of the "Boss". Black has not met the Boss yet, only the runners who delivered the product and collected the money. He had finally gotten rid of his last brick of heroin and he sat in the corner booth, waiting while Cornbread and Do-Dirty waited outside in the Audi with the money. Black took another sip of his vodka and raised his head to see the most beautiful black woman he had ever seen in his entire life. She held the attention of everyone in the room as she floated through the jazz-filled air. Her jet-black complexion was flawless, her diamond-studded earrings gave the café a new lighting that it had never seen. Her breast perfectly round and firm pointed in his direction as her black diamond necklace sat perfectly between them. Her designer jeans were like a piece of fine art that complimented the beauty of nature itself. God had blessed her with the most beautiful eyes that sparkled, complimenting her diamonds. Black couldn't help but stare as his mind had totally left business and was stuck on courting the beautiful woman that stood in front of him. Until now, Black thought that Silky was the most beautiful woman on the planet, including what he's seen on television. But this woman had Silky looking like the singer Seal. There was no way Silky's beauty could compare at all.

"Mr. Black?" she asked with an African accent.

"Uh, yeah, I'm Black and you are?" Black stuttered.

"I am Makeba. It is finally nice to meet you," she said.

"Oh! Damn. It's nice to see you too. Very nice," Black said.

"Do you like the place?" she asked.

"Yeah, this is a nice joint. Not as nice as you though," Black flirted.

"Thank you Mr. Black. I'm flattered," she smiled. "My brother owns this place."

"Oh I see," Black said admiring the place.

"You seem a little on edge. Are you okay?" she asked.

"Yeah, yeah, I'm good. I was just expecting to see a ....."

"A man?" she asked.

"Yeah, I guess you could say that," Black said.

"I figured you would react like this. Well, there's no man. I am the Boss. What you see is what you get."

"Okay, okay Boss. What's good then?" Black asked.

"Everything's a go. My runners are in position and I see your two friends are waiting for you outside," she said.

"Yeah, they're ready when you are," Black said.

"Okay, I'll have my men meet with them."

"Um, Makeba, I'm glad to finally meet you. We're gonna do big things. I got the city on lock. I'm working on Baltimore as we speak."

"I understand, but that is not my concern. I was told that you can handle a substantial amount of product. Is this true," she asked.

"Most definitely, very true. Any amount, I can handle," he said confidently.

"Okay, very well then, but I'm telling you then once the transaction is done we'll start you off with something light; twenty kilos."

"Okay very well then; but I am telling you, I'll be done with them quickly."

"That's fine, just keep my people informed and they'll keep the product coming. There is no limit to this product. I am the Heroine Goddess. I supply 40% of the U.S. I always meet my associates to get a feel of them. I like you," Makeba said, rolling her tongue. Black was erected under the table as his dick rose in his jeans.

"Well, I'm glad we've met. Uh, let me ask you a question.

"Sure."

"This product; is it better than the last?"

"Why? Is it not good?" she asked surprisingly.

"Nah, it's good, but we got competition. The product they have is very good."

"Is that so?" Makeba asked. She knew that the competition was Silky and there was nothing she could do. Silky had her beat. But that has never stopped her before. She would just keep her dope uncut and it would be just as good as the competition. She knew Silky, her father and Chen Ho, but business was business and the truth was, she wanted her dope stamp in Baltimore just as she had done in New Orleans. Makeba, just like Silky, had been born into the heroin business. Her father, Olefumi had passed and she became the Boss at ten years old. Makeba had everything a twenty-five year old could want but power is what she loved. Her drive and control of the drug game gave her a rush. She knew all she needed about Black. He knew nothing about her, she smiled to herself. She would utilize his sources to move her product throughout D.C. and Baltimore. She knew that he would take some time with twenty kilos. She didn't care. As long as her stamp was in the city, she was happy.

"Don't worry Mr. Black. This new product, it is the top of the line. You will have no complaints. In fact I will put these twenty back and tomorrow afternoon my people will meet you with an even better product. I promise. You can hold onto my money if you like," she said.

"Nah, that's yours. You can have them grab it now. I'll call my people," Black said and Makeba gave a signal to her men to retrieve the money.

"Mr. Black, please don't take this as a disrespect, but business is business. My operation runs on loyalty. Me or mine will never lead you astray. We'll be there if you need us; but please don't cross me. Is that understood?"

"Very well understood. I feel the same way," Black said as he stared coldly into her eyes. Black knew what he was dealing with. He too was deadly. Probably more deadly than her.

"Well my time is up here. We will probably never meet again. I hope that your endeavors are greatly achieved. It's been my pleasure, Mr. Black," Makeba said, standing as her perfect thighs came level with Black's face. She turned and walked away as he watched the most perfect fat ass he had ever seen. Her men stood and followed her out of the café.

"Nah Bitch, the pleasure is all mine," Black said as he

downed the Grey Goose and rubbed himself. He needed to get out of there and get some pussy real bad. Whoever it was, she would have to be jet black with an African accent, he thought to himself. "Somebody is going to play the role of Makeba tonight," he said to himself.

CHAPTER TWENTY-FOUR

Prince and Silky sat courtside next to Spike Lee and watched Sin go to work against an older Kobe Bryant and the Lakers.

It was a game to remember because Sin scored a Madison Square Garden record of 85 points. Things had been better than the two brothers expected. They spent a lot of time with each other, both their wives had babies; Silky having a healthy little girl and Tasha having another boy. They were only months apart but Little Prince protected his little brother and sister the same. Prince was full throttle in the drug game and not intentions of letting up, even though Sin begged his brother to stop and become his agent. Prince thought about the idea of getting into the sports business but declined. He had an obligation to run cities on the East Coast and that's what he did. Lately he noticed a few of his customers stopped calling but he hadn't seen a difference in his profits. He heard that a new dope stamp was making a name for itself in Baltimore but word was still out that "Nore" was the best dope in the world. Prince smiled to himself as he and Silky drove to Tasha's to pick up their daughter, Zuri whom Tasha watched while they attended the basketball game.

What's funny Baby?" Silky asked.

"Nah, it ain't important. I was just laughing to myself, these niggas out here is something else."

"Who?" Silky said, smiling.

"They kill me. You know, the ones who know I got the

best dope in the city but rather go up the block and by garbage just because I am from New York."

"Yeah, that's how it always been and that's how it's gonna be. I was talkin to my dad about that. People are so dumb, but that's okay though. Lil Raheem's mother was telling me some D.C. boys were hollering a new stamp. She said it was good because it was free," Silky said laughing and continued. "But she also said it ain't fucking with N.O.R.E."

"I know, but guess what? I'ma drop our shit another number and make this shit even more potent. These niggas was barely eatin, now the gonna starve. N.O.R.E. about to shut down the city, just because niggas wanna hate on me and make history. Why the fuck they hate me? I ain't Alpo, I ain't give them niggas to the feds on a silver platter. All I do is spread love. But now they gonna see how a New York nigga corner the market. Everything they sell for dimes, I'm selling for nickels; Fuck That! I'm coming out in the morning and I'm given 500 samples to everybody and their mamas," Prince said as he swerved through traffic in his spanking brand new Aston Martin Coupe.

"Baby, I never got in the middle of your business or how you conduct it, but just be careful, please. You know sometimes niggas hate can turn deadly. I don't want anything to happen to you. I don't know what me and Zuri would do without you."

"Don't worry ma. Ain't nothing gonna happen to me. I'm just gonna rejuvenate the city like I did when I first got here. I'm gonna have every dope fiend go into their wallet and buy N.O.R.E, circulate the money, and let the niggas know how to start a constant flow." Just as he pulled off the FDR exit his phone rang.

"Yo, who is this?" Prince said angrily.

"Damn son you a-light?" Lil Raheem asked.

"Oh shit, what up Lil Rah. Yeah my bad Lil . I'm good. How about you?"

"Yeah, I'm good. As a matter of fact I'm low on gas. You already know what it is. I told you I ain't fuckin with your boy no more," Raheem said referring to Ralo.

"Yeah, I've been hearing some things. I gotta look into them though?

"Yeah, That's what up?"

"There's a change in the game plan. I'll be back in town on Monday. Just lay low until I get there. You good with food to eat until I get back right?" Prince said referring to how much dope Raheem had left.

"Yeah I'm good until Monday, I hope. You already know my family is greedy."

"Yeah, I'm hip. Just be easy. I'll holla at you in the A.M.

"Okay Big Homie. Ay yo, P.I.?"

"Yeah what up?"

"I got my driver's license in South Carolina this week. Everything on the same day."

"Oh word?"

"Yeah and I got the dough to buy that Maserati from you too. You sellin it?" Raheem asked.

"Hahaha. Nah Lil, I ain't sellin it."

"Aw come on man. Don't front on me now," Raheem began to wine.

"Nah, I'm not a used car salesman. I told you to get your license right?"

"Yeah, that's what you said."

"Yo hold on," Prince said clicking over and dialing Amir's number.

"Yo dad what up?"

"Hey son. How was the game?"

"It was beautiful. The nigga Sin broke all types of records. He had 85 points."

"Damn!"

"Yo, I need you to do me a favor."

"What's that?" Amir asked.

"Go by the garage, get the Maserati and take it to Lil Raheem for me."

"Oh you gonna let him drive it?" Amir asked.

"Yeah something like that, Dad."

"Okay, no problem."

"Thanks."

"Anytime," Amir said, ending the call.

"Yo, Lil Rah you still there?"

"Yeah, I'm here."

"Yo, when is your birthday again?"

"My shit was Saturday," Raheem said.

"Well happy birthday. Amir is coming to holla at you. I'll see you when I get back, "Prince said, ending the call. He made his first statement by giving Raheem the Maserati. His next statement would be selling nickels of "FIRE", he thought to himself. "Yep, FIRE, that's the new stamp. Bye-bye N.O.R.E., hello F.I.R.E., Prince said to himself as he listened to Jay-Z's Reasonable Doubt at a low tone while his wife slept in the comfortable Aston Martin's heated passenger seat.

"… Yo everybody get in the hole! Stay the fuck in line. If one of yall step outta line, I'ma crack you with this bat. Be easy, there's enough for everybody. This is something new and improved," Prince said as he regulated the crowd, as he was about to pass out samples of his new dope. It was important that his customers saw him for the debut of his new dope, "F.I.R.E". It was the same way when he introduced "N.O.R.E." The dope fiends knew when they saw his face that something good or great was about to happen.

"Yo, this is "F.I.R.E." yall, we gonna be hittin all over with nickels. Yep five dollars yall. Only from us will you get this kind of quality," Prince said as Raheem and his workers handed out the gel caps filled with dope.

"Ooooh shit! These big thangs is for five dollars?" Sheila, an older dope fiend asked as she looked down in her hand. "Yall gonna kill em baby with stuff like this. Can I buy four more right now?" she asked.

"Nah, Ms. Sheila. These are not for sale. We'll be up the block on Bond Street," Lil Raheem said.

"Okay then baby. I'll meet yall up the block," Sheila said as she hurried off to try her new dope.

"Let's go. Let's go. Step up and get this "FIRE" yall," Raheem said as he passed out the free samples.

"Damn we got like 10 left and look at all these people in line," Raheem said.
Prince looked at the line and saw that there were over one hundred dope fiends patiently waiting.

"Yo Ralo, go get some more pills," Prince said lowly.

"Nah, It ain't over more samples. The rest is for sale only," Ralo demanded.

"What? Son, I'm not asking you, I'm telling you! Go get some more pills!" Prince said sternly looking into Ralo's cold eyes. He watched Ralo walk off. He had been hearing a lot of funny style shit about his partner. He noticed a change in Ralo's attitude as of late. He would keep his grass cut low so he could see the snakes when they appear. But for now, Ralo was still a crucial member of his team and he would trust him as such until he solidified what was being accused.

"Yo, give us two minutes, yall gonna get hit off too," Prince yelled as he walked out the trap toward his rental car.

The city was in a frenzy. The best dope the city had ever seen was being sold for five dollars. A tactic that Prince had bought with him from New York City. Raheem's trap was moving so much dope that Prince didn't need any other dealers to buy weight from him. The dope fiends were coming from North, South, East and West. The trap was busy all day long. Raheem would come out at 6:30AM and be done hustling by 11:00AM.

Dope fiends would literally cry and be upset because "F.I.R.E" was closed for the day. No one else was making money unless Raheem's Trap was closed. Prince branched out to a few more local hustlers throughout the city and "F.I.R.E" was burning up the hoods. Prince wouldn't get enough dope at one time. Chan-Ho would send him 200 bricks and that would be gone in less than a month. The Baltimore police were sweeping everyday due to the traffic of dope fiends that flooded the streets looking for "F.I.R.E". Prince, Silky and Amir made more money in one month than they had made in one year. Their accounts were filled with enough money to finance a small country. Ralo had more money than he could count but yet he was not satisfied. He wanted Silky.

CHAPTER
TWENTY-FIVE

Life for Raheem was way better than he could have ever imagined.

Even though Prince gave him the Maserati, it was like a hooptie to him now. He had enough money to buy any car he wanted. However, with the advice of Prince he had to lay low on the flashy things since he was not in a position to show accountability for his money. He had to wait until he was able to clean his money. Raheem's girl Toni had begun to act strange. He liked her alot but that was it. He had bitches at his beck and call. He wasn't committed to anything but his family and pushing "F.I.R.E' on the streets. He moved his family far away from the city to deep in Baltimore county. Therefore he had not seen them as much as he wanted to. He still had an apartment downtown, but he made it a priority of his own to drive out to Essex County every weekend to visit his family. He pulled into the private parking complex and headed to be with his family. It was late so he tried his best not to make too much noise. He tip-toed into the crib and saw his two younger brothers knocked out on the plush carpet in front of the 60 inch plasma T.V. Raheem turned off the television and video game but let them continue to sleep. He walked into the back bedroom and heard the T.V. playing loudly from his mother's room. He peeked in and his heart dropped!

"Ooh shit Ma, wake up!" Raheem yelled as he saw his mother's half dressed, lifeless body spread out on the floor. He saw a pill of "Fire" on the night table and he knew the worst had happened. His screaming woke his brothers who rushed into the bedroom.

"Call 9-1-1, hurry up! He yelled at them as tears freely flowed from his eyes while he held his mother's head in his lap. "Ma, wake up," Raheem said silently as he laid on the floor with his mother's head in his lap.

Raheem watched as the paramedics tried desperately to revive his mother. Thank God, she was still alive; but barely. With the help of his brothers, Raheem was able to clean up the room of any trace of contraband that was visible to the naked eye. The paramedics picked up the empty bottle of sleeping pills that lay on the floor. At least for now, it hadn't looked like a heroin overdose. Raheem gathered his brothers and they followed behind the ambulance to the hospital. They watched as the workers worked on their mother as best they could. It was a lot of movement in which the boys would never understand. They knew that the movement was to save their mother.

"Rah, mommy gonna be okay, right?" Na'im asked, staring into the back of the ambulance.

"Yeah Na', she's gonna be fine just like last time. They're just making sure she's okay, that's all," Raheem said. He drove and watched them working on his mother. Then it happened. The backlight in the ambulance went off. There was no more movement, no commotion, no nothing. He hoped in his heart that his mother had come to consciousness. A single tear fell from his left eye. His mom was dead. A week later the autopsy showed that she had died from a mixture of sleeping pills, heroin and cocaine.

Raheem, Na'im, and Khalif sat in front of the funeral parlor on Caroline Street along with their aunt, Vanessa. She was their mother's only remaining kin alive. Prince and Silky sat behind them for the much needed support.. Ever since they heard about the death they had been by Raheem's side. Prince knew first hand what it was like to lose a parent to overdose. Raheem had dealt with many obstacles but this particular one had broken him. He couldn't bear it. However, he had to be strong for Na'im and Khalif. He would do the best he could to raise them as their mother did for him. The three young men sat dressed in the appropriate clothing of designer dress slacks, matching shirts and Gucci loafers that were bought by Silky. Mary looked beautiful, as she laid to rest in her lavender casket. A lavender rose that sat beautifully in her hair complimented her long hair.

After the funeral service, everybody went back to Mary's for some food and drinks to celebrate the life of Mary Lee. The three brothers were entering the limousine when their aunt approached them.

"Raheem," she said softly.

"Yes Aunt Nessa? Thank you for coming. My moms told me so much about you. She loved you. It's messed up that we gotta meet under these circumstances.

"Yeah, I'm so sorry, baby. We should've had a better relationship. Me and your mom didn't see eye to eye on a lot of things. I hated the fact that she used drugs around y'all; especially after what happened to our mom, your grandmother," Vanessa said and went into many things that Rah never knew. She too left her two kids alone to fend for themselves at a young age.

"Listen Raheem, I can take care of yall. I mean, I don't have a lot of money but my job will do. It's only myself and that big ole' house," she said smiling and continued. "I can give you guys a good life. All you have to do is let me. I mean, Silver Springs is not as fast as Baltimore but the schools are great and the neighbors are really nice," she said.

"Wow Aunt Nessa. I appreciate that. But I gotta do for my little brothers. I've been doing this before mom passed," Raheem said and thought for a second and continued. "You know what Aunt Nessa, please take the boys back with you. I mean, I don't want to abandon them, but I really need the best for them and you can give them that. My father left us some money," he lied. "You can take it and make sure they're okay."

"Raheem, I don't need your father's money. You keep it. I told you, I'm doing okay. We won't live lavishly but we'll be okay," she smiled.

"Nah Auntie, please take the money I don't need it."

"So what about you, Raheem?" She asked, waiting for an answer before continuing to speak. "You ain't much older than them. Who's gonna take care of you?" she asked.

"I'm good Auntie. Me and my girlfriend live together." He lied again. "I'll come down there every chance I get to see them and make sure they are doing the right thing. I promise.

"No, don't promise me anything. Promise that you'll be okay," she demanded.

"I promise Auntie. I'll be fine," he said smiling and kissing her on the cheek.

Later that night, after everyone left, Raheem, his two brothers and their Aunt Nessa cleaned up the apartment and packed a few things they would need. Raheem took his two brothers in the back room to talk.

"Yo listen. Don't think for one second that I'm giving up on yall. Me and Auntie talked about this and it's best for all of us. Silver Spring, Maryland is just like here in the county but better. Yall will have yall own room and everything else yall need. I'm giving her enough money for y'all to get whatever y'all want. But, don't take advantage of the fact that y'all got money. I'm gonna pass through and drop off bread from time to time. Just be respectful and do what y'all have to do in school."

"Rah!" Khalif cried.

"What up Lil bro ."

"Why can't you come with us?" he sobbed.

"Because Lil Bro, I gotta take care of business out here. I

gotta make sure me, you and Na'im are good for the rest of our lives. All we got is us, our mom and dad are in Heaven."

"We got Aunt Nessa too," Lil Na'im said.

"Yeah, and we gotta protect Aunt Nessa just like we did with mommy," Raheem said.

"Raheem, do Aunt Nessa do drugs like mommy?" Khalif asked.

"Nah, Lil Brother. Those days are done. She is strict though. Ain't no messin up in school, ya heard?"

"Yeah," they both said in unison.

"I'm getting all A's," Khalif said.

"Me too," Na'im said.

"What about you Rah?" Na'im asked.

"You know what, I'm getting my G.E.D. too." Rah smiled.

"Yeah!" both brothers yelled and hugged their older brother.
Aunt Nessa peeked in the room and saw the Kodak moment. A tear fell from her eye as she knew her life would be totally different from this night on.

"Aunt Nessa, they're ready and packed up. Here's the money I was telling you about."

"Oooh my goodness Raheem. Is this a mistake? Are you sure this check is not supposed to say One thousand?" Vanessa asked, looking curiously at the check.

"Nah, Aunt Nessa, that's correct. It's one million dollars. It's legit. T.L.C. is a clothing company owned by Silky and Prince."

"Yeah, but I thought you said your father left you the money?"

"Yeah, but he left us cash. It's better this way since you know where our Pops money came from. You don't need the headaches," Raheem said.

"Okay. Now what am I supposed to do with all this money?" she asked nervously.

"I look at it like this Auntie, you can set up a college fund for us; clothes, food, whatever else you need and. Split it up evenly, three hundred a piece for us and one hundred for you if you want," Raheem said.

"Boy, I don't know," she said hesitantly.

"Auntie Ness, trust me. I ain't gonna put you or them in harm's way. The money is legit. It couldn't be in better hands. When they graduate high school, get them any car they want."

"Boy, you make me nervous," she said, folding the check, looking around and quickly stuffing it in her bra. Raheem laughed at her nervousness and then gave her a hug.

"Thank you Aunt Nessa. You just saved our lives. I appreciate that."

"Baby, what was I supposed to do" You're the only family I have. I'm obligated to step up to the plate. Anything else would be uncivilized," she said smiling and continued. "Now you know I'm responsible for you too. You better bring your behind down there in that fancy car and visit us every chance you get; and call Everyday!! If you need us we'll be there. You understand?"

"Yes ma'am. I understand clearly. Hey Auntie, you want anything outta this apartment? After tonight, I ain't coming back here." Vanessa looked around and saw a few things she could use. The boys already packed all four televisions and their mom's personal items.

"No baby. I don't need anything out of here. You have given me enough already," Vanessa said as the boys dragged their belongings through the door.

"Oh yeah Aunt Nessa, one more thing. What kind of truck is that you are driving?"

"Oh that is a Ford Flex, baby. Or yall would call that the fake Range Rover. Yeah I watch BET too," she said soliciting hard laughter from Raheem.

"Here you take these keys and let me get the fake Range," Raheem said, passing her the keys to the Maserati.

"Boy are you sure?" she asked.

"Yeah, I'm positive Auntie. It's yours, "Raheem said.

"Well, how are you gonna get all this stuff to my house?" she asked.

"Don't worry, my man got a truck. We'll load it up and he'll follow you. You won't have to lift a finger."

"Well in that case, tell them to pick up this Cartier China, those end tables, that sofa, this stainless steel refrigerator, this dish washer......" She went on and on until the apartment was empty. Raheem laughed, they hugged again and Na'im and Khalif were on their way to a beautiful suburban life. All set up by Raheem himself.

Prince was furious! He was infuriated! Silky had gotten the confirmation he needed that Ralo was pushing Black's dope under the same stamp as him. Prince and Amir rode in the Aston Martin and blew purple haze while the two "REAL" partners talked. Amir was more shocked than anyone because he had sanctioned Ralo from the very beginning. No matter what Ralo and his new friends tried there was no stopping the flow of "F.I.R.E". It was moving close to 2,000,000 dollars a week.

"Damn son. That's my bad. I would have never thought that he would betray *you* of all people. I mean before you put him in position, he was riding a raggedy pedal bike, selling nickels of powder cocaine wherever he could. But you know what they say? You can only trust yourself." Amir said.

"Yeah, but I don't believe in that saying Dad. I believe in giving everyone a fair shot. Just like niggas gave me a shot.

"He needs one right in the back of his head. Punk Bitch!" Amir yelled banging his hand on the plush dashboard.

"Nah, he ain't worth these bullets. We'll just cut him off. He'll feel it. Trust me. After all, soon we'll be the only ones in this city who eat. Everybody else gonna have to fuck with us."

"You know what's crazy Prince? I can't see why. If I was a hustler I would wanna fuck with the best. Especially for these prices," Amir said.

"Yeah but it's only because I'm from New York. A nigga will let his pride empty his pockets. That's the crazy shit. A nigga rather be broke than cop from me, just because I'm from New York. The crazy shit is I'm surprised these haters didn't already tell on me."

"Yeah you're right. Son, I think it may be time to give this shit a break. Our security has been compromised," Amir said.

"Nigga is you crazy? I'm married to this shit. Ain't no fallin back. My hands ain't touch drugs in five years. Lil Raheem took Ralo's spot, he met Chan-Ho on Friday. It's funny because Chan-Ho said he loves Raheem's vibe."

"Yeah he is a good kid. It's sad that he lost his mamma. She used to be a fine mamma-jamma back then."

"Damn dad, you hit that too?" Prince asked looking in Amir's direction.

"No man. That's my daughter's friend," Amir said.

"And?"

"You're right. Don't mean shit. But nah. I respected her husband way too much to fuck his wife. It never even crossed my mind. After he died all she did was get high, but she's about the only one I didn't hit in the street. Why you think I'm so hard to find. Because I am always lost in some pussy.

"You's a funny nigga, Dad," Prince said and they both burst into laughter.

"Oh shit Prince, you saw that?"

"Nah, what was that?" Prince asked.

"Circle the block. Speakin of the devil! I just saw both of them on the other side of the street."

"Who?"

"Ralo and Black. They were standing in front of that Audi." Prince circled the block and just like Amir said, he had seen Ralo's new Audi R8 parked with the music playing from it.

"Yo, I'm going over there. I gotta let this faggot see me," Prince said as he maneuvered his Aston Martin with matching pistachio seats.

Ralo looked up nervously and surprised and nonchalantly walked over to the car.

"Yo, what's jumpin P.I.? What up Amir?" Ralo asked.

"Same shit," they both said at the same time.

"Yo, where yall going?" Ralo asked.

"Nowhere. Just chillin. How bout you," Prince asked.

"Aw man, I'm just chillin. I'm just here talkin shit with a few old friends I ain't seen I a while."

"Oh yeah? What's going on with' Black?" Amir asked.

Black looked up and saw Amir and headed towards the car.

"Ay Pops, what's good?" Black asked.

"I ain't your Pops. This is my only son right here. You and my daughter ain't never been married," Amir said.

"Yeah, you're right Amir. So is this the man of the hour. The Fresh Prince of Baltimore?"

"Ay-yo, that stamp "Nore" you can keep it, aight?"

"I don't know what you talkin about Homeboy. But I ain't one of your workers either," Black said intentionally disrespecting Ralo.

"Yeah, I hear you. I guess I don't pay niggas enough to be loyal. I'ma see you around Big Fella. Oh yeah my wife sends her regards," Prince said infuriating Black.

"Okay, tell her I said what up," Black said and stepped away from the luxury car.

"You heard anything from Chan. We're getting low ain't we?" Ralo said.

"Nah, we already took care of that. Lil Rah made that move. Yo Son, your services are no longer needed. Feel me?"

"What?" Ralo said loudly.

"You hear him Nigger! You're fired! Do we have to get any clearer than that? "Amir said inching his hand on the 357 Magnum.

"Yo, what's that about?" Ralo said as if he was worried.

"Yo man, I ain't with all that verbal gymnastics. You know what you did. I hope you prosper with Black, cause we done."

"Damn, after all I've done for you P.I. This is how you do me?"

"Nah, I didn't do anything to you. You did this to yourself. Never bite the hand that feeds you," Prince said putting the powerful V-12 in gear and pulling off leaving Ralo at the curb. Cornbread walked over to Ralo.

"Yo man, fuck them niggas. You don't need em'. We could've murked them niggas right here," Cornbread said.

"Yeah fuck em," Ralo said. But he knew if he couldn't get his hand on "F.I.R.E" to mix with Black's dope, he wouldn't have a chance in that city. His hand was exposed. Now he had to play it to the best of his ability. Even if it meant murder.

◆ ◆ ◆

".....and Sin King hits another three pointer to tie the game. What an awesome player. This kid has got some good game! He's by far the best player on the planet. Excuse me Mr. D Wade, hello, Sin King," the announcer said excitedly through the plasma screen. Prince watched proudly as his brother scored basket after basket, while he sipped on Absolut Vodka. He had so many things running through his mind, mainly Ralo. "How could this nigga violate? What is his motive? It can't be money." Prince thought to himself. He couldn't figure it out to save his life.

"Ooh my goodness, girl where is your diaper?" Prince laughed as he saw his daughter run past him butt naked. She looked at him, raised her hands and shrugged her shoulders as to say "don't know, don't care." Prince got up, grabbed his nine-month-old daughter and gave her a kiss on her face. She smiled with glee as she was the happiest baby in the world.

"You want a bath?" he playfully asked her. She shrugged her shoulders again saying; "who cares?"

"Where did you learn how to do that girl? Huh?" Prince said and again she shrugged her shoulders, soliciting laughter from her father. He took her in the bedroom, gathered some things and took her in the bathroom to bathe her. After a long and playful bath, Prince oiled her down with Johnson and Johnson Baby Oil, put on a new pamper and t-shirt. Afterwards, they both were exhausted and seconds later they both were ready for sleep. Prince laid down with his daughter glued to his chest.

Silky came back from the market to see the most important people in her life sleeping in her bed. Tears of happiness streamed down her face as the Kodak moment touched her heart. She grabbed her phone and began to take pictures of her family sleeping without a care in the world.

"It's time to leave the game Daddy," Silky whispered in her husband's ear as she began to clean up the mess that her husband and daughter made.

Black waited for the traffic light to turn green so that he could proceed home. He was stressed. He had taken the consignment from the Africans and couldn't get rid of it. He sent a few keys down south but it wasn't selling fast enough. At first Ralo allowed him to mix "Nore" with his dope and things were going very well. But since "F.I.R.E" hit the streets, his dope career had come to a complete stand still; at least in Baltimore City. Black had no where near the money he owed the Africans.

"I should do the bitch just like I did Silky," he thought to himself and drove.

Prince and his crew became a problem in the streets of Baltimore City. He didn't even realize that putting Lil Raheem in position would be such a great benefit. Lil Rah was loved by the entire city and his team was loyal. He took on a leadership role that gained him and everyone around him, money and power. Everybody began to buy "F.I.R.E" and the stamp was everywhere. Chan-Ho began to double the orders and yet, it wasn't enough. The city was on "F.I.R.E".

"Yo Bread, meet me at the spot in a half."

"Aight, I'm ten minutes away. I'll wait for you," Cornbread said, ending the call.

Black knew if he wanted to continue to shake in Baltimore, he would have to remove the competition. Lil Rah was the man on the street. He refused Black's proposition and Black knew that was a problem. But now the problem would have to be eliminated.

"Dudes don't respect nothing but violence," Black said to himself as he pulled in front of the spot.

"Yeah, we gonna kill em in the morning with this shit," Cornbread said as he, Do-Dirty and Black chopped up chunks of raw dope to hit the streets. Black decided to come out with the raw chunks and step up his game. Cornbread gave the sample a test run and according to his behavior, the dope was ready to be distributed. They sat in the hide-out where they stashed money and drugs that would all be profit; since Black decided not to pay the Africans what he owed. Do-Dirty and Black went into the back room to sneak a hit while Cornbread bagged up the dope. They would be there all night preparing for a grand opening in the morning.

"One to Two."

"Two to One, go."

"We got one in the back room nodding off. The other two are still in the front packaging drugs."

"Okay, we'll hit 'em from the back. You watch the front door." The masked uniformed men gave his back up the silent count and kicked the door in. Do-Dirty rose from his nod to a glock in his face, while Black and Cornbread laid face down in the front room/ Each man was plexi cuffed and taken into the back room.

"Listen," a voice of a black man came through the mask. "We can make this easy or hard. Where the rest of the shit?"

"Man what yall see on this table is what yall get. It ain't nothing else in here. Where's the warrant?" Black said raising his head and noticing D.E.A. across the masked man's jacket.

"Warrant? What warrant nigga? There ain't no fuckin warrant. If you don't tell me where the shit at, yall gonna be signing a death warrant. Now you know this is a robbery, let's not turn it into a homicide. Now where's the rest of the shit?"

"Jack Pot." Another masked man said as he lifted the floorboard and pulled our numerous kilos of raw heroin and two duffel bags of money. Cornbread and Do-Dirty didn't even know that much shit was in the spot. The robbers took all the stray money that was stacked on the table along with the already bagged raw dope and every loose cent that was in the spot.

"Two to One."

"One to Two, go."

"How are we lookin out there?"

Everything is quiet! Just walk right out the front door. We right out front," One said.

"Aight cool. We hit the jackpot in here. It's going to be a good Christmas. What do you wanna do with these Lames?" The notorious professional stick up kid, Wayno from Harlem, NY said.

"Let em live," Ralo said to Wayno as he placed the radio in his lap and watched his assembled team walk out the door. They had pulled the robbery of the decade; almost 15 kilos of heroin and 5 million in cash. At least it felt like it. He wished he could've done this to Prince, but Prince's operation was impenetrable. But Black and his two sidekicks were like taking candy from a baby. They were careless. Ralo had other plans. It would be a matter of time before he and Silky would live happily ever after. "Fuck these dusty ass kids, this dusty ass baby mama of mine and her begging ass family. "Just me and you Silky. Just me and you," Ralo smiled and pulled off in the unmarked police car.

CHAPTER TWENTY-SEVEN

"Happy Birthday Princess," Prince and Silky said to their beautiful one year old daughter as soon as she awakened.

"Happy Birthday to you dada," Princess said, eliciting laughter from her parents. Their baby was one year old and today they planned a private party with just the family and a couple of immediate friends. Sin, Tasha and Lil Prince were on their way. They had called and said that they were an hour away.

"Come on Baby, let's get you a bath so you can eat and get dressed. Ay, Prince what time are you going to get the cake?" Silky asked.

"I should go get it now so I can get it outta the way. It's been ready since yesterday. The clown called too. That Bozo will be here at 3 o'clock," Prince said trying to make a joke and getting a chuckle out of Silky.

"Dada"

"Yes Baby?" Prince said, answering his daughter from another room.

"appy irthday!" Princess tried her best saying it.

"No, Happy Birthday to you. How old are you now?"

"Two," she said.

"Girl you ain't two. You act like you're two. You're only one."

"One?" Princess asked.

"Yeah. Say I Am One Years Old," Prince said.

"I am old," Princess said, trying her best to repeat her

father.

"I'll be right back, okay?"

"Can I go, Dada?"

"No, come on Baby let's take a bath first." Silky knew that Prince messed up. She would not let him leave the house without crying until her father got back.

"Damn," Prince said to himself, catching on to Silk's hint.

"Go?" Princess asked.

"Yeah, you go with me later," Prince said. He tried to leave the room and Princess started crying.

"Nigga, you may as well wait. She hip to you now and she's gonna cry until you get back," Silky said laughing.

"Aight, just wash her up. We'll all go together and make all the runs. I'll call Sin to let him know we'll meet them later. Silky gave Princess a quick bath; they dressed the birthday girl and left the condo. While in the car, Prince called and informed everybody about the party. To their surprise they looked up and saw three carloads of family members. Prince's mother, Lily Bird, brothers, sisters, along with Sin and his family in tow.

"Hey Prince!" everybody yelled as they jumped out of the cars.

"Hey Silky. Happy Birthday Princess," was all you heard as it looked like a million people were jumping out of a clown car. Prince put the Aston Martin in park and he, Silky and Princess jumped out. They were both happy and surprised to see everybody. It had been a while since he'd seen any of them. He looked behind Sin and Tasha; and there was his son looking exactly like him running in his direction. He turned to his left and saw another major surprise. It was his team from New York City. Kah, Darren and Big Boi were parking the Range Rover HSE. They jumped out and the family reunion started in the underground parking lot. Prince and Silky hugged and kissed everyone and gave them their security codes to the elevator and apartment. They informed them that they had to pick up some things from the store. From the looks of things, extra food and drinks. They tried to pass the baby girl to her family, but she refused to leave her father' side.

"Look yall, go upstairs and make yall selves at home. We'll be back in a half hour," Silky said as Prince and the birthday girl jumped back in the Aston Martin.

Lil Prince, you wanna go?"

"Nah Dad, I'm going to play XBox," he said.

"Aight. I'll be right back to smash you," his father said.

"Prince!" Ms. Ronnie yelled out.

"Yeah Ma," Prince said, trying to back out. He knew that they wouldn't let him go.

"Why don't you stay with us and let somebody else go. I wanna talk to you. I've been having these crazy dreams about you Baby," Ms. Ronnie said.

"Aw Ma, I'ma be alright. I'll be back in twenty minutes, I promise. I gotta make a few pit stops. Don't worry, I'm safe out here."

"Okay Boy. You hurry back, you hear?"

"Yes Ma.. I'll be right back."

"Don't worry Ms. Ronnie, we'll take good care of him," Silky said.

"Okay, y'all be careful."

Prince pulled out and saw Sin as he was getting something that looked like a wrapped present out of his trunk.

"Yo Bro, you did this didn't you?" Prince asked.

"Man, it's my niece's first birthday. You know we gotta do it BIG. You lucky I couldn't get the permits for Dru-Hill Park," Sin said.

"Yeah I thought about that too, but this is beautiful right here with just family."

"Aight man, go ahead. I'll entertain the guest until y'all get back. Yo Prince?"

"Yeah, what's good Bro?"

"I love you man," Sin said. Prince put his car in park, got out and hugged his brother.

◆ ◆ ◆

Black and Ralo sped up on the highway towards Essex County in Ralo's R8. Ralo had given Black an entire scenario about how Prince and Raheem could have set him up to get robbed. They were on their way to Lil Raheem's house to kidnap him for ransom. Ralo confirmed that Prince would pay anything to get his young soldier back. Little that they knew, Lil Raheem had relocated him and his family to a new and improved down low spot.

"Yo man, I need bread and I need it bad! I gotta get outta town. I got this African Bitch callin my phone. I don't know why she keeps calling, she ain't getting shit. Plus, I gotta pay these two crazy motherfuckers. They hounding me for bread," Black said, referring to Cornbread and Do-Dirty.

Yeah, this shit is gettin' crazy. How they get the drop on you anyway?" Ralo asked unconcerned.

"Man, if I knew, I would tell you. Them niggas was professional as fuck. I thought they were the real deal. I looked up and they were standing over me on some Navy Seal shit. If I didn't know any better, I would have thought that nigga was the D.E.A.," Black said. The truth was, they were professional. They decided to use the D.E.A. tactic because it was the easiest. I was like taking candy from a baby.

"Well, it had to be Prince and them. Who else could it be? I mean, the whole city is rollin with them niggas now. And this nigga, Prince, Reign Supreme at the top, hell no!"

"Yeah, He shining'. But not for long. Niggas is gonna start paying with their lives for this one, starting with this lil nigga Raheem, then your boy Prince after we get the stash house. Yo, you mean to tell me you been with them niggas all this time and you don't know where they keep the stash?" Black asked.

"Nah, I made the initial pick up. Then I would drop it off to another nigga, he would drop it off to another nigga and that nigga would drop it off to Prince. He didn't trust anybody. Only he knows where the stash lands," Ralo said.

"Damn," Black said, banging his hand on the $179,000 dashboard of Ralo's Audi R8.

◆ ◆ ◆

"Yes, we are here for the birthday cake for Princess."

"Oh, I spoke to you earlier right?" the baker asked.

"Yeah, that was me," Prince answered.

"Yes, I have it right here. This is a huge cake for a one year old," the baker said, reaching around and grabbing the birthday cake that was beautifully decorated with all types of Sesame Street characters, balloons and accessories. Prince gave his credit card for the cake and he and Princess walked out of the bakery. Silky was in the liquor store getting a few more bottles for the unexpected guests that arrived at their house. They had more than enough food but they were short on alcohol.

"Damn Ma, how much liquor do you need for one year olds?" Prince said and they both burst out laughing. They watched the store worker put two boxes of liquor in the back of the Aston Martin. Silky tipped him $20. "Can't have enough liquor," Silky said as Prince began to pull off.

"You like cake Ma-Ma?" Silky asked the Princess.

"Yeah, I want cake," Princess said pointing at the box from the car seat where she sat.

◆ ◆ ◆

"Man, I don't give a fuck about what this nigga Black is talkin bout. Somebody gettin' left leaking with holes today. I'm broke as hell," Cornbread said to his brother who was driving.

"Just be easy Bro. We're gonna rob a few traps and get a couple of dollars. We ain't never gonna be broke."

"Yo, you think Black was lying about Prince settin' up the spot?"

"I don't know man. It's something fishy about that nigga Ralo too, but Prince definitely had his hand in it too."

"But why? He's filthy rich. He doesn't even be out like that. Why would he take such a stupid risk?" Cornbread said beginning to use logic and reason, something he rarely did.

"I'll tell you why. To do what he planned to do; cripple the team. You see how we riding around looking for gas money. He did this to keep control of the power. Without money we have no power. Them New York niggas is real slick. Don't ever underestimate them niggas. That's why we supposed to murder them as soon as they hit the city and try to set up shop."

"Word! I'm definitely feeling that. I should've pushed his shit back when I had the drop on em."

"Well, here's your chance right now. Just as they were speaking, Prince and Silky pulled up at the stop light right beside them.

"Ooh shit Bro. That's the bitch ass nigga right there," Cornbread said anxiously. Prince and Silky bopped their heads to the music not paying them any attention.

"Yo follow them Bro."

".....Yeah Sin, meet me downstairs. We got a lot of shit. You know how my wife is," Prince said.

"Aight, bet. We'll be there in two minutes," Prince said, ending the call.

Minutes later, they pulled into the underground parking and right behind them was Do-Dirty and Cornbread. Prince pulled in front of the elevator and didn't notice the two brothers creeping beside the Aston Martin.

"Yo, I like this city." Kah said, as he Sin, Big Boi and Darren rode down on the elevator.

"Yeah, it's good, but it ain't no place like New York," Sin said.

"Yeah, you ain't lying," Boi said and just as they reached the parking garage they heard gunshots.

"Oh shit, you heard that," Darren said as he heard Kah tell Sin to stay to the side while he, Boi and Darren reached at the same time for their guns.

When the door opened Prince's lifeless body laid on the ground with blood oozing from everywhere. They looked in the car and saw Silky's body slumped over the baby's seat as if she was trying to protect her baby when she was shot. Kah looked up and saw two men casually walking towards their car.

"Ooh my God! Oh My God!" Sin said as he saw Kah, Darren and Boi head towards the shooters. Cornbread and Do-Dirty hadn't seen the three men with guns.

"Pop-Pop-Pop-Pop," the 40-caliber rang off splitting both brothers' skulls. Their car slammed into a column and was sprayed with shots until all clips were emptied. Sin sat on the side of his brother's car with his head in his lap waiting for the ambulance to arrive. Since they lived in a respectable condominium, the ambulance was there rather quickly. Prince and Silky were rushed to the hospital. They were still alive. Boi pushed the bodies of the two dead men aside and drove off in their car as Darren and Kah followed. Everybody ran to the crime scene to see what happened. Ms. Ronnie fainted and everybody else stood there staring at the bullet ridden Aston Martin.

CHAPTER TWENTY-EIGHT

"Heaven Calls"

It was Beautiful. It was something that she had never seen before.

The sky was filled with beautiful colors; the air was fresh and clean as if the world was sprayed with Febreze. The people were all smiling and pleasant. There were billions of people, but no cars, no planes, no buses, no traffic. Everything ran smoothly. Only white beautiful horses with solid gold shoes glided through the air. Everyone wore the purest of white clothing. The T.L.C. brand shined on their clothing tags. Silky had never experienced anything like it. She wanted to go beyond the golden gate. She wanted in. She wanted to enter Paradise. She tried to wake up out of the dream; she couldn't. If she didn't know any better, she would think she was in Heaven. She looked up at an approaching horse and there she was. She was the most beautiful woman Silky had ever seen; a younger version of herself. Her hair blew freely in the windless air, her caramel complexion complemented her hazel eyes. As she approached the golden gate, her face was now clear. Zuri stared directly into her daughter's eyes and smiled.

"Mommy?" Silky said nervously.

"Yes Baby, it is me," Zuri said.

"But I thought you...."

"Passed on?"

"Yes."

"Yes my time on earth had expired, but my soul lives on. This is Heaven my beautiful child."

"Can I come in with you?"

"No, Silky. God is not ready for you yet. He has other plans for you, "Zuri answered.

"And what about my family; my husband, my baby?" Silky asked.

"God is ready for them Silky, but he is not ready for you. I promise, they're in the best hands now."

"No mommy. Take me. Leave them on earth," Silky said with much anger.

"I'm sorry Silk, but this is God's orders," Zuri said as two more white horses arrived. Silky watched as her husband and daughter glided in the air without noticing her.

"Prince! Prince! Baby, wait for me!" Silky yelled to deaf ears.

"Mommy Please! Take me with them," she begged.

"It's not my call Silky. God has made his ruling. They'll be here when you come back and you'll live an everlasting life with them Remember John 3:16; For God so loved the world that he gave his only begotten Son, that whosoever believeth in him should not perish, but have everlasting life."

"No mom, I don't want to hear that! I want my family," Silky begged as she saw her mother fading away. Everything that looked and smelled beautiful began to disappear. She blinked her eyes and thought she saw "the light". She looked and saw many lights and sounds of machines.

"Silky?"

"Mommy please," she began to say as tears flowed freely down her face.

"Silky? Silky?" Amir cried, as he couldn't believe that his daughter had awakened from her coma.

"Thank you God," Amir said, looking up towards the Heaven above him.

◆ ◆ ◆

The street was blocked off. Every major person that respected the game was in attendance. They all agreed that one man tried to unite the city and make them all rich at the same time. When they began to deal with Lil Raheem, using Prince's blueprints and product, they all became very wealthy. In the front row sat Silky, who was bound to a wheelchair. Next to her, her father Amir, Ms. Ronnie and her children, Sin, Lil Prince, Tasha and Lil Raheem with his family. Behind them were Prince's friends from NYC; including his old basketball buddies. It was Silky and Ms. Ronnie's decision to bury Prince in Baltimore and not New York. After all, this is where Prince grew into the man he always wanted to be. Prince laid peacefully in a beautiful casket dressed in a white suit, while his daughter lay close to his breastplate. It looked as if they were sleeping. Everyone wept while the Reverend gave his eulogy. Surprisingly to all, Lil Prince stood headed towards the casket. He looked just like his father. His black two-piece site fell gracefully over his tiny Gucci loafers.

"Dad? Mommy said you're going to Heaven. I wish I could come with you so we could play XBox, but Mommy said I couldn't go yet. I bought you some toys so that you can play with Princess." Lil Prince darted back to his seat to get his Spider Man book bag. "I'm back Dad. My bad. This bag is kind of heavy. It has nine dollars in it. Sin told me it was your money. You're probably gonna need it to get you and Princess some McDonald's. Get Princess a Happy Meal; she likes the toys. Oh yeah, Dad, since you're leaving and going to Heaven, can Sin be my daddy too. I like having two daddies; one in New York and one in Heaven. Yall both give me everything I want. I got mad toys dad. My new sister's name is Sihri; she is with Grandma in New York. She loves you too Dad; but nobody loves you more than me," Lil Prince said as Sin rose and approached the casket to stand beside him.

"Hey Big Bro! Hey Little Princess. You both look beautiful," Sin said breaking down to his knees. He couldn't talk. His body shook uncontrollably. He had to be removed by Kah and Darren. This was his third breakdown of that day. Silky unlocked the brakes to her wheelchair and gave Amir the head nod to push her to her family. She sat and watched everyone pay their respects to her husband and daughter. She had no idea of what she would say. There was so much she wanted to say. Amir pushed her in front of the casket and backed away.

"Hi babies. Wow, I can still remember the first day we met. It seems like yesterday. You were sooo cute. You with your flowers," she said with a faint smile as tears flowed down her face. "I wanted to tell yall so many things. I mean, both of yall made my life complete. Just not too long ago we were living the life of Riley and look at our baby. She looks just like you Prince, in her pretty dress. Look at her yall," Silky said back at the mourners. "You see how many people are here Baby?" she said, beginning to cry hysterically and beginning to cough. Amir hurried to his daughter's side and she waved him off.

"I saw my mom. She spoke to me. I saw yall too. Yall looked peaceful, but lonely without me. I'm lonely without you. To be honest, I don't know if I'll make it without y'all. I'll try my best. You always told me, Silky no matter what, stand on your own two feet. Now I can't stand at all. How ironic," Silky said, referring to her inability to walk.

"Baby, I promise you this, if there is anybody else behind this I swear," Silky whispered through clenched teeth. "I swear, they will not only pay with their life, but their bloodline is gonna feel my raft. Baby, I'll meet you in Heaven. I'll be there sooner than you think. I promise. I love you Daddy. I love you Princess," Silky said, blowing a kiss and wheeling herself away from the only man she had ever loved, the only child she had ever bared, her family. Amir got behind her to put her back in her spot. "No," she said and pointed towards the front door. When they were exiting the funeral home, she saw commotion. It was Chan-Ho and his security preventing Ralo from entering the service. It was Amir's order; at least until they got to the bottom of Princes and his daughter's murder.

"Why do you cry mommy?" a one year old asked.

"That's your daddy baby. That's your daddy," Coco said holding her son against her chest tightly as she sobbed for the man she fell in love with the first day she had seen him. Coco and Silky had gotten pregnant on the same day at the same time.

"That's your daddy baby. That is your daddy."

After the services, everybody paid their respects to the family. Tasha and Sin asked Silky if she needed them to stay. She insisted that everybody leave. The private facility where she stayed for rehabilitation was suitable for any celebrity. After all, she was, thanks to T.L.C. whose stocks had gone through the roof after she was shot and it went public. Amir and Chan-Ho refused to leave her side, no matter what she said. They gave her around the clock security as if she was the President. It was clearly the roughest day of her life. She watched her only love and her precious daughter lowered into the ground and covered with dirt. She had lost her soul. She was only flesh; there was no inside to her. Her mind; thoughtless, her heart; frozen. She would not sleep until someone felt the way she did. She sat in her room and stared at the picture she took of Prince with their daughter asleep in bed. They looked the exact same way when they laid in the casket. She smiled at the innocent faces and re-membered the story Prince told her about their baby running around naked without a pamper.

"You make sure you keep that pamper on Ma-Ma." Silky said to the picture, showering it with kisses. Amir and Chan-Ho watched as their only reason for living sat there like an empty shell waiting to be crushed. Someone destroyed their baby's life. Someone will be destroyed.

CHAPTER TWENTY-NINE

"Oh My Goodness."

After a year of intense therapy it had finally happened.

Silky had walked on her own. With the support of her family, she had begun to come around. Not a day passed when she didn't think about her husband and daughter. Her beauty never left, but after a year of rest, she was more beautiful. Her hair fell to the center of her back and her skin glowed beautifully. Her figure had taken a turn for the better, which made her even more attractive. Sin, Tasha and the rest of her immediate family visited frequently giving her the support she much needed and deserved. It was hard for Silky though. Looking at Lil Prince, a spitting image of his father and watching Sihri grow, made her miss her family even more. But today amongst family and friends including Amir and Chan-Ho she had risen and taken her first steps. It had actually been the first time in a year when she had truly been happy. She thought every day about walking again, so she could move on with her life. However, she also thought, "What was moving on?" She could never see herself loving another man and starting a family. Therefore, she would live and be alone for the rest of her life. However, at the moment she was glad her family was there and without them she couldn't imagine where she'd be.

"Look at you girl," Tasha said as she took her first steps.

"Naw, that's my baby," Amir said smiling as she stepped slowly.

"Oh my God!" Silky said again as she began to catch a rhythm and move about in her room without any complications. "Ooh My God. I'm walking. I'm walking. Look at me yall," Silky cried with happiness.

"I knew you could do it sis," Sin said as tears flowed from his eyes.

"I couldn't have done it without y'all. Somebody's watching over me. I know somebody's watching over me," Silky said as she looked out the window towards the beautiful clear blue skies. "Thank you Prince. Thank you Princess I love and miss you guys." Silky said to her family in Heaven.

◆ ◆ ◆

Meanwhile, back in Baltimore

"R.I.P, R.I.P. Get ya R.I.P. yall," the corner men yelled out the powerful dope's name that was turning the city out. Raheem had been passed the torch and he led the city like a true general. After the funeral he and Amir decided to change the "Fire" stamp to "R.I.P." in memory of his brother, his mentor, Prince. The city loved Raheem. His loyalty to the game attracted many who would never think about clicking up. But that is what it was; an organization. Ninety percent of the hood used the "R.I.P." stamp that was backed by the best dope the city had ever seen. Chan-Ho moved to the U.S. to stay close to Silky and he and his men kept the city flooded with the best heroine. Even though Silky didn't need any help. Lil Raheem made it his business to give Silky sixty percent of his earnings. Silky wanted no more of the game. T.L.C. (The Linen Closet) made her a rich woman. Chan-Ho dealt with Raheem and Amir was merely a consultant.

Lil Raheem and his team hugged the block and watched the Trap serve customer after customer who wanted to buy R.I.P. Even though Lil Rah's power status had changed, he was still unable to leave the block alone. This is where he had risen and this is where he became a "Trap Star". He knew the block is where he felt most safe and comfortable. He had corner men watching four ways and gunmen on standby for any unwanted drama. Raheem and his team passed the purple weed and forth as they all watched their money stack up.

"Up Broadway," the corner men yelled out as he had seen an unfamiliar car screeching in their direction. Raheem's gunman took position as the approaching car got closer. Once the car was in sight, Raheem knew the driver. Ralo pulled in front of Raheem in his Audi R8.

"Yo, what up Lil Prince. How you?" Ralo asked sarcastically.

"My name is Raheem. I guess since you went broke you caught amnesia too, huh?

"Yeah, I hear you're the new king of B-More, huh?"

"My nig, if you already know, then why do you ask?"

"You know, I'm just rapping with you, Lil Bro . That's all."

"Oh yeah, that's what you call it, rappin?"

"I'm sayin Lil bro , it ain't no hard feelings is it?"

"I don't know. You tell me. I mean, Prince did give me your position in the hood. I don't think D-Wade would like to ride the bench when LeBron is averaging thirty a game," Raheem said, getting a chuckle from his homies.

"Let me tell you something, you bitch ass nigga. Prince could never put me on the bench. I made him successful in this city. Nobody would buy his product if it wasn't for me," Ralo spurted out.

"Yeah, I guess you're right. So, is that why you crossed him? Is that why you switched sides? Or is it something personal?" Raheem asked.

"My nig, it's never personal. Business is business. Before you were able to come off the stoop, I was a Trap Star and now you got the nerve to question my loyalty. It's never personal, always business.

"Never personal; always business? What's that supposed to mean? You had something to do with that?" Lil Rah said, referring to the murders.

"Nah, I would never do that. You know where that comes from. But I ain't mad at dem niggas either. This is our city. You don't let a nigga from another state come out here and take what Baltimore niggas built," Ralo said.

"Oh, now I see. You were jealous of Son. He did in four years what you were trying to do your whole life. That man put you in that R8 and all you can do is sit here and talk greasy about him? You a coward," Raheem said raising his voice and his gunmen beamed in on the situation.

"Nah Lil bro , I'm not a coward; a genius. See, while your dumb ass is sitting around here mourning a nigga that didn't care if you live or die, I'm gonna continue to stack paper. I ain't nobody's flunky," Ralo said.

"Yall niggas kill me. When Prince was alive you would suck his dick. Now that he is dead.....," Raheem shook his head as Ralo cut him off.

"Fuck that nigga. Fuck his cripple bitch and fuck everybody who mad that I said it," Ralo's voice had risen as he seen a police car coming in their direction.

"Coming up Broadway! Time out," the corner men yelled alerting the workers in the Trap making everybody disperse quickly.

"Man shit, my trap doin just as good as y'all. Come through West B-More and see for yourself, "Silk Tears" that's the stamp and it's one you'll never forget. Silky Tears in the building and she's here to stay," Ralo said, chuckling and pulled off.

"Yo, this nigga named the dope after Silky, Silky," Raheem's right hand man said.

"That's what it sounds like. That's what it sounds like," Raheem said shaking his head in disgust.

CHAPTER THIRTY

"Count it, it's all there Big Dawg. That's sixty cent right there shawty."

"Come on man, we've been doing business for over a year. You think I don't trust you?"

"Nah it ain't that. Business is Business."

"Yeah, I guess you're right. I hope we can continue to do business."

"Man that's on automatic! As long as you keep this good coke, we gon continue to do business shawty!" Rico said in his deepest South Carolina accent.

"Aight then. You know how to get at me. I ain't going nowhere. The coke is there."

"Bet. This is already sold. So I'll be hollering at you in a few days."

"You do that," Black said as he let Rico out the apartment and locked the door behind him.

"Damn, if I'd known the money was this good, I could've left Baltimore," Black said to himself. He counted his money that was supposed to be sixty grand. He had doubled his profit that quick. Black had moved to South Carolina after the shooting and had been living the "Good Life". Everything in South Carolina where he lived was inexpensive. Therefore he lived like a king in the Southern state. He had it all, cars, jewelry, women and a nice piece of property.

"Knock! Knock! Knock!

"Man, this nigga left something," Black said looking around the apartment before opening the door.

"Yo, what up Ric....," Before he could finish his sentence,

he was being pushed into the apartment with a Desert Eagle pointed in his face. Since moving to South Carolina, Black moved cautiously. He changed residences frequently, so no one could pinpoint him. "Damn, this nigga Rico set me up," Black thought to himself and shortly after he was hit across the temple with the butt of the Desert Eagle knocking him out cold.

Silky sat behind her mahogany desk for the first time in her Harborview office overlooking Baltimore. She dreamed of The Linen Closet and now her dreams were being manifested. On her desk, sat a plague with "Silky (no last name)" President and CEO. Next to her was a picture of Prince and Princess as they slept in their bed. It was impossible for her not to grieve at times, so she decided to try to and run her corporation to keep her mind occupied. She had no more ties to the streets, neither did Amir. They were too busy running a multi-million dollar business selling linen suits.

"Uh excuse me Boss you have a call on line #2," Silky's assistant said over the intercom.

"Thanks Lanae, I'll take it in here," Silky said answering line #2.

"Good morning, The Linen Closet. Silky speaking."

"Hello Silky?"

"Hello? Who am I speaking to?" Silky asked.

"This is Makeba, Silky. I really need to meet with you at your earliest convenience," Makeba said.

"Makeba?" Silky said, puzzled.

"Yes. This is Makeba. Do you not remember me?" Makeba asked.

"Of course I remember you, but I'm trying to understand why you're calling me," Silky said.

"I may have some important information for you that may give you closure to your family's death," Makeba said.

"My family's death" What do you have to do with my

family?" Silky asked.

"I don't think I need to say anything else! Do you remember where we used to meet?" Makeba said, referring to her and Silky's prior business meeting.

"Yeah, I remember."

"Can you be there in an hour?"

"Yeah, I'll be there."

"See you then. Goodbye."

Okay, bye," Silky said, hanging up and quickly dialing her cell phone.

"Dad, can you meet me at the house in a half hour?"

"Yeah, of course. You okay?" Amir asked.

"Yeah I'm fine dad. I just need to meet with you and Chan. It's important."

"We'll be there in five minutes. In fact, we're on the way to your office right now. Be downstairs in two minutes.

"Okay dad," Silky said, ending the call.

Silky, Amir and Chan-Ho walked into Lisa's funeral home. This is where her and Makeba had last met. They both had connections with their friend Lisa who could disperse any and everything that needed to disappear, including bodies. They were met by Makeba's men and led to the back where Lisa did her job.

"Hello Silky."

"Hey," Silky said softly.

"Damn," Amir and Chan-Ho said in unison as they both looked upon the beauty that Makeba's features displayed.

"First, let me say this. I am deeply saddened about your loss of loved ones. I will not, and cannot lie, I envied everything about you Silky. I wanted what you had so bad. You are the Queen of this city.

"Was. I'm done," Silky said softly.

"You will always reign as Queen. Your husband may or may not have told you, but one day I approached him in New York City. He was in that gigantic toy store on 5th Avenue. I was taking my nephew shopping and if you must know he didn't accept any of my advances. He was so into his son," Makeba said,

"Thanks for telling me." Silky said and thought about what Prince said about the prettiest woman he had ever seen flirting with him while he was at the toy store in New York City. She remembered clearly. She also remembered the episode they had with the two porn stars when he arrived back from New York also. "Is that why you called me? To tell me that?" Silky said getting agitated. Makeba motioned to her men to pull back the sheet on a gurney where Black laid tied up.

"What the fuck is this nigga doin here?" Amir asked.

"Well, this piece of garbage is one of the main reasons your granddaughter and son-in-law was killed. He along with a young fella named Ralo. They were both determined to destroy Prince. Just as I was jealous of you, they were of Prince. However, they had different motives. Our friend, Black here's motive was greed. His partner Ralo's motive is you," Makeba said pointing at Silky.

"Me?" Silky said surprised. "Why would he want me?" Silky asked.

"Well, according to our friend laying here," Makeba said, referring to Black before continuing. "Our friend Ralo is obsessed with you. He and Black formed an alliance so they both could have what they wanted. See, Black went into a cocoon after you were shot. He hid down in the Carolinas. The two men who shot you were his men. The day before you were shot, Ralo and friends robbed Black. He made it look as if your husband was responsible for the robbery. I can't make this shit up. I heard this from Black's mouth.

"And why are you of all people telling me this?" Silky asked.

"Good question. Silky, you and I are similar in many

ways. I watched you become the Queen you are today. I also watched greed and jealousy take an innocent child's life. I watched this man destroy your family. I am giving you this information with my deepest condolences. I am giving you closure."

"You know what Makeba; you are so right. I always thought about who's, what's and how's every single day and I can finally close this chapter," Silky said, removing her Gucci shades and wiping her tears dry. "Is he still alive?" Amir asked. Makeba ordered her men to wake Black.

"Yo, what da fuck?" Black said after getting slapped in the face.

"Hey Black. How's it been?"

"Yo Silky. Man, you know I ain't do shit to hurt you. It was that nigga Ralo," Black said.

"Oh, you wouldn't huh? But you could hurt my husband? You could kill my family over some drug dealer's dream? You go fuck yourself Black! You were in Prince's same position but your greed got in your way of being successful. Look at you now laying on a fuckin gurney."

"Silky, listen, I'm telling you, I didn't...."

"Shut the fuck up nigga. I don't wanna hear you bitch up. Man The Fuck Up nigga! I don't wanna hear your voice. I wanna hear my husband's voice. I wanna hear my baby call for her mommy but that will not happen. Why? Because of you and your stupid ass dope fiend friends. I knew that was you I saw on that day going to the airport and you had that bitch Ralo with you too, huh? So this was all in your sick plans. Eliminate my husband and you can have me and the city back, huh?"

"Silk please. Don't do this," Black pleaded.

"Do what Black, kill you? The same way you did to my family? I can't let you live baby boy. You lived on these streets. You know how this thang goes. I made a vow to my husband. I gotta keep my word, Honey. I told him that everyone would pay," Silky said, beginning to break down and cry. Amir and Chan-Ho moved in close as they saw her losing balance.

"Silky, please. Don't let this African bitch fool you. This bitch is crazy. She is a liar. She wanted your spot too. How do you know she didn't have nothing to do with it?" Black said.

"I don't know, but I'm 100% sure that you had your hands in on it. And I believe her and not you. Why? Because she never crossed me before and you did." Silky motioned to get the 40-caliber handgun from Chan-Ho. He passed it to her. Makeba already had a Desert Eagle handgun in her hand, pointing it at Blacks' head. Both women emptied their clips in Black's body. Black shook uncontrollably as the bullets entered his thick frame, making him into swiss cheese. Silky handed the gun back to Chan-Ho and walked over to Makeba.

"Thanks girl. The city is yours," Silky said kissing her on her pretty lips and walking out of the funeral home.

"Where's Ralo?" Amir asked as they walked to the Range Rover.

Lisa walked in her work area and began to clean up the bloody mess. Black's body was cremated to ashes and not a trace of him would be found. Lisa just cleared 100 grand.

CHAPTER THIRTY-ONE

"The Cemetery"

"Y ou gonna be okay Silky," Amir asked.

"Yeah, I'm fine, Dad. Wait here. I won't be as long as I was last week. We had a lot to talk about. That Princess was going on and on." Silky said getting out of the Range Rover and heading in the direction of her family's burial site. She looked around at the beautiful flowers that sat neatly against the tombstones. The white rose she held in her hand was for her family. She arrived at the grave site that said:

Prince Dennis Mapp
&
Princess Denise Mapp

"Hey y'all. I told yall I was coming back. I miss yall both so much. I was watching a video of you playing basketball. Prince, you were sooo good. I remember the first time, we didn't know Sin was your brother," Silky said and smiled. "Well, I'm working on finding those responsible for your death. Shit, one of your killers fell right into my lap. Baby could you believe Ralo? I mean, all this time he wanted you out of the picture so he could have me? Now what makes him think I would spit on him, much less talk to him? Baby, he's gonna pay, but first he's gonna he's gonna feel like he made me feel. I promise you this. So, how's our baby doing up there? I know yall is with my mother. Tell her said hi. Well, I guess you already know Prince, you won't be by yourself for long. I have to go Daddy. Kiss our baby for me. Please hold my spot. I'll be with you soon. I promise," Silky said, as rain drops began to lightly fall from the sky.

"Don't cry Baby, don't cry," she said to her husband as she laid down her flowers, kissed the stone and walked off.

CHAPTER THIRTY-TWO

"Hey Boo!"

Ralo navigated his way home from a long week of fun and pure satisfaction.

He smiled as he swerved his Audi R8 in and out of traffic avoiding anything that would stop him from reaching his destination. Home is a place that he hadn't seen in almost two weeks. His time away consisted of a lot of politics, hustle and an enormous amount of fucking exotic women. He smiled and thought to himself about the morning he'd just had. He had everything a man in his late twenties could want; money, cars and lots of thirsty women. After eliminating all competition, he was the new "King of Baltimore". He even thought about changing his name to King. He was a legend in his own mind. He thought about calling his family and letting them know that he would be there shortly with gifts he brought for everyone; especially his complaining baby-mama. He couldn't wait to get home and play with his eighteen-month-old daughter; after all, she was probably the only one who cared about him. Everybody else was just hanging around waiting for the money to pour in. To him, his family was okay. He didn't mind taking care of his mother, grandmother, sisters, brothers and any stragglers in the same house. He was rich! They were a close-knit family and when Ralo skyrocketed, he purchased a home big enough for them all. But even with all this, he still moved with caution.

".... The streets are not only watching, but they talkin

now, they got me circling the block before I'm parking now."
He sang the Beanie Sigel song as he passed the luxury homes in
his neighborhood. Just as he sang, he circled the property before pulling into his driveway. He saw the cable guy working,
he waived, they both head nodded and he walked through the
front door.

"Hey Boo!

"Yo, what the fuck...." was all Ralo could release from his
mouth before he was blindsided by Chan-Ho, who relieved his
9mm that he held in the middle of his back.

"Da-Da!" Ralo's daughter yelled excitedly from Silky's
lap, as Silky lightly brushed his daughter's hair.

"Yo, what the fuck is going on Silk?" Ralo asked nervously
looking at half naked Silky in a see through lace nighty. Her hair
hung low over her shoulder and her face and body were splattered with human blood.

"What do mean Ralo? Isn't this what you wanted? Me,
right?" Silky said brushing his daughter's hair, who also had
splats of blood on her.

"Yo Silk, you buggin. Look I know you lost your family, I
mean I lost a friend also. Don't you think it hurt me to see Prince
lose his life like that," Ralo said beginning to weep.

"I'm buggin huh? So, that is what it is, I'm buggin the fuck
out? Maybe you can help me understand. Let's see. I lost my
husband and my daughter two days before our wedding anniver-
sary. I couldn't walk by myself for over a year, and I'm buggin'?"

"Silky, what does all this gotta do with me? And why are
you sitting in my living room naked with blood all over you?"

"Because you wanted me baby. Right? Me and you could
be a family? I mean, this is what you wanted right? Isn't this
what this is all about? Me, you over little Princess right here.
She's so beautiful," Silky said, rubbing her face while she began
to fall asleep. "I mean, we are all we got, I ain't got no family, no
mother. You just lost yours...."

"Wait, hold up. Yo, where's my mother at?" Ralo weeped.

"Uh Dad, you didn't happen to see Ralo's mother did

you?" Silky yelled into the back room playfully, unintention-
ally waking Ralo's daughter.

"Uh yeah, She'll be with yall in a sec, sweetie pie!" Amir
yelled back playfully as he walked into the living room holding
Ralo's mother's severed head.

"Yo, what da fuck did yall do, Bitch?" Ralo yelled running
in Amir's direction and Chan stepped in his path, stopping him
in his tracks.

"Yo, where is the rest of my family, Silky? Where is my
family?" Ralo said as tears fell freely from his face.

"Ooh wow, you do have a heart. You're crying like the
bitch that you are. Um Chan-Ho?"

"Yes Boss?"

"Will you please go get Ralo's family? Silky asked. Her
voice began to tremble somewhat of a scary tone; the sound of a
demonic person, a stone cold killer.

"I don't have to go get them Boss. They are right here,"
Chan-Ho said bending down, reaching into an oversized black
duffle bag.

"Uh, I think this is his brother's arm. I'll never forget that
watch. It's a Yacht Master, isn't it. It looks like the one Prince
said was stolen from his car. And here is a torso with a Coppin
University t-shirt on it. I think this is his sister. Man, they all
look alike when they're chopped up. My people in the Philippians will enjoy boiling them.

"Nisha!" Ralo yelled as he noticed his sister's t-shirt.

"Nisha!" Silky mimicked Ralo calling his sister loudly.

"Yo, what type of weirdos are yall? Man fuck that shit,
kill me now. I don't give a fuck. Just kill me!"
Laughter erupted in the room as everybody responded to Ralo's
last statement. Silky put the little girl down and she began to
run about the house looking for toys.

"No, no, no we ain't gonna kill you," Silky said, giving
Chan-ho's men the signal to tie him up. "We want the truth
and your daughter will walk outta here alive. That's if you care
whether she stays alive or not.

"The truth about what, Silk? I don't know shit," Ralo said.

"Wrong answer! Nigga why you had my family murdered? Why did you hate him so much?"

"Yo Silky, I swear to God, I never hated Prince. He was like a brother to me. It fucked me up when y'all didn't let me pay my last respects."

Silky motioned to Chan-Ho who immediately chopped off Ralo's right hand.

"Ugh, ugh, FUCK." Ralo yelled in agony and pain as blood gushed from his wrist.

"Now you got a better answer?"

"Silky please. I'm telling you, I never hated him!"

She motioned again to Chan-Ho who cut just below his elbow, removing his forearm. Ralo passed out instantly and was reawakened by Chan-Ho.

"Ralo, I think you are losing this game. As you can see, it ain't no more room in that duffle bag. Now are you gonna stop lying?"

"Aight listen. I hated the motherfucker. I hated the fact that you went to New York City to find a nigga to put in a position that was supposed to be mine. I was always in love with you, but you wouldn't even look at me. I swear to you though, I didn't have anything to do with those murders."

She motioned to Chan-Ho again and he chopped off his left hand.

"Ugh! Fuckkkk you bitch!" Ralo yelled.

"You fuckin liar. Who told Black that Prince robbed him? Who told Black that lie? You did!"

"I swear to God Silky. I never thought they would kill Prince."

She motioned again and Chan-Ho swung low, cutting his leg just below the kneecap.

"Ugh God! Please, no more. Kill me please!"

Uh-uh, don't call God now nigga. Did you call God when my daughter was laying in the casket?"

"Yo Silky, please. I'm sorry. I'll do anything. Please just

tell this crazy nigga to stop," Ralo said looking at Chan-Ho.

"Stop? We have just begun, Baby. I thought you wanted to fuck. You wanna fuck me right?" Silky said motioning them to drop his pants.

"No please, No please," Ralo said as Silky began to lightly rub his dick making him erect. Chan-Ho stepped in with one quick swipe and Ralo's dick laid lifelessly on the floor. He passed out again and he was quickly awakened. Ralo sat there tied at the waist drained of energy and blood. They had sliced off all his limbs by now. Amir beat his eardrums in, causing him to lose his hearing. He only had two senses left, taste and sight.

"Hey Boo, you are still with us," Silky said in a low harsh tone. Since she found out about Ralo being the reason for her family's death, she had not been the same. Her only sense of reasoning was kill, kill, kill. Her way of avenging her family was torture.

"Why don't you just fuckin kill me?" Ralo asked in a funny way. His lips moved but the sounds that came out sounded, as a deaf person would sound when trying to speak.

Silky motioned for them to fetch his daughter who was in her room playing with toys. Now she was all cleaned up in a beautiful dress. Silky brushed her hair into a ponytail and sat her on her lap. She had thought time after time, pertaining to this situation. Up to this point, she had killed everyone in the house. She motioned to Chan-Ho to turn Ralo in her direction as she placed both hands on the baby's head about to snap her neck. The front door opened and Ralo's baby mother walked in.

"Ooh my God...." She said as she'd been grabbed in the middle of her sentence. She was tied up and put next to her daughter. Rachel sat in shock looking at scenery.

"What's going on here? What did I do?" Rachel cried hysterically. "Why are you holding my daughter?"

"Oh, you didn't know? Your daughter's father killed my family, so I killed his."

"Please, Amir. What's going on here? What are you doing?"

"Um do I know you young lady?" Amir asked surprisingly.

"Yeah of course you know me. I'm the pregnant girl that was in the car with Raheem a few years ago. I was also with him when you gave him the Maserati from Prince. Remember? Do you remember when you said I look just like your daughter?" Rachel said. Amir quickly remembered looking at her. She did look like Silky.

"Please Amir, fuck this nigga. I came to get my shit and my daughter. This is not his baby. Doesn't she look like Lil Raheem? You can call and ask him. This is Rasha. Me and Raheem are not together because I was with Ralo. I just got the DNA results back today. It's right there in my purse. This is not Ralo's baby. We are not his family. He just fucks me, that's all," Rachel said. It was a reason the little girl had lived that long. Now they all knew. It was fate.

"Now I have to ask a question, Miss. You see all of this. Why should we let you live," Silky asked.

"Please, I'm from the same place you're from. Fuck all of these people. All I care about is my baby. I don't care if any of them live or die," Rachel said. Silky smiled and motioned to Chan-Ho to empty the duffel bag full of body parts in front of her. Ralo's entire family was spread out all over the floor in the living room. Rachel immediately threw up everything she had eaten that day.

"Now that's disgusting," Amir said looking at the chopped up pieces of pizza.

"Listen," Silky said, closing her robe. First give me those DNA results." Chan-Ho passed her the paper and Silky held them in front of Ralo's eyes. Ralo read the results and couldn't believe that Lil Rah had gotten the best of him. He sat there limbless, but yet he was hurt by the DNA results. The reaction was enough to satisfy Silky. She walked over to Rachel and passed her the machete.

"Go ahead, finish him," Silky ordered.
Rachel quickly rose after being untied and swung the machete

recklessly with two hands with all her force severing his head, knocking it in the middle of the pile. He was literally at the center of his entire family.

"All right. Enough," Silky said. She grabbed the machete. "Today is your lucky day. We're gonna clean this mess up. You're gonna be okay. After today you'll never have to work a day in your life. I don't know how you and Lil Raheem will turn out, but make certain he knows his daughter. You see that money right there?" Silky said pointing at the stacks of money on the leather sofa. "That's Ralo's life savings. There's three million. I'm gonna see that you get five more million. You'll have a job waiting for you at T.L.C. . My dad is gonna keep an eye on you for a little while. If anybody questions you, you let us know. Understand?"

"What? You said eight million?" Rachel asked, forgetting everything else.

"Yeah, eight million."

"Well, I ain't got shit to say. Shit, I killed him. He was a dead man walking anyway. He knew that. It's crazy how this nigga wanted me to be you. He called me Silky when he fucked me. I didn't know what the fuck he was talkin about.

"Yeah, I know. It's sickening. It's over now. Are you sure you're okay?" Silky said.

"I'm fine." Rachel said as Chan-Ho and Amir escorted her towards the cable truck.

CHAPTER THIRTY-THREE

Amir walked into his plush condominium after a long and exhilarating workout.

He finally checked his mailbox, something he rarely did. He saw a letter from his daughter; Silky. He hadn't heard from his only daughter in over a year. She wanted to leave the country for a little while after being faced with so many tragedies back to back. Amir had given Silky her space. He let her move about the world without any interference. He removed his sweaty clothing, took a hot shower, got dressed in comfortable clothes and grabbed him a shot of Ciroc Vodka straight. He sat in his favorite Lazy Boy chair and began to read Silky's letter. To his surprise, the letter looked as if blood had been splattered on it. He quickly gulped his first shot of Vodka and refilled. He didn't realize how much his hands shook as he read the letter in his hand. His body began to tremble as a cold chill had run through him. It was a chill that he had become familiar with; the chill of Death. He sat back in his chair and began to read.

"Dear Dad:

By the time you get this letter, I hope that you and Chan-Ho are in the best of spirits and health. I am actually having the time of my life. I wish yall was here (smile). This past year, I've been able to do everything I've ever wanted and more. I finally made it to Africa. I climbed the mountain at Kilimanjaro in Tanzania. Of course I had some help. But, the feeling when you reach the top is unexplainable; Heaven-like. I felt like I conquered the world (lol!). I finally went skydiving too. Now, that was crazy!! Dad, when I jumped out the plane my parachute wouldn't open. I peed all over Australia's beautiful skies. I went skiing in Germany and drank some of the best vodka in Sweden. I wanted to know if they really made Absolut in Sweden; they do. I'm smiling as I write this letter because when I used to talk to Prince about these things, he used to smile and daydream about taking trips.

Dad, you know that nigga would never leave the United States (lol). I went to Haiti, right after the earthquake. Man, you should see the strength of those people. It was overwhelming how positive their attitudes were. Even after losing everything, (which wasn't much) they still continued to be optimistic about life. There was a ten-year-old boy who had been trapped under rubbish for twenty-nine days. When they found him, he raised his arms in triumph. Shit, I would've asked for something to eat! LOL!!! I started a Prince-Princess foundation and we donated five million to help build schools in Haiti. I met Wyclef and he told me that one day he'd become President. We should pray for him Dad. He really loves his country.

I went across the border to the Dominican Republic. It is beautiful. I may be wrong, but the hotels don't like to give out towels. I guess since everybody walks around naked on the beach, no one needs a towel. Dad, the water is clear and the sand is white. You know I had to get my scuba dive on!! Yep, I went scuba diving and the scenery down there was mesmerizing. You wouldn't believe it. Daddy, I don't care how much money you have, don't go to Russia!! Blacks are not allowed! Even though I don't look black, they followed me around like I was in a Korean store. I said fuck em' and flew outta there that same night.

My last trip is here in the Philippines. This is where I write this letter, Dad, mom is an icon here. As soon as I got off the plane, I was at home. Immediately, I was recognized as Zuri's daughter. It isn't hard because her pictures are everywhere. Schools are named after her.

Dad, she has the Zuri Platter in the restaurant. It's the house special. And guess what? There's a shrine that is totally dedicated to mom and thousands of people visit it everyday. No wonder she loved it here, she's a goddess here. I can actually feel her spirit.

Well Dad, this is the end. I don't wanna confuse you but this is the end Dad. I'm going to be with my family. They're ready for me. I fought with this every single day. Today is the day when I return to them Dad, don't you worry, I'm at peace with my maker. I've completed my entire bucket list. I've explored the world, I've done all that I could have imagined doing; but yet I'm not complete without my husband and my daughter. Enclosed is a full confession of every murder I've committed. I take full responsibility for the deaths that came from NORE dope stamp and any others unsolved. I take full responsibility for killing Black, Ralo and his entire family. It gave me great pleasure to kill them too. But my favorite was murdering Cornbread and Do-Dirty. So the homicide detectives can stop asking around. Silky Mapp is the sole killer and I accept the consequences. Also, enclosed in the ownership rights of T.L.C.. Dad, I made you and Prince's mom partners in the one hundred million dollar enterprise. I just signed with Louis Vuitton, Gucci and True Religion. We're gonna see our line decorated by Gucci and Louis Vuitton. I haven't seen Chan-Ho since I've been here, so I assume he is back in the United States with you. He dedicated his entire life taking care of mom. When she died, he did the same for me. Make sure you tell him I love his crazy ass. Well Dad, I know you're probably on your third or fourth glass of Ciroc. Don't rush to the Philippines, because by the time you arrive I'll be gone and my ashes will be with mom. I love you Dad. I'll see you in Heaven. We'll be waiting for you and then, just then, our family will be complete.` `

Love Always, Your Daughter, Silky XOXO

Amir couldn't believe what he had just read. His eyes were filled with water after reading Silky's suicide note. Guilt began to set in as he thought about the day she left and he talked Chan-Ho into not following her. Chan-Ho was ready to follow Silky, but Amir talked him out of it and now his daughter was dead. It was her blood that splattered the letter, the affidavit and the ownership papers. Amir quickly called Chan-Ho and informed him of the latest news. Chan-Ho broke into tears. The two important women in his life were gone. Now his life was like a penny with a hole in it, worthless. Chan-Ho and Amir quickly arrived in the Philippians to find out more and just as Silky had written, she had been in Heaven for almost a month. She slit her wrist after writing the letter and was found lying in the tub of the hotel room in her wedding dress. She paid someone to make sure that she was cremated and her ashes put with her mother.

THE FINAL CHAPTER

"One Life, One Love, One Eternity"

Ⅰt was beautiful. It was like something you could or would never imagine.

That is why it was called what it was called. The colors were brighter than bright, redder than red, bluer than blue, greener than green, pinker than pink. There was no ceiling, no floors, no doors, and no walls. Everyone smiled; nobody frowned. They were ecstatic to be there. The horses were all colors with shoes of clear-cut diamond. Silky stood at the entrance of Paradise; they were there; the most important people in her life; her reason for living; her reason for dying. They stood there all dressed in T.L.C. linen. Little Princess opened her arms and ran towards her mother. Their bodies clung together. They spun in space as if they were high on ecstasy. Prince watched them. He would soon join them, but not before he cherished the moment. These were the two people he loved the most. Their souls united, they became one soul, one life one love, one eternity, and one family. Once again, as promised, Silky's Tears had been happy ones. Her life was complete. She had finally made it. **Heaven it was!**

"Excuse me, miss?" Raheem said with confidence.

"Yes?" the woman answered in her deep African accent.

"I noticed you standing there, and I must tell you, that you are the most beautiful woman I've ever seen.

"Oh, thank you. That was really sweet of you," the African woman said blushing from ear to ear.

"Do you mind if I ask your name?" Raheem asked.

"Makeba," she answered as every syllable slid off her tongue beautifully. "And your name is?" she asked.

"Raheem, but you can call me Rah."

"How are you today, Rah? Nice to meet you," Makeba said, sticking her hand out.

"Nice to meet you too, Makeba. Do you mind if I give you these flowers?"

"Awwwww these are beautiful, Rah."

"Got her," Raheem said to himself. He finally tried it and it worked. He remembered how Prince had met Silky. He remembered the entire scenario. He promised himself that he would try it one day. Now he stood in Safeway, repeating what he had learned from his mentor. She smiled and they exchanged numbers; he left. Rah jumped in his Aston Martin and watched Makeba walk towards a burgundy Phantom Rolls Royce that was flanked by her men. Raheem's life would change from that day on. He was the new King of Baltimore, whether he believed it or not.

To be continued...

Thank You!

From the bottom of my heart, I would like to thank everyone that supported me in this journey.

For book orders please email me at: Black Squares Publishing

info@theblacksquares.com

(862) 227-1471

Made in the USA
Middletown, DE
17 January 2021